I0417861

LIBRA ASCENDING

ZODIAC GUARDIANS 1

TAMAR SLOAN
TRICIA BARR

Copyright © 2020 by Tricia Barr & Tamar Sloan

All rights reserved.

No part of this book may be reproduced in any form or by any electronic or mechanical means, including information storage and retrieval systems, without written permission from the author, except for the use of brief quotations in a book review.

BRIELLE

L iving with guilt isn't easy. Guilt is a stain on the soul, an anchor on the heart. Even worse is when the guilt you carry isn't your own.

For the full seventeen years of Brielle's life, she's been inexplicably burdened with *seeing* the misdeeds of those around her, and of *feeling* their guilt over those wrongs. Her first instinct when the visions invade her mind is to ignore them, to shut them out. She doesn't enjoy knowing the intimate details of someone's life, whether that person is a stranger on the street, or one of the kids who bunk with her in the orphanage. She's a firm believer in the right to privacy.

But curses are called curses for a reason.

The visions aren't just sight and sound, but emotion, too. Raw, powerful, overwhelming. When Brielle was young, the guilt she experienced was too intense to hold in, and the only way to unburden herself was to confess, the words flowing out like a tidal wave.

This is why the Brady Bunch are currently glaring at her as she walks to Sister Agatha's office. All blonde, they act like siblings, defending each other against anyone outside their tight little circle. Brielle has never been part of that inner sanctum, and not just because her long wavy hair is the color of milk chocolate.

Brielle's an outsider everywhere she goes...forced to look in no matter how much she wants to be on the other side of the invisible wall.

The door to Sister Agatha's office is open, and as Brielle steps inside, Marie—the oldest of the Brady Bunch—shoots Brielle a threatening glance over her crossed arms from her seat besides Sister Agatha's desk. It's a glance that tells Brielle she'd better keep her mouth shut if she knows what's good for her.

Brielle swallows the nervous lump in her throat, the large room suddenly feeling stuffy. "You asked to see me, Sister?" she asks in a quiet voice.

Sister Agatha is a plump and stern middle-aged woman, her floral print blouse buttoned high up her neck. If she's ever committed any sins, she mustn't feel guilty about any of them, because her slate has always been cleaner than the floor she forces them to scrub every night. This is why, despite the nun's stringency, Brielle enjoys her company.

"Yes, Brielle." Sister Agatha braids her fingers on top of her desk and puffs out her large bosom, pretty little crucifixes glinting at her collar. "Someone broke the sacramental wine bottle in the church last night, and as Marie has a fresh cut on her palm, I suspect she was involved." She leans forward, her eyes drilling into Brielle. "Do you have any knowledge of this incident?"

"I don't even know why you're asking her," Marie complains, throwing her hands up in exasperation. "I didn't do it. It's not like Brielle would even know." She crosses her arms over her chest and purses her lips.

But Brielle *would* know. And the moment the denial leaves Marie's lips, Brielle knows she's lying. Another addendum of the cur :. Brielle always knows when someone is lying, with or without the visions.

Whether she wants to be saddled with that knowledge or not.

Brielle's nervous eyes dart from Sister Agatha's stony gaze to Marie's warning glare, quickly flashing away to the window where the light from the early morning sun pours in. It's the safest place to focus right now.

If she doesn't look at Marie, doesn't come any closer, she might avoid the vision.

"Brielle?" Sister Agatha prompts. "And please, sit down and stop hovering in the doorway, it's rude."

Brielle knows better than to roll her eyes or sigh or show any kind of sass in response to Sister Agatha's orders, meaning she has no choice but to sit in the empty chair next to Marie.

It doesn't matter that Brielle's holding her breath, or clenching every muscle in her body, or mentally willing her mind to be a fortress. The vision seeps into her skull like venom, fogging her sight and gripping her soul for a split second.

In flashes, she sees Marie kissing a boy in the shadows of the alley behind the orphanage, hears the boy whisper that they should try to steal some sips of wine, sees the two of them sneak into the church. She can feel Marie's hesitation as the vision follows them to the altar, witnesses the boy removing the wine bottle and struggling to open it. And she feels Marie's shock and horror as the bottle slips from the boy's hands and shatters on the floor. Marie slices her hand frantically trying to pick up the glass, but the vision dissipates with the two abandoning the mess and fleeing the church.

Except guilt from the memory lingers, coiling in Brielle's belly like a snake.

If only it were just the visions that clung to her. It's the person's knowledge of their wrongdoing that grasps her consciousness and doesn't let go.

Brielle clenches her fingers begrudgingly around the arms of her chair as she lowers herself into it, cursing her second sight. If she tells Sister Agatha what she saw, the Brady Bunch's hatred for her will only grow. She'll continue to be known as the freak who knows things she shouldn't. But if she doesn't tell, she'll have to live with Marie's guilt, a constant itch in her insides that will never subside. Is it worth keeping Marie's secret? Suffering for her just to be accepted?

Marie slides a glance at Brielle, the brief glare slashing through her. Marie already hates her. Why is Brielle even bothering to fight for acceptance? It's a lost cause...

Brielle shakes her head. "I'm sorry Sister, but I don't know anything about how the wine bottle broke." This is Brielle's first lie ever, and she internally applauds herself for how well she pulls it off. She hopes her voice and posture are as convincing as she thinks they are. She clears her throat. "Besides, I'm pretty sure I saw Marie in her bed last night. Kinda hard to miss her snoring."

Marie visibly relaxes, and Sister Agatha frowns as she leans back in her chair. "Very well, you may go, Marie." She dismisses the girl with a wave of her hand.

Marie eagerly stands up and skips out the door, throwing Brielle a knowing smile as she passes.

But Brielle didn't do it for her. Well, not just for her, anyway.

"Thank you for your honesty, Brielle," Sister Agatha begins once they're alone. "I know I can always count on you to tell me the truth. I'll miss you when you're gone."

Brielle docsn't point out Sister Agatha has said that the past five times adoptive parents showed an interest in her.

"If I go," she adds, unable to keep the tone of self-doubt out of her words.

"Oh, come on now, your chances of getting adopted this time look very good," Sister Agatha chides. "Are you ready for the Pierces' visit this afternoon?"

"As ready as I'll ever be," Brielle says with little confidence but ample determination. "I hope they like me."

"They already like you." Sister Agatha smiles warmly. "That's the reason they want to meet."

Yes, she and the Pierces did seem to click right away when they stopped by for the Meet and Greet last week.

After the fiasco her last potential adoption had turned into years ago, she'd been metaphorically benched from these events for some time. And now that Brielle's seventeen, she'd all but given up on getting adopted. So, for last week's Meet and Greet, she'd opted to help the nuns keep the snacks and drinks stocked.

While she was pouring more lemonade into the dispenser on the snack table, there was a tap on her shoulder. Thinking it was one of the nuns, she turned around to see a handsome couple. The man looked like he was in his forties, with brown hair, green eyes, and a warm smile. He was tall, and his beige suit fitted him well. The woman on his arm was about the same age, her straight dark brown hair cut to just below shoulders left bare by her spaghetti strap dress.

"Excuse me, but what can you tell me about those girls?" the man asked, pointing to three of the Brady Bunch girls chatting against the wall. Clearly, he thought Brielle worked there.

Rather than correct him, she went along with it. "Well, the tall one is Marie. She's a great conversationalist, but she can be prone to mischief. Ella is the short one, and she's a wiz with numbers. And Sasha, the...er...voluptuous one"—she struggled to find a nice way to say fat—"she's very sweet and loves all forms of art, especially painting."

The couple both nodded, appraising each of the girls.

Brielle saw no reason to slander them. Just because they excluded her didn't mean they deserved to be adopted any less than she did, and she wasn't about to damage their chances. She had enough guilt to deal with without creating her own.

"Can I ask what you're looking for?" After she asked the question, she felt stupid. They weren't shopping for a piece of furniture, they were scouting a potential child to make a permanent part of their family.

The couple chuckled and exchanged uncertain glances.

"Well, we don't really know," the woman said.

"We just know that there's something missing in our lives." The man shrugged. "I guess we'll know when we find it."

The woman cocked her head at Brielle. "You seem young to be working here. Are you a volunteer?"

"Not exactly. I'm...one of the orphans," Brielle confessed, her cheeks burning. "But I'm about to age out of the system, and I like helping, so I offered to help the nuns with the event."

After that, the couple introduced themselves as Frank and Beatrice Pierce and talked to Brielle for the duration of the gathering. It was only an hour, but they...clicked. Mr. Pierce had a very corny sense of humor, and Mrs. Pierce seemed indulgent and affectionate. Brielle felt something she hadn't felt in a long time.

Hope.

And the more days that pass, the more desperately she hopes things go well at their next meeting. This afternoon.

She'd been in this orphanage her entire life. She'd never known family. After watching the fellow babies she'd arrived with each find their forever home, she'd stopped making friends with the other residents. It was just too painful. Sister Agatha was the closest thing to family she'd ever had. Not quite like a mother, but maybe a very strict aunt, which is about as lame as it gets.

Brielle wants a family more than anything in the world. And she's not going to screw things up.

Not this time.

"I'll do my best to make you proud," Brielle says, forcing her lips into a flat smile.

Sister Agatha scoffs. "If you want to do that, stay on as a nun." She laughs, her belly bouncing with each rolling breath.

Brielle sucks in air through her teeth. "Not even as a last resort."

Sister Agatha laughs even harder, so hard even the tight gray bun perched on her head wobbles. When her laughter subsides, she wipes her eyes and regains her composure. "Alright, now off to school with you. Don't want to be late."

"Yes, Sister." Brielle stands, nods, then leaves the office, striding down the hall striped with the morning light coming through the vaulted windows. The orphanage is old, converted from a convent that's been here since the eighteen hundreds. All brick and mortar on the outside, and polished dark wood on the inside. It made for a very cold and dark childhood.

The instant she rounds the corner, she nearly crashes right into Marie, who's been waiting in the hall for her with arms crossed and hip swayed to one side.

"For your information, I don't snore," Marie says, eyes narrowed at her.

"I'm confused. Did you want me to cover for you or not?" Brielle never can keep the sarcasm from slipping out. It's her defense mechanism against always telling the truth. "Because

I'm pretty sure that without that comment, you'd be in massive trouble right now."

Marie steps closer and lowers her voice. "What I don't understand is how you always *know* these things. You shouldn't have to cover for me. I know that no one told you about the wine because I didn't even tell anyone, and I highly doubt a goody-two-shoes like you was out of bed after hours. So how do you always know?"

Brielle avoids the question. That's her specialty. "So you want me *not* to cover for you from now on? Got it." She walks around Marie, hoping to escape any further conversation.

But Marie's hand shoots out and grips tightly around Brielle's upper arm, locking her in place. "You're a freak," she hisses. "And if Sister Agatha accuses me again, of anything, I'll make your life here a living hell."

Brielle jerks her arm free of Marie's clutches. She knows she needs to get back to her room and get ready for school...but that itch in the pit of her stomach is demanding to be scratched. She may have covered for Marie, but she can't stand keeping this guilt completely to herself. Maybe if Marie confesses, the guilt will dissolve.

Lowering her own voice as well, Brielle whispers, "You'll feel better if you tell Sister Agatha yourself."

Marie looks at Brielle as if she thinks she's insane.

"Seriously, I know you feel bad about it," Brielle continues. "Tell her it was an accident. Tell her your boyfriend pressured you into it." The more Brielle speaks, the less the guilt nags at her.

Marie gasps. "You really are stupid. Trying to steal a few sips of wine from Communion is one thing, but Sister Agatha would burn me at the stake for sneaking a boy in! I swear, if she ever finds out, you'll be sorry!" And with that, Marie storms away down the hall toward the cafeteria.

Oddly enough, Brielle's guilt is totally gone. She didn't confess to the person to whom it mattered, but maybe just saying it out loud is the key.

Either way, she's even more desperate now to be on her best behavior with the Pierces this afternoon. She hates this place. Marie just voiced what all the others think: she's a freak.

She can't ever let the Pierces find out about her visions. She wants a family. She wants a home.

And she'll do whatever it takes to get it.

2

TRISTAN

"First day." Tess's bright voice spears through the fog of sleep blissfully wrapped around Tristan.

He rolls over, groaning. The fact she's his adoptive mother means he didn't inherit her morning cheer. "Which one is this, again?"

A new school every few months makes it hard to keep up. It seems like he just gets used to the bed in whatever place they're in and he's in a new one.

"Mirror Point, remember? In New York." Tess enters his room, placing a stack of clean clothes on his dresser. "I reckon the name is a good omen. Mirrors, Geminis, both reflections of each other and all that."

Footsteps thud past the open door. "You said that about Star Passe," Zarius calls out as he continues to the kitchen.

Tristan hauls the covers over his head. "And Twin Buttes," he mutters loud enough to be heard.

"Stop it, you two," Tess admonishes, the smile apparent in her voice. "It's important to be optimistic."

Because they haven't found anything that resembles a

clue that other Zodiac Heirs exist. That any of them actually made it to Earth.

But Tristan doesn't say it aloud. The last time he said something along those lines, the edges of Tess's smile had wilted.

Over the years, Zarius has gotten frustrated, slamming suitcases shut as they packed to move to the next city or town. Tristan has become impatient, knowing they're going to run out of time eventually.

But Tess has never lost hope. *"Fate brought Zarius and I together so we could raise and love you. Fate will bring us the other Heirs,"* she's always said calmly.

But the recent flicker of light in her eyes had been far more concerning than the dead ends or stones that refuse to glow, no matter how many hands they put them in.

Tess is worried.

And that's never happened before.

Tristan pushes himself to a sitting position, the covers falling to his waist. "Fate had better hurry up or I'm going to kick its ass."

Tess grins. "I've seen your new moves, but I'd put my money on fate." She heads to the door. "Breakfast in ten. You don't want to be late."

Tristan flops back onto the bed, staring at the ceiling. This is one of the nicer places they've stayed at. The paint isn't peeling. You can't hear the neighbors through the walls. It's actually a house and not an apartment. And it's not because they can't afford it. The pod Tristan arrived in was loaded with precious metals and gems. If they wanted, they could live off the radar the rest of their days.

But they can't.

They have twelve other Zodiac Heirs to find, considering two are Gemini twins. The Universe depends on it.

So they move from one place to another, taking whatever accommodation is easy and convenient. Searching. Hoping.

So far failing.

The sweet smell of hot sugar has Tristan hauling himself out of bed. Tess always makes waffles on the first day of school. She says it's so he can start on a positive note. Throwing on a shirt, Tristan heads for the stairs. First days no longer make him nervous. He's seen too many plus he's learned they're more of a recon mission. But there's no way he's messing with this tradition.

Waffles are waffles.

He's just at the top of the narrow stairs when he grips the bannister, his head spinning. Tristan frowns, his other hand coming to his temple. Maybe he got up too fast.

He hasn't had a vision in ages…

The cream walls and stained carpet fade away like they were never real. He locks every muscle, knowing what's coming next is impossible to stop.

"Tristan?" It's Tess, her voice full of concern.

But it's too late. A new reality has gripped him.

One painting a future that has yet to come.

It must be night time because everywhere he looks, it's black, right down to the mist at his feet.

There are two girls. One, a blonde, is sprawled on the floor, the other girl, this one a brunette, has collapsed on all fours. It's clear she's distressed. For a split second she looks up and it feels like their eyes meet. Tristan gasps. She can't see him, can she? But then her mouth is moving as if she's talking to someone. Someone who must be standing right where he is.

Glancing over his shoulder, Tristan is met by nothing but darkness. When he turns back, he scans the area, knowing there's more. The visions are always about Skins.

And if there are too many of them, it could mean they've

already been found. If that's the case, they'll be leaving sooner than he thought.

But when he sees them, Tristan's eyes widen with horror and he has to stop himself from taking a step forward and plunging down the stairs. He doesn't get to change what happens. He's nothing but a spectator.

There are many of them, littered around like statues. Frozen. He can tell they're Skins. He always can in the visions. A black aura surrounds them, the evil stain that is Chardis.

The brunette lifts her arm only to collapse as if a weight was just pressed on her. She struggles, but it's obvious that whatever it is, it's too strong. Her hand reaches out as if he's there, but before Tristan can scream, she stills. A pool of blood blooms on the ground around her head, forming a crimson halo.

The vision dissolves, leaving him surrounded by black and his own heavy breathing. But Tristan waits, heart battering his ribs. There will be a second vision.

There's always a second.

This scene unfolds like the first. The brunette on the ground, talking to whoever's in front of her. But this time, when she raises her hand, something changes. The mist recedes. She pushes to her feet.

The vision evaporates just as quickly as the first. The darkness falls away, the morning light suddenly feeling foreign. What the hell just happened?

As consciousness filters in, Tristan finds he's still standing at the top of the stairs. He has to unclench his hand from the bannister, the skin on his knuckles white and stretched.

"Tristan." Tess reaches out carefully. She knows it's hard to shift back to the present. "Are you okay?"

Tristan nods even though his gut is churning. It's always

like this—the disorientation, the jumble in his head, the nausea. It will pass...eventually.

And then he'll have to decide what they're going to do with the two alternate realities he just witnessed.

Zarius is halfway up the stairs, watching them. Everything about him says he's on alert and ready to move if needed. Zarius was sent to Earth along with baby Tristan. His role is that of protector, and he takes his job seriously.

Tristan pulls up a shaky grin. "I haven't vision-walked in years, you know."

Although, if he'd taken the step forward that he'd wanted to in the vision, the tumble down the stairs would've been inevitable.

Zarius relaxes. "You don't remember the time you almost ran into traffic because you saw that Skins were about to find us."

Tristan jogs down the last of the steps. "Good thing the first vision wasn't the one that came true that time, huh?" He slaps Zarius on the shoulder as he trots past.

Heading to the kitchen, he imagines the head shake Zarius is probably still engaging in. Then he'll glance at Tess. She'll smile. And everything will be right for him again.

His heart rate already dropping, Tristan draws in a deep breath. Someone died in the first vision. Death hung in the air.

He shudders. He's never seen anyone die before, let alone several.

Unless it's the second vision that's the true one...

That's the crux of Tristan's visions. Two futures. Only one that comes true. And he never knows which one it is.

Trying to find some equilibrium, Tristan flops onto the chair, drawing the stack of waffles toward him. Tess's right. This is definitely a perk in a life that involves a revolving door of first days at school.

Tess and Zarius join him, sliding in across the table. Tristan focuses on picking up the maple syrup and pouring it over the waffles like it's ketchup.

Zarius's chair scrapes as he pulls himself in. "He's not talking. It must've been a big one."

Tess rests a hand on her husband's arm. "He'll tell us when he's ready."

The first bite of fluffy, crunchy waffle has Tristan closing his eyes. Honeyed sweetness floods his senses, sweeping away the remaining horror of the vision.

Although, this one was more of a nightmare. There was blood, and wide, frightened eyes.

Another few mouthfuls and Tristan's ready to talk. A person's death is something they need to prevent.

As succinctly as he can, and with as little emotion as possible, he tells Tess and Zarius what he saw. Two girls, one possibly already dead. In the first vision it looks like it becomes two fatalities. In the second vision, something changes. He doesn't know how it ends, but it sure as hell feels more hopeful than the first.

Zarius and Tess glance at each other. Zarius frowns. "Was there anyone else there? Did you get a look at the Skin?"

Tristan shoves another forkful of dripping waffle into his mouth, shaking his head as he chews and swallows. "That's a negative on both counts. You know how the visions are. They're like tunnel vision, only showing me a slice of what's going on."

Zarius strokes his chin. "Skins don't usually work alone."

"There were others there, but they weren't moving." Tristan chews on another mouthful. "The brunette, she was talking to someone, but I couldn't see who. Maybe it was another Skin."

"This vision was different," Tess says quietly. "More

dangerous. Deadly." She lifts startled eyes to Zarius, then Tristan. "Do you think one of them was a Zodiac?"

Tristan rocks back in his chair. "That would explain why the blonde girl was on the ground." Possibly dead. "Skins don't usually attack humans in plain sight like that."

Zarius pushes to his feet, pacing across the kitchen and then back to the table. "The only way we can know for sure is if we find them."

This time, Tristan loads up his fork. Training with Zarius most days means having a hearty appetite isn't an issue for him. The hours of running and weights and self-defense mean he can eat what he likes when he likes. On top of being able to kick a Skin's ass, it's a nice little bonus.

It also means with his mouth full, he won't point out that trying to find the other Zodiac Heirs is what they've been doing for years.

Tess draws in a breath. "What if she's the Gemini Twin?"

The waffle turns to dust in Tristan's mouth. His soulmate. The other half of him.

Quite possibly the key to defeating Chardis.

Zarius starts pacing again. "Let's not get ahead of ourselves, love. We need to find these girls first, then we can see if a stone glows in their hands."

Tristan starts chewing again, but the sweet, crispy goodness in his mouth has lost its appeal. He puts his knife and fork down, starting to think strategically. "I'll scout around school. Then afterward, I'll find out where the local hangouts are and check those out, too."

Zarius nods. "It's a start. The girls could be at any school in this area, though. The visions are always of somewhere nearby."

"I'll transfer next week if I don't find them," Tristan adds, consciously working to not grit his teeth.

Suddenly the haystack this needle is hidden in doesn't feel

any smaller. So far all they know is that some poor girls are going to be lying on a dark floor somewhere, their lives hanging in the balance.

"And there was nothing about the location that jumped out?" Zarius strokes his chin. "That could be a place to start."

Tristan's hands grip the table in frustration. "No. It was black as night."

Of course, it was. So far their hit rate has been zero. And that's in over seventeen years.

Why would this be any different?

"We'll have to keep an eye out then, my guess is you'll know it when you see it," Zarius says, frustration grinding his words out.

Tess begins clearing the plates and cutlery. "I'll start wandering the malls, see if anyone fits the bill." She smiles brightly. "We have the description of the two girls, that's something."

Zarius slips a finger through the loophole on her jeans, tugging her onto his lap. "You're amazing, you know that?"

Tess giggles, holding the plates up high but not making a move to stand up. She leans in, the intent to kiss obvious.

Tristan makes a point of scraping his chair back as loudly as he can. "Way to make the waffles come back up, guys." He throws his hands in the air as he heads to the stairs, grinning to himself when their chuckles follow him up to his room.

He makes an issue of their loved-up ways, but they know it's a token objection. Zarius and Tess became his carers when they were quite young, and their life has focused on keeping him safe whilst finding others like him. They deserve the joy they find in each other.

Plus, it's meant he's grown up surrounded by their love. Nurtured by it. Inspired by it.

It gives Tristan hope that he'll find his own soulmate. The second Gemini Twin…

Grabbing his clothes out of his suitcase—he decided long ago there's little point in unpacking—Tristan pauses. Could one of the girls in his vision be a Zodiac Heir? Could she be the other Gemini?

What other reason would there be for a Skin to so blatantly murder someone?

Telling his heart to calm the farm, Tristan quickly gets dressed. A cursory glance in the mirror has him combing his fingers through his hair, which is more than he usually does. But it is his first day, which means he has to make a good impression.

And for the first time in as long as he can remember, it feels like fate might be on his side.

Maybe he won't have to kick its ass after all.

3

BRIELLE

It's a sunny, clove-scented day as Brielle rides her bike to school. Mirror Point is a quaint little suburb on the outskirts of New York City. Brielle's often grateful she didn't end up in a group home in the city. She's heard awful rumors about those places. Grace Orphanage is one of the last nun run orphanages in the country, and given her curse, she prefers the company of nuns.

On many mornings like this, she imagines how different her life would be if she'd grown up in the city. She'd likely have ended up in a nut house. New York's full of shady people. She'd be plagued with visions everywhere she went, and probably so overrun with guilt that she'd...

She pushes the thought out of her mind as she stops at the intersection. Yes, Mirror Point is comparably a great place for someone like her. Simple people with simple lives. And enough parks and even a lovely cliffside where she can escape the crowds when she feels overwhelmed.

The light turns green and she rides forward, hoping the school day passes quickly and without a hitch so she can get to her meeting. This is her last chance to get adopted. So much hangs on her making the best second impression she can.

She just has to act normal.

The parking lot of Mirror Point High is flooded with the usual vehicles full of parents dropping off kids who are eager not to be seen with them. Brielle envies those kids. What she wouldn't give for that kind of life. Something so simple, so ordinary. Something that just about everyone takes for granted.

As she rides up, she lets herself fall into the daydream of a morning in the Pierces' home. Having breakfast with them. Being dropped off before they head to work, wherever that is. Unlike her fellow students, she wouldn't fight off any hugs or kisses or whatever form of affection they'd like to give her. She'd savor it, and probably end up late to class for it repeatedly.

A loud screech from behind jerks her out of her fantasy, and she looks over her shoulder just in time to see a shiny silver Mercedes rapidly coming toward her, frantically attempting to swerve. She hastily tries to steer out of harm's way as the driver blares the horn. The bike topples over and Brielle crashes against the curb.

The Mercedes slams to a halt and the passenger window slides down.

"What the hell is wrong with you? Ride your bike on the sidewalk like a normal person!" Cassandra Sinclair yells at her from the driver's seat, her cell phone firmly in one hand propped above the steering wheel.

"The sidewalk is for pedestrians," Brielle yells back. "Maybe if you weren't on your phone all the time, you'd see when you're about to run someone over!" But her words are wasted, as Cassandra rolls up the window and speeds into the parking lot.

Brielle pushes herself up, the action making her realize

that her palms are scraped and her favorite pair of jeans ripped at the knee. Great. So much for making a good impression.

The first bell rings, and Brielle pushes her bike to the stand to lock it in place. At least it made it through with less damage than she did. She knows she should get to class, but she's not going to let Cassandra get away with almost killing her that easily. That girl is the definition of a spoiled brat, and more people need to stand up to her.

Cassandra gets out of her car, and Brielle stomps toward her.

"You do realize that you almost flattened me," Brielle accuses.

Cassandra rolls her expertly mascara-ed blue eyes and slings her purse over her shoulder, her perfect golden curls falling around her beautiful doll face like a lion's mane. Then she fixes a sneer on Brielle, looking like a feral cat about to strike.

"Don't be so dramatic. You're fine, aren't you?" she retorts. "Besides, if you were driving a car instead of a bike like a normal person, that wouldn't have happened." She tilts her head and pouts her glossed lips. "Oh, that's right, you don't have parents to buy you one."

Brielle's hands ball into fists. Cassandra loves to remind her that she's still an orphan. The irony is, Cassandra used to be one, too, at the same orphanage. It's hard to believe now, but they used to be good friends.

Before Cassandra got adopted.

Brielle lets Cassandra pass, muttering only to herself, "I guess the grass isn't always greener on the family side of the fence." She shakes her head, feeling sorry for her former friend. There are worse things than being an orphan.

The second bell rings, and Brielle tries to shake the bitter taste of the altercation as she rushes to class.

Her first period is English. Mr. Brown begins to read Macbeth, and his monotone soon lulls half the class to sleep. But Brielle has too much going through her mind to either sleep or listen to the story. With the parental visit this afternoon, and the confrontation with Cassandra, she can't keep the memories from invading her mind.

They were eleven, all primped up for the annual Meet and Greet. The Sinclairs had turned up. Sister Agatha had said they were rich and prominent. Brielle had no idea what that second word meant, but she knew it was a good thing from Sister Agatha's tone. At first sight, they were beautiful, like the bride and groom on top of a wedding cake. But up close, even at eleven she could see that they were just as plastic, and just as hollow.

They'd asked to take a stroll through the garden with Brielle, and she was so excited at the prospect of a family that she eagerly agreed. Mr. Sinclair was charming and well-dressed, and Mrs. Sinclair looked like a supermodel, with fine glittering jewelry hanging from her ears and around her neck.

But as soon as Brielle got close, it happened.

Horrible images flashed in her mind. Mr. Sinclair beating one woman after another. Brielle saw it all from his youth to now in a flood of brutal scenes. The first time he hit his high school girlfriend. Then college girlfriends. Worst of all was the stripper he'd left for dead on a bender in Vegas.

Brielle returned to reality with a gasp, hopping away from Mr. Sinclair as if he were about to strike her next. What would happen to her if he adopted her?

She knew in that moment, no matter how badly she wanted a family, she couldn't go with him. She somehow knew that he had yet to hit his new wife, but abuse was his addiction, and it was only a matter of time.

The most disgusting part about it was that guilt wasn't the only alien emotion assaulting her, but so too was satisfaction and urgency. Mr. Sinclair enjoyed hurting women, got a thrill from seeing the fear in their eyes before his fist came down.

Brielle felt all of it inside her, and it made her physically ill. She couldn't keep it in, not just because it affected her so terribly, but because Mrs. Sinclair deserved to know what she was in for.

Still shaking from the vision, she'd grabbed Mrs. Sinclair's wrist and, right there in the middle of the rose garden, pleaded, "Get as far away from this man as you can. He'll hurt you."

Mrs. Sinclair's mannequin smile faded, confusion barely pinching her botoxed face. "I beg your pardon?"

"What are you talking about, girl?" Mr. Sinclair's charming façade melted, an edge in his voice feeling like a threat.

Brielle couldn't take it. The guilt and shameful glee and need overwhelmed her, coupled with her own fear and desperation to prevent future brutality. Tears streamed down her face as she turned on Mr. Sinclair, her vision blurring.

"How could you?" she cried. "What kind of person could enjoy hurting others like that? Especially those who trust you and care about you? If you adopt me, will you beat me, too?"

Mr. Sinclair's face was a mask, but Brielle could see the terror and rage in his eyes. He looked at his wife, whose concern and confusion were evident in her wide gaze. Grasping her arms, his face had softened. "Darling, I assure you, I have no idea what this girl's talking about."

Sister Agatha strolled toward them, her smile faltering as she approached. "Is everything alright here?"

"What sort of orphanage are you running, Sister?" Mr. Sinclair barked. "I thought I'd have better luck finding a respectable child at an old-fashioned orphanage than a group home, but your kids seem to be just as perverse."

Sister Agatha looked at Brielle, who was frantically shaking her head in denial, and her thick brow furrowed in concern. "What happened?"

Mr. Sinclair straightened his shoulders and adjusted his tie.

"*This girl accused me of doing terrible things to women. I shudder to think how she even knows of such things. If you have no more wholesome young girls at this institution, I don't think—*"

"*Slow down, Mr. Sinclair,*" Sister Agatha cut him off. "*While I can't account for whatever Brielle said without further investigation, I can assure you that we raise these children with the utmost care and discipline. If adoption is truly something you want to pursue, I can't in good conscience let you leave without at least speaking with some of the other girls in need of a good home.*"

Mr. Sinclair smoothed his suit over his torso. "*Very well. And how will you punish this one for making outrageous accusations?*"

Sister Agatha regarded Brielle with a look of curiosity, and Brielle couldn't tell whose side the Sister was on.

"*I will speak with her in private, but I think for now the missed chance at being adopted is punishment enough,*" Sister Agatha said. "*Brielle, wait for me in my office. Mr. and Mrs. Sinclair, if you'll follow me back inside, I think I know just the girl who would be perfect for your family.*" She waved an ushering hand toward the orphanage, inviting the Sinclairs to follow her.

Brielle had rushed to Sister Agatha's office as instructed, preparing her words of protest and explanation.

When Sister Agatha finally entered the room and closed the door behind her, she sat beside Brielle rather than on the other side of her desk. Her face was stony and unreadable, and Brielle was certain she was about to be punished. It was so unfair!

"*Sister, I don't know how to explain it, but I know what he did.*" Brielle's words came out in a high-pitched flood. "*He's a bad man! You can't let him adopt any of the girls here, please!*"

Sister Agatha put a comforting hand on Brielle's shoulder. "*I'm only going to ask you this once, and I need you to be honest with me.*" Her eyes locked on Brielle's to stress the importance of her question. "*Did Mr. Sinclair hurt you or touch you inappropriately?*"

Brielle frowned and shook her head ever so slightly. "No, but... Sister, I saw him hurt others."

"What do you mean you saw?" Sister Agatha asked. "Did he hurt any of the other children here?"

"No, he hurt his girlfriends," Brielle insisted. "I saw him do it, in my head. And if he adopts any of the girls here, he might do the same to them."

Disappointment deepened the wrinkles on Sister Agatha's face as she closed her eyes and sighed. "I don't know where this is coming from, Brielle. But I think it means you're not ready to be adopted. And it's unfair of you to try to take that same chance away from others."

"Sister, that's not what's happening," Brielle protested, getting more and more desperate. She couldn't explain how she'd seen what Mr. Sinclair had done. It was crazy. No one would believe her accusation without proof. But she couldn't just sit by and let someone else fall into his clutches. "I want to be adopted more than anything. You know that. Which is why you have to believe me when I say that Mr. Sinclair is a bad man."

"How do you know that, Brielle? Have you ever met him before today?"

"No." She shook her head slowly.

"Have you seen or read anything about him in the news?" Sister Agatha continued.

"No, but—"

"Then how do you know?"

"I just know," Brielle shouted, slamming her hands on her lap. "Please, you have to believe me. You know I wouldn't lie."

Sister Agatha looked at her for a long moment, then rose and rounded the desk to sit in her usual chair on the other side of it. "I'm sorry, Brielle. The Sinclairs are a very prominent couple, and they can offer some needy orphan a good home. Without proof they are unfit parents, legally, I can't do anything to prevent them from adopting her."

Her? Oh no, they've chosen someone.

"Who?" Brielle asked, mouth suddenly dry.

"Your friend, Cassandra."

The bell rings, and Brielle gratefully comes back to reality, eager for a more engaging class that would keep her from reliving the past. She'd quarreled with herself over that incident for years. Should she have not said anything? After all, her actions came to no avail; the Sinclairs still adopted her friend. If she'd just made them dislike her without upsetting them or Sister Agatha, maybe she wouldn't have lost Cassandra as a friend. Maybe she would have saved Cassandra from him. She might even have been adopted years ago because Sister Agatha wouldn't have excluded her from events in fear that she'd scare off other parents.

Brielle shakes her head as she walks down the hall to her next class. No, things couldn't have gone any other way. Because warning people about who Mr. Sinclair really had been the right thing to do, and Brielle always tries to do the right thing, even if it costs her.

But none of that matters anymore. She has a second chance. The Pierces are interested in adopting her.

She just needs to be...normal.

4

TRISTAN

Mirror Point High looks like so many of the other high schools Tristan's seen, he doubts he'll even remember it once they leave. Multi-storied and square. Brown brick and narrow windows. He scans it, thinking of his vision, but nothing about it feels familiar...

Of course it's not. There's no way it would be that easy—rock up to school, find a Zodiac Heir, take them home to proudly show Zarius and Tess.

Feel like they've actually got a chance at winning this.

Standing in the parking lot, Tristan hears the screech of tires. He holds still, pretending he hasn't noticed as his body goes on high alert.

Zarius's voice whispers through his mind. *Skins are everywhere.*

Chardis chooses his vessels carefully, infiltrating their minds and taking control of their bodies. The possession blackens their hearts until it's the same pithy void as Chardis's soul. Unfortunately, it also gives them unnatural strength.

And the ability to turn invisible.

You drop your guard, you're dead.

Zarius hasn't sugarcoated the truth during their training. Some days, his words are as brutal as his kicks. But he can't afford to. If Tristan isn't ready for anything, anytime, his days end.

And so does the Universe.

But someone shouts, there's a brief argument, and it's over. The usual bustle of students resumes around him, one or two glancing at Tristan, most too preoccupied with each other or their cell phones to notice the new kid.

Tristan doesn't mind. It gives him time to scope out the place.

He strolls toward the entrance, looking casual and self-assured. He's learned this whole process is quicker if he hooks up with the right kids from the get-go. He just has to find them...

There's a wide set of stairs that lead up the front door, pale and stained. To the left, Tristan notices a bunch of kids on the other side, prowling in the shadows. The Outcasts, as he likes to call them. They like to wear black boots and too much eye-liner. They're too busy perfecting their blank stares and life-sucks attitude to know what's going on in the school.

They're worth keeping a note of as it's possible some of the Zodiacs have struggled to assimilate, especially with their powers unchecked, but they're not the people Tristan wants to talk to right now.

Someone sweeps past him, and Tristan registers the sharp scent of soap. Three teens, clothes neatly pressed, stride up the steps, books in hand. The High Achievers. They get the best grades, love to talk about books and Anime, and generally come from well-to-do families. Usually intact families. Odds are, they're not a Zodiac. Plus, they spend too much time in the library to be of use.

Tristan hears a tinkling laugh and he slows, knowing he's getting close. A bunch of kids are hanging around the doors on the right, laughing and chatting. All girls, their hair straightened and glossy, their midriffs peeking between their leggings and tees. Two of the girls crowd in close, lips pouting. Tristan waits for it. Yep, there it is. The requisite selfies.

They lean back, scrolling through the multitude of photos they just snapped. "Do you think it works? Maybe we should take it again?"

Tristan blows out a breath through pursed lips. He's fallen for this before, thinking these are the people he needs to integrate with. It wasted days when they could've been moving onto the next school.

These guys are the Fringe Group. The Wannabes, the Second-in-Line. The Popular Clique would never question their selfies. Even if they hated it they know you don't show that sort of insecurity right on the front steps of the school.

The Popular Clique knows you look like you're having fun. Always.

Reaching the bottom of the stairs, Tristan leans against a concrete column. If he's found the Fringe group, then it's only a matter of time. The next part is inevitable.

It happens only a second later. The glance, the cute little wave. The frantic patting down of hair.

They're here.

The group is smaller than he's seen in other schools, but then again, Mirror Point High is one of the smaller places they've been to. Generally, Zarius and Tess prefer to hit the bigger schools. More butts for your buck as Zarius likes to say. Tess doesn't bother to correct him anymore—"bang, Zarius, we're not buying backsides!"— because they get the gist. More teens to check out in one location.

But desperate times mean desperate measures.

Three of them—two boys, one girl—are waiting at the

end of the pavement beside the parking lot. A girl sashays towards them, pressing the button of a remote over her shoulder as a silver Mercedes flashes its indicator lights behind her.

A blonde girl.

Holy pitch. *The* blonde girl.

She joins the others, rolling her eyes and laughing at something they said. "I know. I never would've got the smell of poor out if she'd hit."

They walk past him, secure in their knowledge they're lords of this kingdom. Tristan's heart is hammering. It's the girl from his vision. Less bruised, far more conscious, but definitely the same girl.

The thought flashes through his mind before he can stop it. *Could she be a Zodiac Heir?*

Could she be the Gemini Twin?

Shaking his head and telling himself to get a grip, Tristan picks up his books. Just because the girl was in a vision doesn't make her one of them.

But it does mean he needs to find out more about her. Especially if her life could be at stake.

Good thing he's done this a gazillion times before.

Falling behind them, Tristan flicks up his collar.

One of the guys, tall with shoulders almost the width of the stairs, throws a small red ball up into the air and catches it again. "Coach reckons I can go from defense to offense next game."

The other girl, sleek black hair and caramel skin, scoffs out a laugh. "You said that last week."

The blonde girl is absorbed in her cell, not even noticing when one of the Fringe girls waves. She's frowning as she chews on a fake nail that perfectly matches her pink skirt.

The big guy throws the ball against the wall, above the head of one of the Outcasts as he tries to slink through the door. The Outcast flinches but doesn't bother to turn around or look. The guy catches it, grinning. "Yeah, well, he saw me when I got that fast break."

Tristan comes up beside him as they enter the school. "You were trying to get an unsettled clear? That ain't easy."

The guy turns around, frowning when he doesn't recognize Tristan. "Ah, you play lacrosse?"

"Nah, just prefer it to football."

The dude's eyebrows hike up like they usually do. It's always one of the two—football or lacrosse. You figure out the school sport, find the jock, and you're in.

They're outside the lockers and the guy slows to a stop. The others crowd around him, except for the blonde. She's still glued to her cell.

The big guy grins. "People think football's rough."

Tristan rolls his eyes. "I've never seen a guy knocked for a loop in football like I have in lacrosse." If this were a different school Tristan would be swapping the sports around. "Although it's not all brawn. You need brains, and a mean throwing arm."

"Damn straight you do." The guy flicks the ball above the lockers, angling it so it comes straight at Tristan.

Even if he wasn't expecting it, Tristan's reflexes have been honed from years of training with Zarius. Considering Skins can go invisible, a lot of it's been done with a blindfold.

You can tell a lot from the sound of rubber hitting brick, from the *schlurp* of the ball collapsing in on itself, the *crack* as it recoils.

Tristan doesn't need to look to catch the ball as it comes straight at his head. His hand darts up and the ball lands in his palm with a *slap*.

The smart ones test you. That's good.

The smart ones have all the info.

The big guy's eyebrows shoot up. "Whoa!"

He says it loud enough that several others turn around to see what's going on. Tristan grins at each curious face, not minding the attention. The more people he can smile at, the more people will be happy to talk to him.

What's more, it gets the blonde's attention.

She looks up from her phone, an irritated frown marring her smooth skin, glancing around to see what the fuss is. Her eyes skim Tristan, registering he's no one she knows, and she goes to look away. As a general rule, the Popular Clique doesn't give the common student the time of day.

But then she stops. Her eyes dart back to Tristan.

His grin expands as he gives her a short, jaunty wave.

Her eyes widen, vivid blue seeming to dominate her face, but she quickly recovers. She scans Tristan from head to toe, a slight challenge in the assessing tilt of her chin. Being easy on the eye has its advantages…

Tristan waits, deciding he likes her already. She's got qualities a guy would like and she knows it. When her eyes return to his, he nods. "Hey, I'm Tristan."

He leaves a question mark at the end. Knowing the blonde girl's name is the first step.

Her pink lips tip up. "Cassandra. First day, huh?"

"Sure is. Was hoping someone could translate this for me." He holds up a slip of paper with his schedule. From what he can tell, he has English first. It's finding someone to sit with that's the goal.

She steps in close, her eyes twinkling. Plucking it from his hands, she puckers her lips as she scans it. "Advanced English first." She looks up and Tristan registers her perfume —floral yet spicy. "With me."

He arches a brow. "Now that's lucky."

Before Cassandra can answer, a solid *thwump* hits Tristan between the shoulder blades. "The name's Zayn. And our team is always looking for reserves…"

Bingo. Tristan is now *in*.

He absorbs the slap, knowing it was supposed to put him off balance. "Depends. What do people do for kicks around here?"

Zayn slams his locker shut. "Play lacrosse, obviously."

The dark-haired girl rolls her eyes. "Watch Netflix while your parents think you're studying. My name's Suki, by the way."

Cassandra leans in a little closer. "Go down to the local fro-yo cafe—Creamy Dreams."

"Cool name," Tristan states with an arched brow. He turns to Zayn, holding his hands up in apology. "Sorry man, fro-yo will win out every time."

The bell rings followed by a chorus of more lockers clanging shut. Zayn snaps a glance at Tristan's midriff. "It shows, too."

Tristan laughs—he had a six pack when he was fourteen —glad that at least he'll like these people. It makes a necessary task enjoyable.

Cassandra flips her hair over her shoulder. "Let's get going. We don't want to give Ms. Grotberg an excuse to give out detention."

"Ms. Grotberg?"

Suki rolls her eyes again and Tristan suspects it's her thing. "And saying her name like that is the best way to get one. She's also the vice-principal."

He follows them down the hall, scanning the students as he goes. He's found the blonde from his vision, now to find the brunette.

That one who looked at him like he was just there, like he was real...

The curious glances continue, and Tristan makes a point of smiling or saying hi. No one fits the image he saw. He tells himself he needs to connect with his inner Tess.

Patience, Zodiac boy. You've found one girl already. You'll find the second.

Cassandra and Zayn take a left into a classroom and Tristan follows them. Luckily, the tables are grouped in bunches of four, meaning he easily sits beside his newfound friends. Students file in, taking their places.

None of them the brunette.

When Ms. Grotberg enters, the entire room falls into silence. Elderly, with a beak-like nose, she surveys the room. Her gaze falls onto Tristan, not looking pleased to have a new addition.

Tristan stands, smiling as if he's the one welcoming her. "Good morning, Ms. Grotberg. My name's Tristan Ayers and I just recently transferred from Twin Buttes."

There's a snigger and Ms. Grotberg's hawkish gaze snaps left, trying to locate it. She's greeted with silence and blank faces.

"An unusual name, I know," adds Tristan, widening his smile as he lifts his brows. "But quite unforgettable."

Ms. Grotberg's jaw slackens for the briefest of seconds. She shakes her head. "You're one of those, huh?" She waves a hand dismissively. "Take a seat, young man. Page eighty-four in your textbook."

Tristan sits back down and Zayn leans in. "Whoa, your head's still intact," he whispers, clearly impressed.

Tristan grins. Who knew the name of that place would actually come in handy after showing absolutely no Zodiac Heir potential, no matter what Tess said. "Good thing, too." He taps his temple. "I need to get up to speed."

Zayn frowns. "Get up to speed?"

Cassandra leans forward, her twinkling eyes narrowed. "You mean you want the goss."

Thwump. Another blow lands between Tristan's shoulder blades. "Then you've come to the right place."

Tristan makes a show of looking curious yet surprised. The Popular Clique are always the ones in the know. "I really have hit the jackpot then," he murmurs.

Keeping their voices low, Cassandra and Zayn progressively work around the room, describing each student. Cheerleader. Chess champion. Works at Creamy Dreams and will give you a discount if you compliment the purple hair. The longer they talk though, the more intimate the details get. She lost her virginity at camp. He got caught by the principal trying to graffiti the news in the boys' bathroom.

Throughout, Tristan asks his strategic questions. "What did his parents think about that?"

Zayn chuckles. "They're hoping to hell his younger brother only follows him in looks."

So, not adopted. Mentally, Tristan scratches another kid off the list.

He tilts his chin at a girl with ink-black hair slouched in the back corner. "Now, she looks like someone who could lift tables with her mind."

Cassandra snorts. "The only thing that gets high is her."

No special abilities then. Scratch another one off.

The period is almost coming to an end when Tristan brings the conversation back to Cassandra. "What about you? What's your favorite fro-yo flavor?"

Start small and innocuous, a little flirtatiously. Then work your way up.

"You're kidding right?" Zayn scoffs. "The daughter of the great Mr. Sinclair would never eat fro-yo. She's too busy getting straight A's, winning national debates, and getting gold for the track team." He nudges her shoulder. "And looking slim, trim and terrific, to boot."

Cassandra scowls at him. "Shut up, Zayn. For the hundredth time, I don't like fro-yo."

So, pretty *and* a high-achiever. They sound like qualities one would want in a Zodiac Heir.

"Your parents are the Sinclairs?" Tristan doesn't actually know who they are, but he makes a note of doing some research. "Is your mom as pretty as you?"

Cassandra rolls her eyes, no doubt used to compliments. "We're both blonde, if that counts."

So, possibly not adopted. Squashing the disappointment, Tristan wishes he could just come out and ask these questions.

It would save a whole lot of time.

He opens his mouth to probe about siblings when the bell rings, sparking a flurry of movement. Cassandra scoops her books up. "Electives next. I'm off to Global Economics, Zayn has Sports Science. You?"

Tristan ignores the second punch of disappointment. It seems the talk with Cassandra is going to have to wait. He makes a show of pulling his schedule out of his back pocket even though he's already memorized it. "Classic American, whatever that is."

Cassandra's smile turns coy as she pauses at the door. "Make me something good."

Zayn snorts. "She's not going to eat it, though."

Eat it?

Classic American is a cooking class?

Without warning, Zayn pitches the ball at Tristan again. He doesn't blink as he catches it and lobs it back.

Zayn inclines his head with a grin. "Not bad."

Tristan winks. "Get that ball up the field so you can get more offensive players in the attack zone."

Zayn throws the ball across the hall, making several people duck, then catches it. "That's the plan, m'man!"

Cassandra shakes her head. "Your classroom is down the hall and to the left. See you at the cafeteria?"

Tristan lets the happiness those words spark shine from his smile. "Looking forward to it."

He finds his class easily enough—not only is Mirror Point High too small to get lost in, but Zarius has had Tristan navigate every new house or apartment they've been in blindfolded. Tristan could easily follow the smell of cheap cleaning spray and burnt cheese.

Cooking class. How the hell did he end up in cooking class? Tess usually deals with the enrollments and class selection. She knows Tristan's generally ahead of the curriculum thanks to the home-schooling, and also needs to be in a diverse set of classes so he can connect with as many kids as possible.

But cooking class?

Admittedly, the title Classic American doesn't really say food technology.

Straightening his spine and telling himself he can't afford to miss an opportunity, Tristan eyes the teens that pass him on the way down the hall. Any of them could be a Zodiac Heir.

And if they don't find one soon…

Kids file past, tall ones, short ones, smiling ones, frowning ones. Tristan tries to stay focused even though they start to blur together. How many teens has he scanned, wondering if there's some way to distinguish a Zodiac just by sight? How many times has he thought he had a lead only to come up empty-handed?

Right now, talking to Cassandra is his best bet. It's the closest they've come so far. Lunch can't come fast enough.

Tristan slips into the classroom, bright pictures of fruit and vegetables lining the wall. He suppresses a shudder. Chardis's lair probably looks like this place.

As he waits for the teacher to look up from her computer, he scans the room. His eyes stop at a girl in the far station across the room. Her head is tilted so her chocolate-colored hair falls over her face. This is a girl who doesn't want to be noticed.

But for some reason Tristan notices her.

In fact, he can't look away.

She's a brunette, but so is half the school. It doesn't mean anything...

She looks up and two words slam through Tristan.

It's her.

The girl from the vision.

The one who looked at him in a way no one has.

The one who's staring right back at him like her world just stopped, too.

5

BRIELLE

Cooking is one of Brielle's favorite classes. Not just because making food gives her a focus that nothing else does, but because it's the one class she has with her best —and kind of only—friend, Adalind.

The snarky brunette is already sitting at their station when Brielle enters the room, the streak in her hair dyed pink this week. Adalind's bored expression perks up as Brielle comes to join her.

"How was your weekend?" Adalind asks, smiling at Brielle like she's the only person in the room.

Brielle loves this about her, how she puts her full attention on her, and truly is interested in what she has to say. What she loves most is that Adalind is one of the only people she's never had a vision of. What more could she ask for in a best friend?

"It was okay," Brielle shrugs. "I spent the whole time stressing about today."

"You shouldn't worry," Adalind says, flipping her pink streak over her shoulder. "That couple will love you, you're awesome! You just have to be yourself, and they'll see that, too."

Brielle smiles but looks down at the table. Adalind only thinks that because she doesn't know Brielle's freak side, and if Brielle has anything to do with it, she never will.

Adalind came to the school at the start of the year, a military brat, and for whatever reason, she latched onto Brielle instantly. Brielle isn't the best at making friends. Ironically, being forced to see the private details of everyone else's lives has made her very closed off, so she doesn't put herself out there as much as she should.

But that didn't seem to matter to Adalind. From the day she arrived, Adalind had gravitated toward Brielle like a magnet, and Brielle didn't mind one little bit.

Adalind sighs dramatically. "I wish you had a cell phone. Then we could text each other on weekends."

Brielle smirks. "You mean, as opposed to actually talking in person, like they used to in the old days?"

Adalind rolls her dark eyes. "You know what I mean. And trying to hang out with you on weekends is tough because that creepy nun interrogates me at the door every time."

Brielle snickers. Sister Cora is kind of a scary old lady.

"You should just let me buy you a phone," Adalind offers for the umpteenth time. "Just because you don't have parents doesn't mean you have to live without modern day necessities. I could be like your sponsor, you know."

"Okay, fine, if I don't get adopted this time around, then I'll concede and let you buy me a phone," Brielle says.

Adalind shrugs. "Fair enough."

Smiling wide, Brielle shakes her head and rolls her eyes, and when her eyes fall, the sight they behold makes her heart trip.

A guy is walking through the doorway. A new guy as

she'd remember someone who looked like that. A guy she can't look away from.

His golden brown hair is mussed in casual spikes, and his blue t-shirt hugs his Adonis physique in a way that would make any girl drool. But it's not just his good looks or lean grace or the fact he's new that has Brielle's heart doing somersaults; it's the way his cerulean eyes are locked on hers, and the frozen way he stands just past the entrance of the class, staring at her.

Looking like she feels—like the world just...expanded and imploded at the same time.

"Ah, you must be Tristan Ayers," Ms. Brom greets.

He falters and turns to her, and Brielle's arms prickle with a chill at the loss of his gaze.

"Yes, ma'am," Tristan says, readjusting his backpack slung over his shoulder.

Miss Brom scribbles on her attendance sheet and nods. "Alright, Tristan, you can take the empty seat at station four."

Brielle's eyes widen and her heart just flat-out stops beating.

That's her station!

Brielle and Adalind had been happy not to have a third person at their station, it gave them the freedom to chat about personal stuff during class without having to include anyone else.

Tristan approaches, checking the numbers on counter-tops he passes. When he spots the number four sticker on the edge of her counter, he once again puts those intense, bright blue eyes on her and smiles, and a sizzle surges through Brielle's nerve endings. As he takes the empty stool to her left, she's happy to give up that third seat and the privacy its vacancy had previously afforded.

Brielle hardly notices the other students settling into their seats around her. All she can do is feel the heat of the solid male body right next to her, smell the sweet musky scent of his body spray, and try like heck not to look in his direction lest she be paralyzed that way for the duration of the hour.

"Hey," he says in a way that draws out the single syllable, making it impossible not to look. "I hope you ladies are good at cooking, because I sure as hell am not." He grins again, and Brielle is mesmerized by how soft his pink lips appear as they lift to reveal straight white teeth. "Sorry you got the short straw."

Brielle blinks. That's the last thing she's thinking right now.

"I usually ride Brielle's coattails, so I guess you'll be hopping on that bandwagon, too," Adalind says, reminding Brielle that there are other people in the room besides her and Tristan.

"Right," Brielle says, coming to her senses. "Yeah, I don't mind."

"I'm more than happy to help, cooking just isn't my forte," Tristan says. "I have no intention of letting you do all the work." He winks at her, and she hardly notices the heat radiating up her neck. "I'm Tristan, by the way," he says, leaning closer, the warm skin of his upper arm grazing hers.

"I'm Brielle," she says, mouth suddenly dry. She swallows. "And this is Adalind."

Adalind gives a half-hearted two-finger salute in greeting.

Tristan opens his mouth to say something, but is interrupted by the teacher.

"The lesson for today is one of my favorites, but it's not easy." Ms. Brom claps her hands in front of her plaid apron, a far too eager smile on her plump face. "They're round, sweet, and everyone's favorite treat—donuts!" She raises her arms high up over her messy bun like her announcement is the best news any of them has ever heard, only to receive sighs of exasperation from the class.

"Donuts," Tristan breathes like he's just found water after a week in the desert. He looks at Brielle, hope bright in his eyes. "They can't be that hard to make, right?"

Brielle glances at the deep fryer filled with oil on the counter in front of them, figuring they must be making fried donuts rather than baked. "You'd be surprised."

Ms. Brom begins her demonstration at her station, and Brielle, Adalind and Tristan measure out the ingredients accordingly.

"So Tristan, what's your story?" Adalind asks, frowning in disgust at the yolk on her fingers as she cracks the eggs.

"My story?" he repeats as he dumps a cup of flour into the mixing bowl.

"Yeah, like, what brings you to Mirror Point High in the middle of the semester?" she clarifies, washing the yolk away at the sink as soon as she's finished cracking.

"My parents move around a lot for work," he says, waving away the cloud of flour that erupts as a result of his too-hasty dumping. "I've been all over the place."

"Oh, are your parents in the military, too?" Brielle asks. "Adalind's parents are in the Air Force, right?"

"Something like that," Adalind replies. She's always vague when it comes to the topic of her parents, and Brielle assumes they do something classified, so she never presses the issue.

"Kinda. My dad's in defense," he says, ducking his head to check out the recipe. "Sugar. We're going to need lots of sugar."

They put all the ingredients together and Tristan tries stirring, his sloppy motions forcing the mixture to spill over the brim.

"Here, let me." Brielle takes the bowl and whisk from

Tristan and stirs in an even circular motion, smoothing the ingredients together.

"Wow, you're pretty good at that," Tristan says, flaunting that perfect smile once more. "Did your mom teach you how to cook?"

Brielle frowns and shakes her head, not wanting to get into the issue of her parentlessness.

"Is your dad the cook in the family, then?" he asks.

Again, Brielle shakes her head, continuing to stir. When the dough is thoroughly mixed, she takes it out and attempts to roll it. "Wanna try?" She offers the rolling pin to Tristan, and he accepts it with hesitation. "It's okay, you can't really mess this part up." She giggles.

He pushes the pin onto the mass of dough and rolls it back and forth. He's a bit too rough, and Brielle is tempted to guide his hands with hers, if only for the excuse to touch him. What's wrong with her? She's never been this...girly around a guy before.

"So, what do your parents do for a living, Brielle?" he asks, and Brielle bites her lip at the question.

"Brielle is currently in the market for parents," Adalind says, as if they were talking about merchandise and not people. "If her current prospects don't take the offer, I'm considering adopting her myself." She winks at Brielle, and Brielle is super grateful for the save.

"Oh," Tristan says, pausing in his clumsy rolling. He looks at Brielle long enough for her to turn back to the dough, suddenly uncomfortable. Tristan's probably already decided she's a freak. "I get it," he continues rolling, his voice hushed. "I'm adopted, too. I just got lucky."

"Oh." Brielle looks back, surprised. Aside from the kids she grew up with in Grace Orphanage, she's never met another orphan. This time she doesn't break away from Tristan's blue gaze.

Is that why she feels so drawn to him? They literally just met!

Tristan is the first to break away. He clears his throat. "Okay, I think that's good." Tristan lifts the pin to assess his work.

"May I?" She gestures for the pin. He hands it over and she smooths the undulating dough a bit more to make it uniformly flat. "Now we just cut out circles." She hands Tristan the small circle cutter, then proceeds to press the larger one into the dough. "Press that into the center of my circles."

"Ah yes, the holes. The worst part of a donut." He slants a cheeky look at Brielle. "Do you think we can go rogue and not do this bit?"

Brielle has to suppress a smile. "Ah, no. We do this the right way. This will be a *normal* donut."

Tristan winks. "I guess I could try that."

After a few minutes, the dough is cut into about a dozen donuts. Brielle gently slips her fingers around one and lifts it from the counter, offering it to Adalind to put into the hot oil.

Adalind puts her hands up in surrender, backing away. "Ah-ah, I'm not getting anywhere near that fryer."

Brielle chuckles and shakes her head, then carefully drops the donut into the oil. Without saying anything, Tristan begins picking up donuts and doing the same. He drops the first one in too high above the oil and it splashes.

"Here, you have to lower it right above the surface," Brielle says. Without thinking, she puts her hand on his over the fryer.

Static snaps as their hands touch, and they both pause and glance at each other. Tristan's blue eyes look deep into hers, and the electric current coursing from her hand is more than just static, seeping into her chest and bathing her with a delicious warmth.

Brielle blinks it away and looks back at their hands, remembering what they're supposed to be doing. "There, now let it go slowly."

Tristan releases the donut with far more ease and, this time, there's no splash.

"Perfect." Brielle removes her hand and looks everywhere but at Tristan, hoping the moment isn't as awkward as she feels.

The dough bubbles and browns in the oil as they watch.

"Are you doing anything after school?" Tristan asks, the sensation of his eyes on her like the blaze of a spotlight.

She slowly looks up at him. "Sorta. I have a meeting at three o'clock. Why?" Her heartbeat pounds in her ears as she waits for him to answer.

"Well, I heard there's a great fro-yo place down the road. Creamy Dreams. Do you know it?"

Everyone in town knows Creamy Dreams. But as Brielle almost never has money—and few invites apart from Adalind—she's only ever gone a couple of times when she fails to refuse Adalind's insistence on paying for her.

"Yeah, I know it," she replies, tucking her hair behind her ear as she ducks her head.

"Do you think you have time before your appointment to go with me? Fro-yo is better with friends, after all." He flares a sharp brow, looking too handsome to resist.

Holy crap! Did he just ask her out?

Brielle is struck dumb for a moment, the butterflies in her stomach fluttering into a frenzy.

"Not today," Adalind interjects, leaning over the counter to shoot him a quietly hostile glance. "Her meeting is very important."

Shocked by Adalind's interruption, Brielle frowns at her.

"No," she immediately retorts a bit too loudly. Then she turns to Tristan. "I'm sure I can spare a few minutes after school."

Yes, the meeting with her hopefully new parents is massively important, but getting asked out by the hot new guy in school isn't something that happens every day—or ever. What if this is Brielle's one chance at normalcy? Does Adalind really expect her to pass this up? Surely she can do both.

Adalind rolls her eyes but says nothing as she leans back. Tristan's smile looks as if he's just won the lottery.

"Great, it's a date," he says, making her heart spike. "And don't worry, *Mom*"—he casts a teasing glance at Adalind—"I promise to have her home before three."

A date. Brielle's never actually been on one before.

A date and meeting her prospective new parents all in the same afternoon.

Maybe her luck is finally changing.

6

BRIELLE

"I can't believe you're going on a date with the new guy. And right before your parent meeting!"

Adalind taps the toes of her right foot against the pavement, her arms crossed and hip jutted to one side as they stand outside the entrance of Mirror Point High after school.

"You really don't like him," Brielle states, scanning the heads of the students pouring down the stairs, a nervous ball forming in her belly.

Adalind scoffs. "I just don't want him to screw this up for you."

"He won't," Brielle says, adamant. "It'll just be a quick, harmless fro-yo. Twenty minutes tops. Then I'll be back with plenty of time for the meeting."

"I hope so. You better call me after to let me know how it goes! The date and the meeting."

"You know I will." Brielle offers a reassuring smile.

"Okay. Have fun—but not too much fun." Adalind wags a warning finger at Brielle, then smiles before heading off to her car in the parking lot.

Brielle hugs her arms as she stands on the sidewalk, waiting. She turns away from the stairs, trying not to look desperate.

Maybe Tristan just won't show, and she can forget about him and move on with her day. She really shouldn't have agreed to this today of all days, but who could say no to that face? And those biceps! She's never felt this way about a guy before, especially not upon first meeting. What's the harm? And besides, if she'd said no, he might never ask her again. Normal high school girls go on dates. And as she's never been on one before, this is an important milestone.

"What are you doing out here?" a nastily familiar voice chimes behind her. "Don't you have to get back to scrub floors and sew clothes, or whatever it is orphans do these days?"

Brielle doesn't bother to face Cassandra. "Not that it's any of your business, but the new guy at school asked me to go to Creamy Dreams with him."

Cassandra rounds on Brielle like she was prey. "You don't mean Tristan?" She arches a perfectly plucked blonde brow.

Brielle isn't surprised Cassandra knows his name. As Mirror Point High's own resident Gossip Girl, she always knows everything that happens at school.

Cassandra coughs an insulting laugh. "What would a hottie like Tristan see in a filthy orphan like you?"

"Careful, Cassandra, your skin is turning green," Brielle says in a steady tone.

Cassandra narrows her eyes, then shrugs and makes a show of looking at her fake pink nails. "Well, I'm sorry to disappoint you, but I saw Tristan drive off a few minutes ago. Looks like he bailed."

The words are meant to sting. But Brielle knows as soon as Cassandra begins saying them that they're a lie.

She can't let Cassandra see that, though. Cassandra doesn't know about Brielle's lie-detection, and she doesn't need further fuel to torment Brielle. So Brielle frowns and casts a look of disappointment down at the sidewalk.

Satisfied, Cassandra *hmphs*, turns on her heel and sashays away.

"I didn't know you and Cassandra were friends." This time, the familiar voice behind her is a welcome one.

Brielle turns, a triumphant smile spreading across her face. "We're not. She was trying to convince me that you were standing me up."

Tristan shakes his head as he looks in the direction Cassandra just left. "I'd never do that. Even if I had to bail for some reason, I'd let you know. I like to, at least, think I'm a gentleman."

"You might be the only one left in existence," she teases.

He chuckles, then pulls his phone out of his front jeans pocket. "It's two-o-five. We'd better get going."

He nods for her to follow him as he steps off the curb into the parking lot toward a sleek black truck. When they reach it, he opens the passenger door for her. "Your carriage awaits, m'lady."

"Nice truck," she says, the nervous ball in her stomach tightening as she lowers herself onto the leather seats. So this is what he meant when he said he got lucky. His parents must be loaded!

"Thanks," he says, closing the door then jogging around to slip into the driver's seat.

As he starts the engine, their proximity strikes her. She's never been this close to a guy, and in such a private, confined space. A sort of claustrophobia sets in, though not entirely an unpleasant feeling. It's all she can do not to devour every inch of him with her hungry gaze.

"I'm sorry about earlier," he says, a welcome end to the silence. "I didn't mean to make you feel uncomfortable with all the parent questions. I get that the whole topic is a sensitive one, and I shouldn't have drawn it out of you like that."

"It's okay, you couldn't have known," Brielle says with a shrug. "You said you're adopted. How old were you?"

"I was a baby, so I've never really gotten to experience what it's like to be an orphan." He looks at her as he drives down the street, some unknown emotion darkening the blue of his eyes. "I'm sorry you've been one for so long. I imagine it could get quite lonely...." He offers a smile that seems sincerely sympathetic.

She looks down at her lap. "Thanks. But hopefully not much longer. That's the meeting I have after school. With a couple who's considering adopting me." The reality of that weighs down on her once again, making her heart thump against her ribs.

"That's great! I'm really happy for you."

Thanks to her curse, Brielle can tell he means it. She slides a glance out of the corner of her eye. Handsome. Sweet. Nice car. Tristan seems too good to be true. If Cassandra hadn't appeared on the steps of the school with her nasty lie, Brielle would be wondering if she'd stepped into an alternate universe.

The drive to Creamy Dreams is a short one, with the shop being only a few blocks down the road from the school. When they go inside, a handful of the more popular kids are already occupying tables. Tristan fills his cup with chocolate fro-yo, then piles on gummy bears and M&Ms. Brielle opts for blueberry fro-yo with no toppings, conscious of the whispering around them.

"Would you like to sit outside?" he asks after he pays the clerk at the register. "It's a really nice day."

"Sure," she says, happy for the excuse to avoid the stares from her classmates.

The tables outside are all empty, so they have their pick.

Tristan heads toward the one farthest from the sidewalk, and Brielle is grateful for the privacy it offers.

She sits opposite him, putting a spoonful of her fro-yo in her mouth as she frantically debates what to say. Her mind is a complete blank. What do people even talk about on dates?

"What would you say is your special talent?" he asks, ending her debate on conversation topics.

"My special talent?" she asks.

"Yeah, aside from being a wiz in the kitchen. What's your superpower?"

Brielle pauses. She should say there's nothing outside of making a mean cheesecake. But for some reason she doesn't want to evade the question. This is her first date, and something about Tristan makes her trust him. "Okay. Well, I can always tell when someone is lying."

"Really?" Tristan's arms are crossed over the table, his gaze fixed on her, and Brielle notices he hasn't touched his fro-yo.

"Try me," she invites, surprising herself with how flirtatious she sounds.

Tristan purses his lips and tilts his head. "Alright. I'll spout random things about myself and you tell me if they're true or not."

She nods, accepting the challenge.

"I'm seventeen," he says.

"True."

He nods. "I was in New Jersey before I came here."

Her lie alarm goes off. "False."

"Lucky guess," he says. "In fact, I was in Twin Buttes before this."

"Even though that sounds like it would be a lie, that's true," Brielle says with a giggle. "And it's pronounced 'byoots' not 'butts.'"

"I know, it's just funnier that way." He chuckles. "Okay, here's another one: my favorite color is blue."

The signal in her chest goes off again, and she shakes her head. "What is it really?"

"Wow, you're good at this," he says. "Don't judge, but my favorite color is actually purple."

His hand reaches up to his neck and fingers a smooth purple gem that she hadn't noticed hanging from a cord around his neck. Is it her imagination, or is the gem glowing slightly?

"Alright, how about this?" She looks up from his necklace to his face, and though his expression remains playful, there's a serious glint in his eyes. "I'm an alien prince from a far away planet, and I'm here on a mission to find others like me."

Grinning big at his obvious lie, Brielle pauses and stares at him for a long moment, waiting for the lie radar to signal inside her brain. But it never does. Her grin fades. Something isn't right. She replays his words again in her head, wondering if she could have possibly misheard him.

"Wait...what?" she asks, the nervous ball in her gut twisting for a new reason.

He leans closer. "I'm an alien prince on a mission to find others like me," he repeats. "Is it true or a lie?"

Brielle shakes her head and leans back on the bench, compelled by the sudden urge to create distance between them. He isn't lying. That means he truly believes what he's saying.

What has she gotten herself into?

He leans closer still. "You know, don't you. You know I'm not lying."

She clears her throat and looks around, anywhere but at him. "What time is it? I should probably get going."

"This isn't a joke, Brielle," he says, all play gone from his tone and expression. "I really am an alien prince. The Heir to be the next Gemini Zodiac Guardian, to be exact. Seventeen years ago, my planet was attacked by the greatest evil in the Universe, and I was sent to Earth for protection, along with twelve other Zodiac Guardian Heirs. Now it's my responsibility to locate them, and I believe you might be one of them."

Alarm bells were ringing before, but now they're a siren, a cascade of screaming for Brielle to get out of there.

Tristan believes every single thing he just said to her. He's insane! And absolutely not the kind of person she should be involving herself with, not on the eve of her possible adoption. She needs to be normal, and this guy is as far from normal as it gets.

"I really do have to go." She puts her hands on the table and stands up to leave.

"Please, wait." He shoots up and puts his hand on top of hers. "I had a vision about you. You're in danger."

How could his touch burn in the most delicious way even as his words make her want to run?

"Whatever you're involved in, I just can't right now, Tristan," she says, pulling away. "I have to go." She hops over the bench and takes her uneaten fro-yo to the garbage can.

"At least let me drive you," he implores, walking after her.

"No, my bike is at the school, I can get it on my own."

To her relief, he doesn't follow as she walks back toward their school.

How could she have so grievously misjudged him? Tristan's a bucketful of crazy in a charming, handsome package. And she has no room for crazy in her life. She has enough of her own crazy to sweep under the rug.

Disappointment stings Brielle's eyes. The attraction, the date, it had all felt like a sign that things were looking up. That she might deserve to have what others take for granted.

That she could be…normal.

Straightening her shoulders, she shakes off the feeling that this is an omen. At least now she can focus on what's really important. The only thing that had ever been important.

Find a family.

Belong.

7

TRISTAN

D ammit.
   Dammit.
Dammit.

Tristan watches Brielle hurry away, her shoulders hunched around herself protectively. He went in too hard, too fast.

What was he thinking? He's never done that before. There's a formula—smile, connect, ask some questions about their parents, probe for anything unusual.

This time he smiled. She smiled. They connected.

And that's where he lost it.

Because the sense of connection was different to anything he's ever experienced. It threw the formula out. And then she said she could sense lies. Could that be a superpower? Could she be…

Shaking his head, Tristan heads back to his car. The vision this morning has got him on edge. Add that to the growing uneasiness as they keep coming up empty handed, town after town, and he let the impatience get a hold of him.

Until he learns otherwise, it was nothing more than that.

And now Brielle's hightailing it, thinking he's one short of a baker's dozen. Climbing into the car, Tristan grips the steering wheel. It's time to do some digging.

Taking a left at the end of the block, Tristan glances in the rear view mirror. It's a habit Zarius instilled in him from the day he learned to drive. *Always be aware of your surroundings, Tristan. You're not the only one looking for the Zodiac Heirs.*

A group of girls are entering Creamy Dreams and a flash of blonde catches the light. Cassandra. Will she be killed by a Skin? Will he fail to get to her in time?

And why the hell does Chardis go after her in the first place?

Tristan's knuckles turn white as he stops at a set of traffic lights. The public library is only a couple of blocks away—always the first place to check when they arrive in a new town. And today, more than ever, he needs answers.

His cell dings as he parks the car, Tess's name lighting up the screen.

You at the library?

Tristan smiles. Great, he's becoming predictable.

Yep. If all goes well, I'll be getting dirty.

Most people of this generation don't realize that there's a wealth of information that doesn't exist on the internet. It's found in the archives and basements of libraries. Under about six feet of dust.

I'll head over. I've got some photos for you to check out.

And I'll bring brownies.

"I do love you, Tess." Tristan chuckles as he tucks his cell back in his pocket.

Tristan pauses outside the library. It's an old building like many of them are, brick without a lot of windows. But it's not the one from his vision. Not large enough. No sense of familiarity.

Pushing open the door, Tristan breathes in the scent of

books and—he tilts his head—is that cinnamon? And sugar? A soft chime echoes somewhere in the back and he hears the sound of a paper bag scrunching up, then rushed, uneven footsteps.

Seems the librarian has a limp. And they just finished some cinnamon donuts.

Tristan walks through the shelves of books, not really paying attention. Most libraries have the fiction section up the front, people never realizing there's an evil out there far scarier than the ones crafted in the pages.

Because this one is real.

The nonfiction is always relegated to the back, which is fine by Tristan. He's not here to hang out away from prying adult eyes like so many people his age are. He's here for information.

The smell of sugar and cinnamon gets stronger, and the area opens out to reveal a large desk to the left. An older man, tall and slightly gray, is standing with his back to Tristan, stacking books on a trolley.

Tristan approaches the desk, pulling up a smile as he waits.

"Internet computers are to the left," the man mutters without turning around. "Don't forget to fill in the sign-in sheet."

"Thanks, but I wasn't after the computers."

The man turns around, the books he was about to put down still in his hands. Tristan blinks, trying to hide his surprise. The guy has a patch over his left eye.

"I don't validate parking, either."

Tristan recovers his grin. "Well, that's disappointing. I was hoping to spend a bit of time here."

The man's only visible eye narrows slightly. "We close at five."

"Noted, ah…"—Tristan glances at the man's name badge

—"Alden." He dials up the biggest smile he can. "I've got an assignment for school. It's on the history of Mirror Point."

Alden puts down the books with a *thwump*. "The Mirror Point Women's Society has a website with all the information you'll need." He points to the computer bank at the back of the room. "Don't forget to sign in."

Tristan grits his teeth behind his smile. This dude has to be the most unhelpful librarian he's ever met. Tristan checked out that website during math and all he learned was that people didn't like smiling much back then and that cross-stitch classes are on Wednesday nights.

"It's just that I really need to get an A on this assignment." Tristan leans forward. "My parents said if I don't, they'll send me to stay with Aunt Ida for the summer break." He makes a show of shuddering at the thought of visiting his non-existent aunt.

Alden grunts, clearly communicating he doesn't care what Tristan's summer break looks like. "Local history is down there," he indicates with his chin.

"Much appreciated, Alden," Tristan says cheerfully. He needs to keep this guy on his side, even if he's determined to be a cranky pirate rather than a helpful librarian.

The local history section is exactly where Alden indicates, but it still takes Tristan a minute to find it. Not only is it in the bottom corner, it's much smaller than he expected. Most places he's been to, the section documenting the history of the town has any book ever published on the area. And it's placed far more prominently.

A quick scan of the spines doesn't give Tristan much hope. There are only seven books. And three of them are on cross-stitch. Taking the others to a nearby table, he flips through them.

Nothing jumps out as worth investigating further. Established back when most places around here were. Population not worthy of mentioning. Their claim to fame is their annual embroidery fair. Mirror Point has to be the most vanilla town he's ever come across.

Taking one of the books back to the front desk, Tristan figures he can at least have a closer look at the pictures of some of the buildings. Maybe he'll recognize one from his vision. He finds Alden where he left him as if the man turned to stone once Tristan walked away. Alden watches Tristan put the book down on the counter so closely that Tristan wonders what kids have done in here before. Booby trapped a book with a mouse trap? TNT? Frowning dust?

Tristan keeps his posture relaxed. "Who would've thought that many people would travel so far for an embroidery fair, huh?" Alden doesn't respond but Tristan doesn't expect him to. "Are there any other books?"

"That's everything."

"Are you sure? I was kind of hoping to write about something...cool."

Alden arches a brow. "And the art of the slip stitch isn't?"

"Whip stitch was probably the only one that caught my eye, to be honest. Look, I'm more thinking of"—Tristan's eyes light up as if he just thought of something—"something like alien sightings! Now that would be cool."

Alden's brow looks like it might have atrophied up there. "Nope. Sorry. You got the wrong town."

"I read this story once about this alien pod landing in a field. There are a lot of fields around here—"

"Nope. No pods."

"What about downstairs? Are there any extra books—"

"Nope."

Before Tristan can open his mouth to ask about any strange murders or deaths, Alden has turned away. "We're closing soon."

Tristan deflates. You'd think he'd be used to dead ends by

now, but for some reason this one stings even more than they did back in the beginning. It's just that with the vision, with meeting Cassandra so quickly. Then the moments with Brielle.

It'd felt like this time was different.

Tristan turns away. "Thanks, Alden. You've been really helpful."

There's no answer behind him, but Tristan didn't expect there to be. Alden is probably sterilizing everything Tristan touched in case smiling is contagious.

He's just closed the door when Tess rounds the corner. She stops, surprised. "You've finished already?"

"Yeah. Library closes at five."

Tess glances at her watch. "But it's only four thirty."

Tristan flops onto a bench seat facing the street. "Did you know size matters when it comes to your embroidery needle?"

"I can't say that I did." Tess slides in next to him. She passes him a container, several glistening brownies inside. "But now I know who to go to if I'm ever making a sampler."

Tristan takes out a fudgy slice of awesomeness, trying to focus on the sweet sugar dancing over his tongue as he takes a bite. He chews for a few moments, waiting for the buzz he always gets with Tess's brownies. When it doesn't come, he sighs. "I saw both girls from my vision today. They're at the school."

"You did?" Tess presses her hands between her thighs, a sure-fire sign she's excited, but he doesn't look at her.

"I still need to find out whether Cassandra, the blonde girl, could be a match. Brielle, the other one." The one with the hair the color of coffee and eyes the color of rich moss. "She's an orphan."

This time, Tess doesn't move. "And?"

"She said she can detect lies."

"And?" This time, Tess's voice is cautious. She's picked up that Tristan isn't matching her enthusiasm.

"I told her the truth and she looked at me like I needed to be committed."

"Oh."

"Yeah, oh." Tristan's head falls into his hands. "I didn't keep my cool, Tess."

Tess's warm hand falls on his shoulder. "You've never done it like that before, Tristan. What happened?"

Brielle felt…different. Tristan pushes to his feet, his body feeling like a live wire. "Because that vision was a reminder, Tess. We're running out of time."

Chardis is starting to kill.

Tess looks up from the bench, her gaze soft. So full of patience. "She's an orphan, that's one step closer."

"So was Sophie," Tristan points out. And Anne. And Danika.

They were all lovely. And none of them turned out to be a Zodiac Heir let alone his Gemini Twin.

"And she says she can detect lies."

Tristan throws Tess an unimpressed look. "One, you just need to be good at reading people to do that. Two, lie detection isn't the most offensive power when it comes to fighting off Skins."

Three, when he told Brielle the truth, she looked like she'd be happy never to see Tristan again. Not exactly Gemini Twin material. Tristan flops back onto the bench beside Tess. That's what's gotten to him.

It's the fact that it doesn't look like Brielle is…*her*.

"Here." Tess holds out a sheaf of papers. "Maybe this will give us something. I printed any images I could find of buildings in this area that could match. Big. Empty."

Tristan shakes his head, a rueful smile tugging at his lips. This woman is like Flubber, she can bounce back no matter what. He takes the pages, scanning the top one. "Nope." He flips to the second one, barely glancing at it. "Nope."

Great, now he's starting to sound like Alden.

The third, the fourth, then the fifth are all rejected. None of them feel familiar. He passes the sheaf back to Tess and the container of brownies. Even they've lost their ability to lift his mood right now. "Surprise, surprise. Nothing."

Tess slips an arm around his shoulder. "I know this is taking longer than any of us expected. Especially after Zarius found you when you were a baby."

Tristan doesn't point out he's seventeen. That's seventeen years of searching. Seventeen years of zilch.

"But we'll find them, Tristan. I know we will."

The quiet conviction in Tess's voice wraps around him. He straightens. "We have to."

The alternative isn't something anyone wants to consider.

Tess smiles. "What would you normally do next? Those times you've come up empty handed."

"You mean *all* the other times?" Tristan asks wryly. Despite that, he leans back, staring in thought. "Looked for more clues. Didn't give up."

"Exactly." Tess squeezes his knee before standing up. "If you were genetically related, I'd say you inherited your determination from Zarius."

Tristan stands too, drawing her into a hug, realizing Tess's unwavering belief in him has been his foundation his whole life. "I'll take that as a compliment."

Tess pulls back, her hand stroking his cheek before she pulls away. "Speaking of Zarius. I haven't seen him all day. He'll be hungry when he gets back."

Tristan chuckles. Tess's love language is cooking. "Cool. I'm going to drive around for a bit, it helps me think."

Tess nods. "I'll see you back at home."

As Tess takes a right to leave the parking lot, Tristan takes a left. He passes Creamy Dreams, surprised to find the place closed. Small towns aren't big on nightlife, it seems. When Mirror Point High appears ahead Tristan realizes he was unconsciously retracing his steps. The café where he scared off Brielle.

The school where he first set eyes on her.

Even if she's not the Gemini Twin, there's still a possibility she's a Zodiac Heir. Now the challenge is getting her to talk to him again.

Tristan pulls in, noting there are still a couple of cars parked out the front. It looks like he's going to be spending more time in cooking class.

The door to the school opens and Tristan sits up straight when he sees who's leaving. Her hair pulled up in a perky ponytail and her slim figure encased in workout gear, Cassandra skips down the stairs. She looks up, stopping when she spots Tristan.

Her smile grows as she sashays over. "Hey, can't stay away from the place, huh?"

Tristan grins, liking the teasing glint in her eye. "I thought I'd forgotten something." He holds up his cell. "Turns out it was in my pocket all along."

Cassandra's smile grows, telling Tristan she can't detect lies, unlike Brielle's claim that she can. "Good timing, then. I just finished training."

"Oh? What's your specialty?"

Her nose wrinkles as she looks down, twisting a leg one way then the other. "You can't tell from the calves? Sprints."

Tristan keeps his eyes steadfastly up. "Perfectly proportioned, I'm sure."

Cassandra bites her lip, flicking her ponytail over her shoulder as she leans against the open window. "How was the date with Brielle?"

Tristan shrugs. "It was cut short."

"Probably a good thing. You don't want to hang out with the likes of her."

"Oh?" Judging by those words, and the hard edge to them, Brielle was telling the truth—friends isn't how to describe Cassandra and Brielle's relationship.

"Anyone who spends time with her quickly learns it was a mistake."

Tristan keeps his posture casual, knowing he can't look too interested. "Sounds like there's some bad blood there."

"We were in the same orphanage as kids." She flicks her hair as if that's of no consequence. "There's a reason everyone else got adopted and Brielle didn't."

Holy pitch—Cassandra's an orphan!

Staying still and casual is hard work considering his brain wants to whoop out loud, but it seems Zarius has trained him well. Tristan hooks an arm out the window. "Well, if hanging with Brielle isn't a good idea, it looks like I'll have some spare time on my hands."

Cassandra angles her head, her lips tipping up. "It seems so," she purrs. Moving her bag around to her front, she rifles around. Pulling out a pen, she lifts a brow. "I'll give you my number."

Tristan's about to look for a piece of paper when she grasps his arm. Extending it, she leans down, her perfume tickling his nose as she holds his wrist. With eyebrows raised, Tristan watches as she scrawls her number on his arm.

"There." Cassandra smiles as she returns the pen to her bag. She steps back, cheeks a little pink. "I've gotta go or my dad will have a fit."

"I'll call you," Tristan tells her, retreating back.

She glances over her shoulder. "Don't make me wait too long."

Cassandra climbs into a shiny Mercedes—seems she hit

the jackpot when she got adopted—and drives off. Tristan glances at his arm, his skin tingling where the numbers are printed in small, round numerals.

That's two orphans at Mirror Point. And one willing to talk.

Tristan punches the air. "I'd call that progress."

He puts the car into gear, looking forward to telling Zarius and Tess the news, when something catches his eye. Tristan stills, glancing back at the school. The front steps are empty, the afternoon light casting long shadows down one side.

He takes his time scanning. The door's shut, there's no one around.

But still…

Tristan narrows his eyes, peering closer. Nothing moves, there's barely a breeze. Even the shadows are as peaceful as the rest of this town. He's probably overreacting after the rollercoaster today has been. But something keeps him there.

You're not the only one looking for Zodiac Heirs.

Tristan climbs out of the car, closing his eyes as he holds still. The softest sound reaches him. The subtle crunching of gravel.

Then the smell. The scent of a person.

Yet there's no one around.

Tristan's eyes fly open, his muscles flooding with adrenaline. There's no time to call Zarius.

He'll be facing this Skin alone.

8

BRIELLE

I*'m an alien prince and I'm here to find others like me...*
Tristan's words keep replaying in Brielle's head like an annoying song lyric all the way back to the orphanage.

He actually believes he's an alien prince. And what, he thinks Brielle's an alien, too? She's not sure what's more upsetting; that the only guy to ever ask her out thinks he's an alien, or that she's such an outcast that he thinks she's one as well.

I may be a freak who has visions and can sniff out lies like a bloodhound, but I'm certainly no alien. Thanks for the confidence boost, Tristan.

She sighs as she walks up the steps to the front door. She can't let this distract her. The Pierces will be here soon, and she needs to be her best self. She's just going to have to shake the unpleasant encounter off and get ready for the most important meeting of her life.

Getting to her room, Brielle tosses her backpack on her bed and takes the brush off her nightstand, running it through her hair for good measure. She examines her reflection in the mirror, pulling in a steadying breath. Her clothes aren't the most fashionable, but this outfit is the best she's got. At least the pant legs fit all the way down and have no rips like the others, even if they do now have a rip at the knee, thanks to Cassandra. While ripped and frayed jeans may be a fashion trend, they're just too real when it comes to being an orphan.

Before she can debate changing her pants, someone knocks at the door.

"Brielle." It's Sister Agatha.

Brielle turns around, her heart clambering up her throat. She's out of time.

"The Pierces are in the drawing room waiting for you," Sister Agatha says, the eager glint in her eye betraying her serene façade. "Are you ready?"

Brielle inhales slowly and nods, following Sister Agatha out of the room.

"Relax, Brielle," she says softly. "I'm sure you'll do fine. Just be yourself." Sister Agatha doesn't hug, but her kind tone wraps around Brielle, offering the same comfort that an embrace would.

Brielle nods, the walk to the drawing room feeling more like a procession down death row, with the eyes and whispers of her inmates following her as she passes.

Too quickly, they cross the threshold into the drawing room. Frank and Beatrice are sitting on the green paisley loveseat, and the welcoming smile they cast as she approaches helps to ease the tension that has Brielle's shoulders aching.

"It's a pleasure to see you again, Brielle," Frank says, standing and extending his hand.

Brielle shakes it in return, hoping to hell her palm isn't sweaty. "Trust me, the pleasure is all mine."

The couple chuckles at what was apparently a charming remark on her part, and she blushes.

"I'll leave you to your meeting," Sister Agatha says, bowing slightly before she leaves the room.

"Please, sit down," Beatrice invites, gesturing to the armchair opposite the loveseat.

Brielle sits, only vaguely noticing that the cushion is too stiff from lack of use. The drawing room is only used for one thing—meetings between adoptees and potential parents. Children are not allowed to lounge in here, and it's kept in pristine condition, looking as close to a cozy living room as it can despite the dark wood-paneled walls and hardwood floor. This is also the only room in the building with curtains on the large central window, a seafoam green to match the paisley furniture and the ancient rug.

The Pierces seem to look just as nervous as she feels, Frank tapping his fingers on his lap and Beatrice bouncing one leg.

"I'm not entirely sure how to start the conversation," Frank confesses with a laugh.

Brielle chuckles, releasing some of her own nervous energy. "I know what you mean." She bites her lip. "Well, what do you do for a living, Frank?"

"Ah, excellent question." He claps his hands. "I'm an investment banker with Sinclair Trustees, and Beatrice is a real estate agent slash freelance interior designer."

"Yes, so if this is a good fit for all of us, you'll never want for anything," Beatrice says warmly.

Brielle nods with a smile, appreciating the reassurance even though that's the furthest thing from her mind.

"Why don't you tell us a bit about yourself," Frank says, leaning forward and bracing his elbows on his knees. "Your hobbies, talents and goals for the future."

His mention of talents invites the memory of her disastrous date with Tristan. She's not going to make any big confessions with them as she did with him.

She adjusts her position on the armchair, crossing her legs. "Well, I love to cook and bake. I often help in the kitchen around here when I can, so I've learned a lot about classic American cuisine. Perhaps I can make you both dinner sometime?"

Frank and Beatrice exchange doe-eyed smiles, then turn back to her.

"That would be wonderful," Beatrice says, putting her right hand over her chest.

Brielle's smile widens. This is going well!

"And I'm very good with small children," she adds. "I spend a lot of time in the nursery." Babies and toddlers have little sense of guilt, so she rarely gets visions while caring for and playing with them. Not to mention they're too young to follow the gossip of the older kids, who never play with them anyway, so she's always welcome there. "So if you have any, I can be a big help."

Beatrice's smile falls, and before Brielle knows what hit her, a vision flashes. Beatrice and Frank are sitting in what looks like a doctor's office. "You have a uterine tumor," a man in a white lab coat informs Beatrice. "We'll have to remove it before it gets much larger. And I'm afraid, as a result, you may not be able to have children…"

The vision vanishes as abruptly as it had come, leaving behind a guilt that Brielle doesn't quite understand.

She tries to mask her facial features so the Pierces don't think she's just had a stroke.

Frank puts his hand on Beatrice's left knee, looking down at his lap as he says, "Unfortunately, we're unable to have children. That's why we're adopting."

Beatrice casts her gaze to the floor, a look of shame weighing her brow downward.

"I'm so sorry," Brielle says sincerely. Now she understands. Beatrice feels it's her fault that she can't give Frank a baby. Brielle wishes she could comfort her in some way. "Are you sure you want to consider me and not one of the younger children? Maybe a baby?"

Wait, what is she saying? The guilt has the wheel.

Beatrice shakes her head. "To be honest, we're getting a little too old to keep up with a baby." She offers a half-hearted laugh.

"We knew when we came here that we wanted someone older," Frank says. "Most people want a baby, so we're sure they'll have no trouble getting adopted without our help. Our life is more suited to a teenager, and we feel teens are selected less often and would need a home more. Would you agree?"

His words ring so true they sting Brielle's eyes. Babies and toddlers don't stay here long. The older a child gets, the less likely they are to be adopted. As she grew up, watching child after child get picked, she knew her chances were dwindling. It's why Brielle has all but given up.

"That's very generous of you," Brielle says. "I know I'll never be able to replace the child you couldn't have, but I hope I'll be able to make a pleasant addition to your family. If you'll have me, that is."

"We hope so, too," Beatrice says.

After a silence, Frank changes the subject to the kind of TV Brielle likes to watch, and they bond over a shared interest in Stranger Things and other shows.

The conversation moves easily from shows and movies to travel interests to favorite foods. At some point, it strikes Brielle that she feels very comfortable with them. There's no tension in her body anywhere, and their postures are more relaxed as well. No matter how much she tries to tamp it down, hope swells in her chest.

A *ding* has Frank reaching into his pocket for his phone and glancing down at it.

"Man how time flies," he says, stuffing it back in his slacks. "We're out of time for today, but this has been a really nice chat."

"I know you offered to make us dinner, but how about we take you out later this week?" Beatrice offers.

"We don't want to be too hasty about this decision, for both our sakes," Frank says. "We want to make sure you like us as much as we like you."

Brielle's lips are spread so wide it makes her face hurt. "I would love nothing more than to join you for dinner."

"Excellent!" Frank claps his hands again. "Friday night, say 5 o'clock? We'll pick you up?"

"Sounds perfect." Brielle's heart is so full of joy, it could burst inside her chest.

Frank and Beatrice stand to leave, and Brielle follows. Beatrice closes the distance and wraps her arms around Brielle in a motherly embrace. Surprise is quickly replaced by a slow warmth that radiates throughout her limbs. They've moved beyond shaking hands to hugging, and Brielle loves it.

When Beatrice withdraws, Frank comes in for a hug too, and Brielle delights in fantasies of many more such embraces. What would it be like to be able to call him "Dad"...

They say their goodbyes and the Pierces exit through the front door.

Sister Agatha walks up beside Brielle, her eyes twinkling. "That seemed to go well."

Brielle's smile is still painfully yet joyously etched on her face. "They invited me out for dinner on Friday," she manages to say without squealing.

"I'm happy to hear it. Seeing as you may not be around much longer, would you help me set the tables for dinner?"

As Brielle goes around the tables in the dining hall with silverware and napkins, all she can think about is the upcoming dinner with the Pierces, getting adopted by them, going on family outings with them. Her excitement is so overwhelming, she bounces on her heels as she makes her rounds, and nothing can take the smile off her face.

A hand lands firmly on her shoulder and turns her around. Her eyes fall on Marie, who looks angrier than usual.

"What did you do to me?" she hisses.

Despite her confusion and sense of violation at Marie's rough handling, fear stabs at Brielle's gut. "What are you talking about?"

"Don't play dumb!" Marie spits. "You cast some kind of spell on me, didn't you?"

"Spell?" Does Marie actually think Brielle's a witch?

Marie leans forward, her lip quivering. "You did something to me yesterday, when you told me to tell Sister Agatha about the wine. Ever since then, I can't think about anything else. I couldn't sleep at all last night. I keep reliving that night, and all I can see when I close my eyes are the things Sister Agatha will do when she finds out. She would ground me, make it so I can never leave. She might even black ball me from getting adopted, like she did you."

Brielle puts her hands up in a calming gesture. "Marie, it's really not that big of a deal. I mean, yeah, you shouldn't have snuck your boyfriend into the church, but Sister Agatha wouldn't interfere with your adoption chances as punishment. I bet she'll even go easier on you if you just tell her how bad you feel about it."

The vulnerability Marie had briefly displayed vanishes, and she stomps her foot and clenches her fists. "I didn't feel this way until you used your magic on me. You're making me obsess about it until it drives me insane!" Her eyes mist over and she looks like she's on the brink of crying.

"You can't honestly think—"

Marie points her index finger at Brielle's face. "Don't! Just make it stop, or I swear I'll find a way to prove you're doing this and make sure you can never do it to anyone else!" She spins around and storms out.

Brielle stands motionless, staring down at the table she hasn't finished setting. Marie is crazy, right? How can she accuse Brielle of putting some kind of hex on her? It's not her fault that Marie's obsessing about something she did that she clearly regrets doing. And now Marie is threatening to interfere with Brielle's plans.

Just keep your head down, Brielle. Tread lightly. Stay out of everyone's business and you'll get through this.

But even as Brielle shakes her head and continues placing forks and knives on napkins, she can't help but feel guilty.

It seems guilt is a tricky business, even when you know you're innocent.

9

TRISTAN

"Show yourself, you bastards," growls Tristan, taking a few steps further into the center of the parking lot.

Skins stay invisible till the last moment, knowing if someone is seen fighting off non-existent opponents it would raise too much attention.

But that doesn't mean they don't make the most of their advantage.

Tristan holds still, slowing his breathing. He simultaneously loosens his joints and locks his muscles. They'll get close before they reveal themselves.

But there's a reason he's meeting them out here in the open. The parking lot is layered with gravel. They won't be able to approach him silently.

There's a *scrape* to his left. A *crunch* behind. Two always come from the front. That's at least four.

Adrenaline floods Tristan as he spreads his legs, finding his center of gravity.

The blow he was expecting still slams through him like a hammer. His head snaps to the side, the punch landing him squarely in the jaw. Tristan absorbs the pain and the punch, gritting his teeth. A trickle of blood oozes from his lip.

Now he knows where the first one is.

His arm whips out, dealing a punch of his own. There's an *oomph* and a man materializes before him, two more taking shape. There will be another behind him.

A leg flies out and Tristan ducks, his own foot shooting out to sweep the Skin he just punched. As the man crashes to the ground, Tristan leaps up, throwing all his strength into the uppercut that smashes into the next Skin's jaw. The man launches into the air, arcing backward before slamming into the ground.

"That's two down," Tristan growls.

The Skin on his right roars, his eyes black with fury. He leaps at Tristan, his fists at the ready.

As he's about to connect with Tristan's chest, Tristan grasps his meaty fist and jerks. The man's launched forward and Tristan kicks his back so he spears into the hard ground.

"That's three," Tristan pants, wiping the blood from the edge of his mouth.

He expects the man when he grabs him from behind, letting him yank his arms back. The Skin's hands are like hot steel, the power of Chardis flowing through him. Tristan's tendons scream as they're stretched, but he waits.

The Skin will never see the flip coming. A twist and leap, using the man like a fulcrum, and Tristan will have the upper hand again.

Except Tristan doesn't register the blow to his solar plexus coming. He goes to double over except the Skin behind him holds him up. It leaves Tristan open and vulnerable when the next one slams into him, wrenching out a groan. And the next.

And the next.

Pitch. There's a fifth guy. And he's figured he could stay invisible while his four friends were making a ruckus.

The final Skin appears, his broad face twisted with a grin. "Surprise," he sneers.

The next punch slams into Tristan's face, and it feels like it hammers his brain. For a brief moment, pinpoints of pain dance before him. He lets himself sag, wincing when the Skin holding him jerks him upright.

The Skin who pummeled Tristan steps forward and grips his chin. Leaning in, he shoves his face close. "How many are there?"

"Technically thirteen seeing as there are two Geminis," Tristan drawls out, every word tasting like blood.

The crack across his face doesn't surprise Tristan, but it still stings. He grins, knowing the blow was driven by frustration.

"How many Zodiacs are here?" the Skin shouts.

Tristan allows himself two panting breaths. Two shallow gulps of oxygen, hoping it's enough for his battered body to do what needs to be done next.

"Just me." Tristan winks. "Unless you have some royal blood no one knows about."

The Skin steps back, glancing over Tristan's shoulder. "Once we're finished with him we'll bring his sorry ass in. Chardis will know how to get the answers we need."

The gap is all Tristan needs.

He pushes up from the ground, his legs kicking out hard and connecting with the Skin's jaw. The man's head snaps to the side with a *crack* a second before his body crumples to the ground.

But Tristan doesn't have time to see whether he'll be getting back up, he maintains the momentum he gained when he launched off the Skin. He backflips through the air, arching over the Skin who was holding him.

By the time Tristan's landed, the Skin has spun around, his hands raised and ready to fight. Even as he does it, though, his feet shuffle back.

Tristan straightens, knowing he's about to flee. Especially once he realizes three of his comrades already have.

The Skin looks around, his face twisting in a snarl when he sees he's been abandoned. He glares at Tristan. "You won't always win," he spits before sprinting off.

"Says the guy running away," Tristan shouts after him.

He straightens, cataloging the bruised ribs and face that feels like mashed potato. The sooner he gets home to heal, the better.

He steps up to the Skin still lying in the gravel. Although he's the one who inflicted most of the damage, Tristan doesn't take any pleasure from seeing the sharp angle the man's neck is at.

Before Chardis swallowed this man's soul, he could've been anyone. A postman with a family. A staunch vegetarian. A brother, son, father. Maybe all of those.

Swallowing the blood still flooding his mouth, Tristan turns away. There are a lot of things that suck about the war he was born into, but killing Skins is at the top of that list. He jogs back to his car, pretending pain isn't screaming at him to never move again. The Skins will be back. They never leave their dead behind. They don't want any questions asked.

He's glad the drive home is short. Tristan can already feel his face swelling, and breathing is becoming difficult. Each inhale has his ribs feeling like they're cracking all over again.

As he opens the front door, he hears Tess call out. "Zarius, is that you?"

She gasps when she sees Tristan in the hall. "Tristan! What happ—"

She stops herself before she finishes the question. It's obvious what happened. Skins happened.

Tess goes to touch him but Tristan holds a hand up. "Maybe after the nanites?"

Her arms dropping, Tess nods. Face tense, she turns away. "I'll get them."

Tristan lowers himself into a chair in the kitchen, waiting while Tess goes down to the basement. The nanites are kept in a safe along with any other alien technology that arrived with him in his pod.

Like the gems.

Tess rushes back a few moments later, placing a box on the table. "How many?" she asks as she takes out a vial.

"I thought there were only four."

Tess arches a brow. "You were taken by surprise?"

Tristan looks away, glad his face is purple and blue so she can't see his flush. "I'm thinking we keep that between the two of us…"

Tess holds out a glowing vial, the color within shifting from orange to yellow and back again. "Here."

Tristan extends his arm and she expertly injects it. Tess has done every first aid course under the sun. "Thank pitch for microscopic, bio-engineered molecules, huh?"

In a few hours it'll be like the fight never happened thanks to the accelerated healing the nanites will busily carry out.

Tess remains where she is, watching him closely. "Tell me what happened."

"I went back to the school and ran into Cassandra. I sensed them after she left." Tristan frowns. "I killed one."

Tess clasps Tristan's knee. "He would've tortured and killed you without blinking if given the order."

"And he would've done it with a smile, but it still doesn't make it any easier."

"I know," Tess sighs. "We just have to remember their humanity no longer exists thanks to Chardis."

Tristan straightens as he remembers something else, hissing as pain spears through his chest. "Before I finished him, he asked me how many Zodiacs were here."

Tess's eyes widen. "That's a good sign." She inhales sharply. "They think there could be more than one?"

"Maybe?" Tristan looks around, suddenly conscious Zarius isn't here. That Tess asked if it was him when he came in. "Where's Zarius? He'll want to know all this."

Tess bites her lip. "He hasn't come home yet."

"He's not answering his cell?"

Tess shakes her head, worry spilling from her eyes. "I'm sure he's just got caught up with something. You know how he is."

Zarius can be single-minded when he thinks he's found a lead. That could be it. Or he could've come across more Skins…

Tristan nods. "I'm sure he's fine. Like you said, Zarius has probably lost track of time." He picks up the box with the vials of nanites. "I'll put this stuff back, then go for a drive, just in case."

Tess shoots to her feet. "No!" She modulates her tone as she realizes she almost shouted the protest. "You're still healing. Let's give him another hour or two. It's not even dark yet."

Tristan's about to object but the pleading in Tess's eyes stops him. "Sure," he smiles. "Zarius wouldn't want us jumping into anything."

Which is true.

He keeps telling Tristian patience is the one quality he hasn't mastered yet. If Tristan had spent a little more time thinking, maybe the fifth Skin wouldn't have snuck up on him.

Tristan goes to jog down the stairs but quickly stops. Although he's definitely feeling better, it looks like there's more work for the nanites than he thought. Inside the basement, he pauses as he sees his pod.

The shuttle he arrived in as a baby.

Smooth and egg-shaped, it glows with the same muted power the vials do. Thirteen of those landed on the same day as his did. At first, they'd assumed it was in the same general location as his, but as they'd come up empty handed, they'd had to widen their search.

The Skins think there could be more than one…

Could Mirror Point be their break? Maybe Cassandra is a Zodiac Heir.

Tristan's breath pulls in sharply. Maybe Brielle is.

One of them might be his soulmate, and despite Cassandra's flirting, it's Brielle's wide green eyes that fill Tristan's mind.

Shaking his head, Tristan punches in the code to the safe. Inside, another simple black box lies in the gloom. The gems. Not all twelve, seeing as some of the Zodiac Heirs already had theirs, but six of them.

They'll be the only way to truly know if Brielle or Cassandra are destined to join the fight against Chardis. The moment they'll be united with their stone it will glow; their power will be amplified. Tristan grips the purple tourmaline hanging around his neck, aware there's a second, identical stone in the box.

The stone that belongs to his Gemini Twin.

Placing the box with the vials beside it, Tristan closes the safe with a click.

Zarius's voice trickles through his mind. *Patience isn't a weakness.*

"Well, it sure isn't one of my strengths," Tristan mutters.

Thinking of Zarius has Tristan looking around. He's already set up the basement as their command center. The back wall is covered with images and printouts. Most are cut-outs from newspapers, some are articles from alien fan sites. All researching landings of pods around the continent. The side wall has a bank of computer screens, several linked to the surveillance cameras around the house, others scanning the internet for the information they're desperately searching for.

He's about to head back up the stairs when a new slip of paper catches Tristan's attention. It's nothing more than a yellow note, but he knows it wasn't there yesterday. He and Zarius spend hours poring over the information they accumulate, trying to find clues or patterns. If anything seems to be of interest, it gets pinned up on the wall.

Stepping closer, Tristan sees it's an address. His pulse leaps—maybe it's the address of the building from his vision! Glancing over his shoulder to confirm Tess isn't coming down to check why he's taking so long, he quickly slides in front of one of the computers and shuffles the mouse. The screen comes to life and Tristan enters the address into Google maps.

The little red pin pops up in a square of farmland. Zooming in, Tristan discovers it's an old warehouse. Although it's not what he was hoping for, he can see why Zarius thought it might be interesting. Isolated, but not too far away, it looks like an ideal place to hide a pod.

Finding one of the other pods would be pretty cool, but would it keep Zarius away the whole day? With no texts or calls?

"Only one way to find out," Tristan murmurs, heading to the stairs. He goes to take two at a time, but when the first leap jars through his ribs, he slows. The nanites had better work their magic before he gets to Zarius or playing down the fact his ass got whooped is going to be hard.

"All okay?" Tess calls out as Tristan locks the door to the basement.

"Yep. All good," Tristan states cheerfully. "I'm just going to chill in my room, give the nanites a chance to do what they do."

There's no way Tess is going to let Tristan go and look for Zarius straight after the fight with the Skins. Which means sneaking out.

Time to put all those lessons on stealth mode into practice.

Thankful for the carpet in the hall, Tristan keeps himself as light footed as possible as he heads to the back door. Turning the knob slowly but steadily, he waits for the resistance that tells him the latch is moving. He finds it and tightens his grip, slowly twisting it further.

Click. Tristan freezes, holding his breath, but there's no sign of Tess coming down the hall. Slipping through, he repeats the process to close it. Out in the backyard, he pulls in a breath of fresh, calming air. Saying Tess is going to be unimpressed when she finds him gone is an understatement.

But if he finds Zarius, then forgiveness will quickly follow the fierce frowns.

The backyard is little more than lawn and a clothesline surrounded by an eight-foot hedge. Tristan lines up the prickly green fence. He'll be able to clear it, but landing on the other side is going to hurt like pitch.

Stepping into a sprinter's stance, he jams his back foot into the ground. He'll need to gain as much speed as he can before—

"I don't think so."

Tristan's push off is abruptly interrupted by Tess's statement. He stumbles as all the momentum he was trying to launch has nowhere to go, floundering for a few steps before righting himself.

Tess raises a brow. "I'm just going to chill in my room?

Really, Tristan? You never do that, even when we actually want you to."

Dammit. Tristan's shoulders sag. "I found an address. I think that's where Zarius went."

She's already shaking her head. "No. You're not well enough, yet."

Tristan takes a step forward. "But—"

"No!" Tess seems almost as startled as Tristan as she half-shouts the word. She pulls in a breath. "I'm just as worried as you are. I don't need to be worried about you, too."

Tristan snaps his mouth closed on the argument he was about to pose. Tess is wringing her hands, something he hasn't seen her do often.

"If Zarius doesn't come home tonight and we don't hear from him, we'll go searching in the morning. Together."

Tristan nods, not liking the knot of worry that's clenching his gut. "Okay." He smiles. "I reckon he's found another pod and got trapped inside."

Tess's returning smile is strained. "I hope so."

Slipping an arm around her shoulder, Tristan leads her back inside. "Let's get dinner organized. If he finds the emergency exit button, he's going to be hungry when he gets back."

Holding the door open for Tess, Tristan sends out a silent message to the man who's been far more than a guardian and a mentor. Zarius has raised him as his own son.

You'd better be back by morning, Zarius.

Tristan doesn't want to think what it could mean if he's not.

10

BRIELLE

"So the new guy is kinda loopy, huh?"

Brielle and Adalind sit at their station in cooking class before the bell rings, savoring the last few precious seconds of alone time they have.

Brielle nods, keeping an eye on the door for Tristan. "Yeah, I should've known a good-looking guy like that was too good to be true."

"He actually thinks he's an alien?" Adalind's smile is joking, but there's a spark in her eyes that Brielle doesn't recognize.

Brielle doesn't want to be the one to start rumors. She's had her fair share of gossip started about her, and no one deserves to be plagued by them. She shakes her head. "He was probably just messing with me. Some kind of joke to screw with my head."

Adalind purses her lips, then shrugs. "Well then, it's his loss. Some better guy will come along, and he'll be even hotter."

"Maybe. I shouldn't be thinking about boys right now

anyway. The only thing that matters right now is keeping the Pierces' favor."

"I'm so glad your visit went well with them," Adalind squeals. "Just two more days till your big dinner!"

The spark of excitement and glee that Brielle had felt when they left yesterday flares back to life. She can't wait for Friday!

Just as the smile starts to spread on her face, Tristan walks through the classroom door. Brielle straightens her lips and looks away in case he thinks she was smiling at him. As he approaches their station, she's aware that his eyes are on her, the heat of his gaze making her heart flutter and her nerves sizzle even as she tells herself she wants nothing to do with him.

He sits beside her, his sweet, musky scent teasing her nostrils, as if to whisper, "come closer."

She doesn't acknowledge him as he settles into his stool, and the uncertainty over where to put her gaze is almost maddening.

"Hey," he says, nudging her arm with his elbow.

She doesn't want to be rude, so she flicks a glance at him and says, "Hey," in return.

"Listen," he whispers, leaning closer. "I'm sorry about yesterday. I didn't mean to freak you out. Can we just start over? Friends?" He holds out his open hand.

Tristan isn't the kind of person she should be friends with, but she definitely doesn't need any more enemies.

"Sure, friends," she whispers. She stares at his open hand for a moment, debating accepting such a gesture. But the desire to touch him is too strong, and finally, she can't hold back anymore.

She grasps his hand.

Warmth radiates over every millimeter of her palm at his touch, and before she can guess whether or not he feels it too, he gasps. Brielle looks up at him. His eyes are magnetic, a sort of gravitational pull locking hers to them. She's struck by how blue they are, and how comforting it feels to be held by them. She could stare into these eyes forever, curl up into them and disappear into their crystalline abyss.

The classroom door closes, the sound shaking Brielle out of the spell.

She jerks her hand free a little too forcefully and says, "*Just* friends."

He nods, accepting her terms. "You're staying at school all day today?"

Brielle tenses. Please don't let him ask to sit with her at break. "Ah, yeah. But—"

"Good. Make sure you do. It's the safest place for you right now."

Before Brielle can ask what that means, Tristan pushes to his feet. "I'm so sorry, Ms. Brom. But my mom just texted. We forgot I have an appointment."

Brielle frowns. She didn't hear a message, not even the buzzing when a cell is on silent.

Ms. Brom crosses her arms. "I find that hard to believe."

Tristan grins as he walks toward her, holding up his cell. She reads it, her brows low. "You'll need to wait here while she contacts the front office."

But Tristan is already at the door, pushing it open. "I'll tell her when I meet her there. Hope the class goes well."

He's gone before Ms. Brom can say another word. Brielle pulls down the brows that had hiked up. What in the world just happened?

Ms. Brom starts instructing their next cooking assignment—homemade mac 'n cheese—and Brielle almost succeeds in getting through the period without thinking about the boy who is far too tempting, and far too great a threat to everything she truly wants. His weird actions just proved that.

When the bell rings for break, Brielle can't get to the cafeteria quickly enough. She hasn't been able to focus on anything but touching Tristan's hand since this morning, and she needs the mental distraction she's sure conversation with Adalind will give her. Why can't she get this guy out of her mind?

She gets her lunch tray and sits at their usual table, absentmindedly squirting a packet of ketchup onto her burger as she scours the hundreds of faces for the one she's waiting for.

Unfortunately, Cassandra's face is the one she finds, and Cassandra sees her, too. Like a Brielle-seeking missile, she zooms straight through the sea of students to Brielle's table.

Great. Maybe if she ignores her, Cassandra will just go away.

"Hi freak," Cassandra's venomously silky voice chimes over her shoulder.

No such luck.

"Don't you have anyone else to torture?" Brielle asks in as cool a tone as she can manage.

"I heard Tristan ditched you at Creamy Dreams," she says, bulldozing Brielle's calm façade. "What did you do to scare him off so quickly?"

Brielle rolls her eyes, disbelieving how quickly true events become distorted by the gossip wheel.

"Not that it's any of your business, but I was the one who walked out on him."

Cassandra throws her head back and lets out an insulting laugh. "I'm so sure."

The last thing Brielle wants is to put any kind of black mark on Tristan's social life as the new student. "I had to leave to meet with a couple that's interested in adopting me, as a matter of fact." A small tingle of satisfaction swirls in her chest as she confesses this to her childhood rival.

Cassandra's black-lined eyes widen in surprise, then squeeze shut as she buckles over giggling. "Oh, that poor couple! I wonder if they have any idea what they're in for. As a conscientious citizen, I should warn them."

Coming out of nowhere, Adalind pops up between them and pushes Cassandra back. "You'll do no such thing."

Cassandra gawks at Adalind, mouth agape. No one has ever touched Cassandra like that, and she seems just as stunned. Cassandra may be athletic, but she's not the type of girl to get into a catfight. Especially not at school.

Cassandra quickly reclaims both her composure and her catty mask. "You're right, they'll figure it out eventually. It's only a matter of time before they see the truth that I know only too well. No family worth having would ever adopt you."

The statement is like a slap in the face, the words stinging as they assault Brielle's ears.

"Oh and your loss with Tristan is my gain. We're going out this weekend." She winks, the gesture feeling more like she stuck her tongue out, then she saunters away to the table her clique has claimed as their lunch time throne.

In her wake, Adalind is still standing in a battle-ready stance in front of Brielle, flexing her fists at her sides.

"Forget about her." Brielle tugs on the bottom of Adalind's shirt. "Let's just try to enjoy our food."

Sneering in Cassandra's direction, Adalind pulls her tray closer and sits next to Brielle. "What is her problem with you, anyway? I mean, she's nasty to everyone, but why does she have such a target out for you?"

Brielle returns to dressing her burger. "Believe it or not, but little miss perfect grew up in the same orphanage I did."

Adalind's mouth rounds into a perfect O. "What? Seriously?"

"We actually used to be best friends before she got adopted."

Adalind leans in, starving for the juicy gossip Brielle's about to share. "What happened?"

Brielle has been fighting the memory the last few days, but now that it's been brought to the surface, she's helpless not to relive it.

"Sister Agatha told me Cassandra was about to be adopted by some parents I'd just met."

In fact, Brielle had rushed back to the room she shared with Cassandra as soon as Sister Agatha told her the news, her heart thumping with horror.

"Did you hear?" Cassandra's face beamed with the brightest smile as she came up to grab Brielle's hands. "I can't believe it's finally happening. I'm going to have a family, Bri! A real family!"

"Yes, I heard," Brielle said, unable to lift her brow for the deep frown that held it so heavily down. "About that, listen—"

"Maybe they can adopt you, too!" Cassandra went on, so full of excitement that she practically glowed like the sun. "We could be real sisters! Wouldn't that be wonderful?"

Brielle puts her face in her hands. "I found out some stuff... I had to warn her."

Brielle's heart had cracked inside her chest. Cassandra had been like a sister her entire life, and the thought of being sisters legally was truly wonderful. But it couldn't happen. Cassandra didn't know.

"Cass, that's not going to happen," Brielle had said, trying to find the right way to tell her best friend the truth.

Cassandra's doll face pinched in confusion. "What do you mean? You don't want us to be sisters? I know I've been spending a lot of time with Gabby lately, but you know you'll always be my best friend."

Gabby was a new girl at school who had recently been taking up a lot of Cassandra's attention. And while Brielle had to admit she'd been a little jealous of the two getting so close, she held no ill will about the friendship. Cassandra was allowed to have other friends. That was a natural part of growing up. Well, for most people...

"This has nothing to do with Gabby," Brielle prefaced. "Cassandra, I know the Sinclairs seem like they are the perfect parents, but they're not. Please, you can't let them adopt you."

As Cassandra stared at Brielle, her usually sunny amber eyes darkened. Her smile faded. She dropped Brielle's hands and stepped back. Cassandra was well-known for her quick temper, and Brielle had clearly set it off.

Drawing her hands down her face, Brielle looks at Adalind. "She wouldn't believe me. She thought I was jealous."

"Why are you trying to ruin this for me?" Cassandra had accused, her tone deep, angry. "You can't get adopted so you're trying to make sure I don't either?"

"No! I want you to have every happiness in the world. I want you to get adopted just as much as I want it for myself. But the Sinclairs are bad news. I'm just trying to protect you, you're my best friend."

Cassandra's golden curls ruffled around her face as her body tensed. The explosion was imminent. "So that's what this is about. I got a new friend and suddenly you'll do everything you can to keep me around. Even make up lies about my new parents. I can't believe you could be so selfish as to try to mess this up for me!" *Her pitch rose with each word, amping Brielle's desperation higher, too.*

"I love you like a sister, you have to know that," Brielle pleaded. "I swear this has nothing to do with jealousy or selfishness or anything that petty. I would never keep you from achieving the dream we both have, but if you go with the Sinclairs, that dream will become a nightmare."

Cassandra shook her head, stalking closer. "You don't think I know what happened? I heard from the other girls that the Sinclairs were interested in you first, and that they rejected you. I had hoped I could change their minds, plead on your behalf and they'd take both of us. But now... Now that I see you'd go to such lengths to ruin this for me because you ruined your own chances... I'm glad I'm getting out of here, and leaving you behind."

Brielle had no other choice. She had to confess. If she didn't tell Cassandra, so much more than just their friendship would be destroyed.

"You want to know the truth?" Brielle yelled, stomping her foot in aggravation. "They didn't reject me, I rejected them. I saw the horrible things that Mr. Sinclair had done. He hurts women, Cass! He likes inflicting pain. I didn't want to have to live with a father like that, so I outed him and begged Sister Agatha not to let him adopt anyone here. He's dangerous."

Cassandra narrowed her eyes into slits. "What do you mean, you saw?"

A lump instinctively constricted Brielle's throat, her body's natural defense against spilling her secret. She'd never told anyone, not even Cassandra. She didn't want Cassandra to think she was crazy. But now, she had to, to save her friend.

"I get...visions," Brielle confessed, the soft volume of her voice such a contrast to the yelling of a moment ago that her ears rang. "I see the bad things people have done, things they feel guilty about. You know how I can always tell when you're lying? Well, it's not always just a sense. Sometimes, I see the truth, like it's happening to me."

Cassandra's eyes gradually widened as Brielle spoke, her head shaking harder and harder. "You're crazy," she whispered. "The other girls always told me things about you, but I never believed it. I defended you. I don't know you at all." Her doll face furrowed into the nastiest snarl Brielle had ever seen. "You're not my sister, you're not my friend, and I truly hope the Sinclairs

*move me far away from here because I never want to see you
again."*

*The sheer hatred in Cassandra's voice took Brielle's breath
away, and she'd stood frozen, heartbroken, as Cassandra grabbed
the bag she'd been packing and stormed out of the room for the last
time.*

Brielle shrugs. "I think in the end, Cassandra was happy
that they didn't move her far away, because it meant she got
to torture me every day."

"That's awful," Adalind says, the fry she's been holding
during the story likely cold and dry now. "So the folks that
adopted her are bad news? She seems happy with them. Or at
least with their money."

Brielle nods. "I'm glad I was wrong about them. I really
am. I worried about her for a long time. But after a year or so
of the hazing and turning everyone at school against me, I
got over it. I just wish things had gone differently."

"Why? You actually wish you were friends with that
hateful cow?" Adalind throws her fry onto her tray.

"If we'd stayed friends, she might not be so hateful,"
Brielle says.

"Or you might be just as nasty as she is. That's not a trade
I'd make."

Brielle smiles, wondering if Adalind is right.

"How did you know the guy was bad?" Adalind asks, the
familiar spark of intrigue in her narrowed eyes. "Cassandra's
father? You said you found out what he'd done and told on
him, but how did you find out?"

Brielle had vowed to never tell another friend about her
curse, and she isn't going to start now. "Just rumors I'd
heard," she lied. "And when I got close to him, I don't know, I
just sensed he was dangerous. I like to think I'm a good judge
of character."

"Well, no offense, but you don't have such a great track

record so far," Adalind teases. "First, you were best friends with the most heinous girl I've ever met. Then you got the hots for the new guy who's clearly a weirdo."

Brielle chuckles. "You do have a point."

She remembers her burger, whose top bun is still off, so she places it on top of the condiment-smothered patty and takes a bite. Of course, it's cold. Figures.

"I am curious, though," Adalind says, crossing her arms in front of her tray. "Ever get a sense about me?" She flares a playful eyebrow.

Brielle smiles with her mouth full of cold burger, then swallows. "I haven't, but I'm pretty sure you're a good egg."

Adalind puts her hands against her chest and blows out a breath through tight lips. "Good, I was afraid I was going to turn out to be some villain."

Brielle laughs. Adalind is the furthest thing from a villain she's ever known, and she's so grateful to have her as a friend. Glancing over at Cassandra at the popular table, Brielle is sure that the best friend change is an upgrade.

11

TRISTAN

As he strides to the front doors, Tristan knows he just went up a notch on Brielle's crazy meter. Considering he's supposed to pretend such an instrument doesn't exist, making sure she's safe then hightailing it is the last thing he should've done.

At least he didn't mention that humans possessed by dark matter intent on killing anyone they suspect is a Zodiac Heir could be after her...

But he had to make sure she and Cassandra were okay. Cassandra had readily agreed to a date.

Brielle agreed to being friends out of politeness.

Knowing he's done all he can for the moment, Tristan climbs back into the truck.

Tess glances at him, gripping her cell like it might ring any second. "They're both here?"

Tristan jams the truck into gear. "Both accounted for, both at school."

"Good." Tess lets out a breath. "Once we get Zarius back, we can figure out what to do."

Once we get Zarius back.

Pulling out of the school parking lot, Tristan sets his jaw. Damn straight they're going to get Zarius back.

The drive to the warehouse is a tense one. Zarius's cell has gone straight to voicemail since midnight. Tristan knows there's no way he'd let it go flat without contacting them.

If he's not here, they have no idea where he is.

If he is, it's hard not to worry about what they're going to find.

Tess's hands are a tight knot in her lap. She keeps glancing at the map on her cell as they head there, as if she's worried the little red pin is going to disappear any moment. Tristan focuses on the road. No matter what, they're getting Zarius back.

The houses of Mirror Point fall away as green farmland stretches around them. There's the odd tree, a few more cows, but little else. Isolated is good, Tristan tells himself. Less witnesses.

"We're getting close," Tess murmurs tensely.

Dust billows up on top of the rise ahead and Tristan slows. Tess glances around. "What's wrong?"

Tristan points to the particles slowly dissipating in the breeze. "There are others ahead."

And they haven't seen anyone for ages.

Pulling over, he turns the engine off. "I think we walk the rest of the way."

Tess nods, not questioning his decision. They haven't verbalized it, but they've both thought it—this could be a trap.

Parking the car among some bushes, they hike up the small hill. Tristan reaches the top first, and the moment he does, he jerks Tess back. "Skins," he hisses.

Tess nods and they go down to all fours, creeping back up and dropping to their stomachs. Three cars are parked haphazardly around a large warehouse.

That means at least six. The bastards always travel in pairs.

"Zarius," Tess whispers hoarsely.

Tristan scans the countryside, planning his entry. "I'll go down, you have the car ready to go."

Tess opens her mouth only to shut it. She might've learned to defend herself, but she's not an offensive fighter. Her shoulders sag. "Be careful."

Tristan grins. "We both know that's not my strong point."

She narrows her eyes. "Or the waffle tradition ends."

His grin dies. Who knows how many schools he'll have to enroll in yet. "Fine, then," he mutters. "But if Zarius goes full soldier on them, then you can't blame me for any bruises."

Tess relaxes just like Tristan knew she would. Talking about finding Zarius alive is the reassurance she needs right now.

Planting a hard kiss on her forehead, Tristan sprints for the first tree. Heart thumping, he presses himself against the rough bark. But there are no shouts of alarm, no shots fired. Crouching down, he watches the warehouse. There's no movement, but he didn't expect there to be. If there are Skins patrolling the outside, they'd be invisible.

All he needs is a sign…

A leaf flutters toward one of the walls, flicking and dancing on the wind. Tristan watches it with narrowed eyes. It trips up on an eddy then slams to a stop.

Bingo.

The Skin must flick it off, because it flips, trembles and resumes its random flight. One Skin beside the door. That means another on the opposite side. Holding his breath, Tristan counts. One, two.

And the bastard would be around the corner.

Another frantic run and he plasters himself against the next tree.

He waits to discover whether he's been seen. Nothing.

Five. Six. Seven.

Only a few yards to go. Please let these Skins be ambling like he's counting on.

Keeping his breathing under control, Tristan lines up the water tank nestled against the side of the warehouse. Silently, he streaks over the grass.

He reaches it, his whole body wired and tense. Waiting for a bullet to penetrate it. The breeze caresses his hair, cooling the sweat at his temple. Silence.

Holding still, Tristan angles his head. Zarius would spend hours having him stand in their constantly changing backyards, listening for crickets. Once he'd heard one, he'd have to locate it with nothing but sound.

And then he'd have to tell Zarius when it had started munching on a blade of grass.

It means Tristan hears the almost silent scrape of a shoe on gravel. The Skin's coming around the corner of the warehouse.

Slipping a hand into his pocket, he grips the contents.

He leaps, throwing a handful of chalk dust at where the Skin should be and the outline of a broad shouldered man instantly appears. It's all Tristan needs as he slams his arm into the man's neck. The man crumples, becoming visible as he loses consciousness, and Tristan catches him before he can hit the ground.

Dragging him around the back of the water tank, Tristan waits to repeat the process.

Dust. Strike to the neck. Make him disappear.

Another few precious minutes to make sure he hasn't miscalculated and there are more Skins patrolling the outside, Tristan studies the timber door. Probably creaky. Who knows what's on the other side.

Apart from at least another four Skins.

Invisibility sure would be good right now.

Actually, what would be better is his suit.

Every Zodiac Guardian possesses one, stored within their gem with advanced technology Tristan will never understand. Covering him from head to toe in a molded, protective shell, it would mean he could storm this warehouse wearing his own personalized shield.

But Zarius is a soldier, not royalty. There was no time to learn how to unlock the suit trapped inside Tristan's tanzanite gem before he jumped in the pod and left the exploding space station.

Zarius has been able to teach him everything but that.

Turning the door handle slowly and evenly, Tristan waits for the inevitable *creak*. When it fails to fracture the tense silence, he doesn't let out his pent up breath. He needs to get inside undetected first.

Slipping through, Tristan silently enters. And stops.

On the other side of the warehouse, Zarius is tied to a chair. Head drooping as blood drips onto his lap, six Skins circle him. Here in the warehouse, they haven't bothered with their invisibility. Their hands flex as they pace, their backs to Tristan.

They don't know he's here, which is a good thing.

But there's more than he'd hoped. Not such a good thing.

Without warning, one of the Skins steps in, slamming his fist into Zarius's face. A low groan slides through the warehouse and Tristan winces. Things must be bad for Zarius to be showing pain.

"Tell us where the Gemini Prince is," growls the Skin.

Zarius raises his bloody face to glare at the Skin. He spits a glob of blood at the man's feet. "Go. To. Hell."

A second Skin steps in, this time with an uppercut. And then another one. And another. "And once you tell us about his location, you can tell us about the others."

Tristan skims over the wall to a stack of wooden crates and slips behind them. The sound of fist hitting flesh assaults him again and he knows he doesn't have much time.

His only option is to take as many of them out before they know he's here.

He skitters a pebble from the opposite corner of the stack of crates and waits.

"Go check it out," mutters a voice.

Which tells Tristan babkas about how many are heading over.

He's already in fighting stance when a Skin rounds the corner. Tristan grabs his shirt, snaps the man's head back then jerks him down. Pain ricochets through Tristan as he slams the crown of his head into the Skin's nose and the man crumples.

The second Skin rushes around having heard the commotion. Tristan jams the palm of his hand into the man's chin. He collapses on top of his comrade.

There's silence and Tristan knows the other Skins are now suspicious.

Two down. Four to go.

"Dan? Ivan?"

Tristan takes two steps back, allowing him to keep a better eye on the two sides of the crate stack. If they're smart, they'll come around both sides at the same time.

The first man launches from the left, his face twisted in fury.

Angry. But not smart.

Three punches and the man is unconscious.

This time though, two men rush from both sides. Tristan runs and leaps onto the stack, takes two running steps then launches off the other side. The momentum flips him through the air and he lands on the ground on the other side.

Several startled faces stare at him.

Including Zarius. He mouths one word. "Tristan."

Tristan grins. "To the rescue."

From his left, a Skin snaps into motion, running at him. Tristan grabs the man, spins him to gain momentum, then releases him at Zarius.

Zarius's eyes widen as he sees the human projectile coming at him, but then does what Tristan hoped he would. At the last moment, Zarius stands and spins around. The Skin slams into the chair, knocking Zarius over, but also smashing the timber to pieces.

Zarius is on all fours on the ground, but free.

Tristan hears the swing at his head and he spins around, his return strike already in motion. It hits the Skin's chest, yanking out an *oomph* but it's not enough to down him. He staggers back, the desire for retribution twisting his face.

Tristan raises his fists, watching as a second Skin joins the first. The more who are on him, the fewer are on Zarius.

"I'm glad you brought a friend," Tristan growls. "It's more fun this way."

The Skins glance at each other before simultaneously launching at him. Tristan is ready for them. Fists connect with flesh, kicks aim for vulnerable gaps. He lands a few good shots, but so do they. A blow to his ribs reminds him they only recently took a knock from these guys. Pain spirals through his chest but he ignores it. Broken ribs can be healed.

Death can't.

Behind him, Tristan hears the sounds of more fighting. Zarius is up, dealing with the other two. It's only a matter of time before they get to victory dance.

When one of the Skins lands a second jab into Tristan's ribs he grits his teeth. Time to end this. He doubles over like the pain wants him to, seeing the glint of satisfaction in one of the Skin's eyes.

They both move in, faces lighting with the prospect of triumph.

But they never get to taste it, let alone see it. Tristan jumps, spins, and spears out his leg. Both men slam to the ground as, one after the other, as his foot connects with their jaw.

Tristan straightens, breathing heavily. The sound of another body hitting the ground almost has him smiling. Zarius has taken another Skin out.

That leaves one more.

Tristan spins around to see the Skin slowly stepping backward. The coward is retreating. For every step back, Zarius takes a step forward, not losing any ground. His face is swollen and purple and one hand looks like it won't be making a fist any time soon, but he doesn't take his gaze from his prey.

Tristan heads left, fanning out so he has a better chance of coming between the Skin and the door. The guy is going to run for sure.

The Skin glances between the two of them before his gaze settles on Zarius. "He can fight." His hands shift to his side. "You've taught him to protect himself."

"Stay still," commands Zarius.

The Skin stops, only to turn his hollow gaze toward Tristan. "Hello, Gem."

"My name's Tristan." Although Gem's the name he was born with in the Gemini solar system, no one's called him that since he was a baby.

In fact, Zarius only uses it when he's feeling exceptionally sentimental or particularly angry. Usually, it's the latter.

The Skin dips his head in acknowledgement. "I'll let Chardis know you've assimilated more than we thought."

"Enough," barks Zarius. "Put your hands on your head and face the wall."

The Skin cautiously lifts his hands but the slowly spreading smile has Tristan on high alert. Skins aren't smart —hell, sometimes they seem to like the pain—but this guy doesn't look like he knows he's lost.

That Zarius is about to finish him.

It all happens fast. Too fast. The Skin jams his hand into his jacket, yanking out a gun.

But it's not a gun Tristan has seen before. Slick and narrow, it glints blue-black like a shiny, metal bruise. The Skin lifts it, spins his arm wide and aims it at Tristan.

"No!" Zarius is already running, but even he can't run faster than a bullet.

The Skin's eyes blaze as he pulls the trigger.

A split second later, a sharp sting pierces Tristan's chest. He has time to suck in a startled breath before his body crumples.

He expects there to be pain, but there isn't. An icy cold explodes from the site of the bullet, catapulting through his veins and spearing down his limbs.

Vaguely, Tristan registers the *crack* of a snapped neck. He wants to make sure it's not Zarius's but his head feels like lead.

Zarius's freaked out face appears above him and Tristan tries to smile, hoping to give the man who raised him like a son some reassurance.

Except he can't. His entire body is shutting down.

As his muscles lock like they've jumped straight to rigor mortis, Tristan closes his eyes.

Yep, a suit would've been good.

12

BRIELLE

The afternoon sun bastes Brielle with its warmth as she rides to the public library after school. Mr. Jackson, her fifth period history teacher, had assigned a ten-page essay on the Civil War due Monday. Brielle wants to get it out of the way tonight so that she doesn't have to worry about anything during her dinner with the Pierces tomorrow.

And now that Tristan is no longer an issue—apparently dating Cassandra—Brielle has nothing better to do.

As she locks her bike to the rack on the front lawn of the library, she wonders why the thought of the two of them together bothers her so much. She's the one who rejected Tristan. She's the one who insisted they just be friends.

Brielle shakes her head. If Tristan had shown interest in any other girl, she probably wouldn't care. But it's Cassandra. How could Tristan go so quickly from Brielle to her? From sweet and simple to fake and evil?

She clenches her jaw as she ascends the library steps, begrudging the fact that Tristan's still distracting her. *Time to focus on more important things, Brielle.*

Scanning the signs hanging over the aisles of book shelves, she spots the history section. She's decided to write her paper on Abraham Lincoln's politics during the Civil War, then she can use some of his biography to make up the ten pages.

Once in the History section, she narrows in on books about the Civil War. There are dozens of books on the topic. *The Underground Railroad. Slavery in the Civil War. A Chronology of Battles during the Civil War Era.* Nothing stands out except for a biography on Abraham Lincoln, but that won't offer enough targeted information for the paper. She needs information specifically on the President's part in the war.

She tucks the biography under her arm, then goes to the front desk to ask the librarian for help. The desk is vacant, and Brielle looks around. Stacking books on the shelf closest to the desk is the Eye Patch Guy. He's worked at the library for ages. Many of her classmates are afraid of him. He doesn't look like the type of person who would be a librarian. All gray hair and rough edges, and biceps that don't come from stacking books. And there are always new rumors in circulation about how he lost his eye: he was shot in the face during some battle in the military; he was tortured by the mafia and is hiding out here as the assistant librarian; he took it out himself just to scare children.

Brielle doesn't believe any of the gossip, or really care, but the man is intimidating regardless, and she's not thrilled about having to approach him and ask for assistance.

"Excuse me," she announces her presence as she comes up behind him.

He doesn't turn around, or halt his robotic book stacking. "What do you want?"

She clears her throat. "I was hoping you could help me

find some books about President Lincoln's politics during the Civil War."

"Did you look in the History section?" His voice is gruff, and he remains facing the bookshelf. Is he doing that because he knows his eye patch makes people uncomfortable? On second thought, he doesn't seem like the kind of person who cares about what other people think.

"Yes, I did, but it didn't quite have what I was looking for," she says, waving her book in the direction of the History section.

He sighs and looks over his shoulder. His wizened features don't change from the frown they're set in, but the lingering way he looks at her makes her wonder if there is any truth to some of the rumors. He stares at her for too long without speaking, and she's so uncomfortable that she wishes she'd just kept looking on her own.

"Ugh! Where's the librarian?" an irritated high pitched voice complains behind her. Brielle would recognize Suki's nasally voice anywhere, mostly because she can't stand hearing it.

Eye Patch Guy finally surrenders the staring contest to flick his dark gray eye at the desk.

He sighs again before saying, "I can help you find what you're looking for," then struts over to the computer at the desk. Brielle reluctantly follows, stopping a safe distance away from Suki, who gives her an up-down look with her characteristically scrunched nose like everything smells bad.

"I thought this was a public library, not a homeless shelter," Suki says, smiling with pride at her insult. Then she addresses Eye Patch Guy. "I need you to find a book for me."

Suki doesn't usually act this nasty to authority figures, and Brielle is embarrassed for her that she's doing so to Eye Patch Guy. But it's somewhat satisfying to see him respond to her with such disdain, returning the lack of respect she was displaying to him.

"Find it yourself."

She crosses her arms. "But you're helping her!"

"*She's* not a spoiled brat."

The look of outrage on Suki's face is priceless, with her thin glossy lips hanging open in a perfect O. Brielle bites her lip to smother the smile that aches to bloom. This may be Brielle's favorite moment of all time. Maybe Eye Patch Guy isn't so bad after all.

He looks over the screen to Brielle. "The book you want is in the Politics section. *Presidential Letters* by J. Huff. Looks like it's a compilation of letters written from President Lincoln during the war."

"Thank you," Brielle says, unleashing her wide grin.

"Any time." He waves, turns around and walks back to his book stacking, leaving Suki standing there like she doesn't exist.

Brielle shrugs at Suki, who's so angry Brielle can practically see waves of heat radiating from her. Suki makes a high-pitched "humph", then stomps into the maze of shelves. With a spring in her step, Brielle heads back into the rows looking for the sign that reads *Politics*. It's all the way in the back on the right, behind the Social Sciences section. Brielle goes down the first row, scanning the spines for last names starting with H. She goes up one side and down the other, names going from A to F. Must be in the next row.

Brielle rounds the shelf and—

Suki is frantically running her finger over spines at the end.

No, she can't be…

More hastily now, Brielle scours the names, her eyes breezing over the Fs, the Gs, ah, H! She's getting closer to

Suki, who glances sideways at her with the same urgency. Hallaway, Handler, Hopper, Humphrey...

Just as Brielle spots Huff, the book is snatched off the shelf. Suki straightens and steps back, hugging the book. "Not what I came for but it'll do."

"Give me that book," Brielle insists, her anger at a sudden peak.

Suki rotates her torso and the book away from Brielle. "No, I need it for my Civil War paper. And I found it first."

"You didn't even want it until you heard him tell me about it." Brielle tries her best to keep her tone down, to stay respectful of the fact that they're in a library, but every muscle in her body clenches with the desire to throw a fit.

Suki shrugs. "You should have been quicker." She flicks her straight black hair and walks up the row, bumping Brielle's shoulder as she passes and heads to the checkout counter.

Brielle stands still, a storm raging inside her. She had made herself a promise to stay out of the way of others, to not put herself into any compromising situations. But does that mean she can't stand up for herself? Let people walk all over her? Turn the other cheek?

She knows she should let it go. It's just a book. Brielle can find sources online.

But it's not just about the book. It's everything. Cassandra and Suki, everyone, they all treat her like crap. Tristan may be a weirdo, but he's one of the few people who's ever shown her respect, like she was more than some unwanted peasant. She doesn't deserve to be treated this way, and they won't stop if she never stands up to them.

Gathering her courage, she follows Suki to the counter.

"I'm not letting you take that book, Suki," she asserts when she closes in.

"Oh yeah?" Suki rests the book on her opposite hip and

narrows her almond-shaped eyes. "What are you going to do about it?"

As swiftly as she can move, Brielle reaches across Suki's petite body to snatch the book, but Suki is just a split-second faster and swings it up out of Brielle's grasp.

She laughs, her eyes wide and mouth open. "You actually thought you could take it from me?" She laughs harder. "Little Orphan Annie is getting brave."

That word is like a red hot poker stoking the fire of rage inside her. "Enough with the orphan jokes! Don't you ever get tired of it?"

"No." Suki flashes a wicked smile, and Brielle has had it.

The desire to hurt Suki is overwhelming. But rather than lashing out with a shove, a different instinctual response triggers.

Brielle doesn't know how she does it, how she taps into the curse that usually has a mind of its own. Just like hundreds of times in the past, her world blurs and the vision pulls her in, but this time, she's not an unwilling witness. This time, she has the wheel.

From Suki's eyes, she sees her making out with Kevin Carr, the scrawny and nerdy captain of the Audio Visual club. Under the bleachers at school, on various beds and couches, in her car. And every incident is followed by a flash of a lie she tells her boyfriend Zayn about where she's at, and the guilt she feels when she's with him.

The vision fades quickly, for once without the usual sense of disorientation or lightheadedness. Suki's guilt saturates her, but it doesn't feel like such a burden.

Brielle is struck by the fact that she's never been able to turn on the visions before. They usually only come on when the other person is thinking of what they feel guilty about, or something in the present triggers a memory. This is the first time she's ever been able to invite a vision in.

But she has bigger fish to fry. Suki is cheating on the captain of the lacrosse team with arguably the biggest nerd in the school! If her friends ever found out, she'd be humiliated. And if Zayn found out…

Maybe this curse could be useful after all.

"I wonder what Zayn would say if he found out about your stolen rendezvous with Kevin," Brielle says, unsure if she's mastered a threatening tone.

Suki's jeering expression falls harder than the stock market. The hand that holds the book at arm's length drops to her side. She leans closer and whispers with horror in her eyes, "Wh—bu—who told you?"

Brielle shrugs, trying to keep her face as cool as possible. She's not comfortable with extortion, and she's fairly certain she would never actually tell anyone Suki's dirty secret. But finally not being the underdog feels so liberating!

"And I doubt Cassandra would be too happy to hear about it. She and Zayn are friends after all."

Suki releases the book and it bounces on its corners before landing flat on its face. "You wouldn't." Her words are barely a hiss.

Suki's right, but she doesn't need to know that. "Why shouldn't I?" She feels oddly like Cassandra, and the sensation is both thrilling and repulsive.

While Suki's frozen in place, Brielle goes around her and picks the book up off the linoleum floor, then motions toward the checkout counter, acting cool as ice despite the elevated heart rate that has her fingers trembling.

"You have to tell me how you found out," Suki urges in a hoarse whisper. "No one knew. No one but me and Kevin. Did you see us? Did Kevin tell you?" What was fear a moment ago morphs into suspicion as she leans in on Brielle.

Brielle has no qualms with Kevin. He's nice. She doesn't

want any of Suki's rage to fall on him. "What does it matter how I found out?"

Suki is quiet for a few seconds too long, and Brielle glances at her. She's staring at Brielle with a look she knows all too well.

"And I thought Cassandra was just paranoid," Suki says, shaking her head.

Now it's Brielle's suspicion that piques. "What do you mean?"

"She said you know things about people. That you're psychic or something. You really are a witch, aren't you?"

How has this situation so quickly turned against Brielle's favor?

Brielle scoffs and rolls her eyes as she continues checking out the book, pretending the accusation is foolish.

"You're not just an orphan, you're a freak!" Suki's voice gets louder with each word, and Brielle's aware that the few patrons in the library are now staring at them. Even Eye Patch Guy has stopped his stacking.

"I don't know what Cassandra told you, but that's insane." She has to put a pin in this now. "You seriously believe in that stuff?"

"Then tell me how you found out," Suki insists, the snarky curl returning to the corners of her thin lips.

"No." Brielle isn't sure how much longer she can keep up the pretense. She just wants to finish checking out and leave before this gets any worse.

"So what, then? Hmm? If you're not a witch or whatever, then you must go around stalking people, and that's way worse. Either way, you're a freak and—"

"Shut up!" Brielle snaps, and just like the other day with Marie, the guilt from Suki's vision is gone.

Suki gasps, her hands rushing over her mouth. "Omigod!

He's going to hate me." Her face pinched and reddening, she runs out the library doors.

Right past Frank and Beatrice Pierce.

Who are staring at Brielle with confusion plain on their faces.

How much did they see?

Brielle snatches the checkout receipt for her book, puts on a fake smile and goes up to them, feeling like a dog with her tail tucked between her legs.

"Is everything okay?" Frank asks.

"What was that all about?" Beatrice points in the direction Suki went running.

"Yeah, everything is fine," Brielle struggles to say through the stricture in her throat. "Just a misunderstanding with a girl at school." The air is so full of tension that Brielle feels she may suffocate. She almost wishes she would. "I've gotta get home to finish a paper for school, but I'll see you both tomorrow for dinner?" She means for the last part to come out as a statement, but it becomes a question instead.

"Of course." Frank smiles but it doesn't reach his eyes. "We'll see you tomorrow."

Brielle nods and skips away before the two most important people in her life can see her features crack into a deep frown.

She should have just let it go. Why did she have to go after Suki? She thought it would feel good to stand up for herself, to even the scales on the popular girls. But it's only made things worse. Not only does Suki now think she's a psychic or a witch or whatever—and will surely spread that rumor around school—but Brielle may have also damaged any hope of being adopted by the Pierces.

She gets on her bike and races home, desperate to get to her room and disappear into her despair.

There's something else, something that's even more frightening than the threats to her social and family life.

Brielle had been able to control her curse today. She'd willed it to happen with Suki. And then when she snapped at Suki, she'd unloaded the guilt back onto her and amplified it. It's the same thing that happened with Marie the other day. Marie was right. Brielle is the cause of her obsessive guilt.

This curse is growing, getting more powerful.

And Brielle is terrified to discover what else she's capable of.

13

TRISTAN

Tristan knows he's being carried by Zarius because he can hear the thumping of his heart pressed against his ear. The sound of Zarius's breathing is just above. The scent of grass and outdoors registers a few seconds later.

Zarius is getting the both of them the hell out of here.

Except Tristan can hear and smell, but he can't see. And he can't feel a thing.

He has no idea where his limbs are or what they're doing. It's as if he's nothing more than a floating brain.

"Zarius?"

It's Tess. And that one trembling word says it all—she's scared.

"He's alive, but out of it. He was shot."

What? No! I'm here! Tristan struggles against whatever's holding him down. He needs to give them a sign—a moan, a flutter of the eyelids, flick the bird to the Skins they just whooped.

But he can't. Feel. A. Thing.

"Oh, Tristan," Tess moans.

"We need to get him home." Zarius's voice is strained. "You sit with him in the back. I'll drive."

There's the sound of rustling, of car doors slamming, of an engine starting. Tristan pictures his body sprawled across the back seat, his head in Tess's lap. Zarius would be driving like a demon.

"His breathing is regular," Tess states calmly. "Oh god, his pulse! It's so slow, Zarius!"

Tess's voice hikes up and Tristan wishes he could grip the hand that would be wrapped around his wrist. He's not about to kick anyone's ass right now, but he'd give anything to tell Tess he's not two steps away from death.

Whether that's the truth or not, doesn't matter. Reassuring Tess does.

"He's going to be fine, Tess."

Tristan hopes the steely determination in Zarius's voice is enough to dial down Tess's fear. Tess freaks out with the same intensity that she does everything else—baking, fighting, loving.

"Then why isn't he waking up?"

She's holding her comatose son in her lap. They haven't had to deal with anything like this before, but Tess has devoted her life to this little family, one not connected by blood, but woven together by something far stronger—love.

"Tell me a story, Tess."

"What? Now isn't the time to—"

"Now. Tess. Make it a good one."

If Tristan could relax, he would. Zarius's idea is genius. Tess loves to relive their memories. It'll keep her busy.

It'll remind her that they'd never let anything happen to each other.

"Do you remember the time he was five, Zarius?"

"He was five for a whole year. You're going to have to be more specific."

Zarius is pushing her to focus on the details. Clever guy.

Tess huffs and Tristan imagines her rolling her eyes. "The time he had the visions about what we were getting him for his birthday."

The sound of a chuckle filters through Tristan's senses and he wishes he could smile.

"He saw that he got a fighting stick that he'd later use on a Skin—"

"A bō staff."

"That's what I said. He saw you passing a great big stick all wrapped up with a ribbon or an…"

"An avocado." The tension has eased from Zarius's voice. He was hoping to help Tess, but it doesn't surprise Tristan she's easing his mind, too.

Memories of that evening fill Tristan's mind. Without the sensation of his body, it's like he's there. He'd been elated by the first vision. Devastated by the second.

He hates avocados.

Zarius and Tess had no choice but to tell him the truth. He got the bō early and set himself the challenge to see if he could convince them to get him two sai instead.

Getting those batons with their pretty curved prongs coming up the sides had been quite the cherry on his birthday celebration.

"And do you remember the time he was six and he walked in on us, well…"

Suddenly, Tristan wants to bolt upright and tell them he's fine. Of all the stories to tell! This is one he doesn't want to hear.

"I told him I was teaching you the body fold defense."

"Which he then wanted to learn." The eye roll in Tess's voice is apparent.

"So, I told him about the Gemini planets instead."

Tess sighs. "He always loved hearing about them."

The memory of his first time hearing ab ut his home worlds blossoms in his prison of a mind.

"The Twin planets are the most beautiful of all *ie planets I've* *ever been to,"* Zarius had said, sitting on the edge (*Tristan's bed* after tucking him back in. *"Unlike Earth, all the p int life is red.* *There is nothing more beautiful than looking dow* *on a forest of* *red Ocana trees, with their luscious pink flowers."*

"What makes them red instead of green?" Tris *in had asked,* eyes wide with wonder.

Zarius chuckled. *"I never thought to ask that qu stion. Red was* *my normal. Earth's green plants are strange to me. He'd winked,* and Tristan giggled.

"What else is different from Earth?" Tristan aske eagerly.

"Everything," Zarius had laughed. *"Because th: planets rotate* *around each other in the same orbit, they frequen y eclipse each* *other. The planets act as each other's moons, giving each other the* *tidal pull they need to sustain life, and it's so beautif l to see the red* *and blue orb of Gemini II in the sky on Gemini I. Larth's Moon is* *so unremarkable with its plain white. I miss home."*

Zarius looked longingly out the window, as he of en did.

"Will I ever get to see our home planet?" Trist n asked in a small voice.

Zarius looked back at him and smiled. *"I hope so, Tristan. I* *hope we both will."*

"Of course, then Tristan wanted to know about the Gemini Twins," says Tess fondly, snapping Tris an out of his reverie.

He always asked about them. Even back hen, Tristan felt...incomplete. The words Zarius spoke that night have always stayed with him.

Twin orbiting planets. Two separate bloodlines. One moment in time.

For thousands of years, the Gemini Heirs were born at the exact same second. They weren't only destined to become the Gemini Guardians, to wield the powers of their ancient stones, but were also fated to be soulmates.

And when their forces combined, no power in the Universe could defeat them.

"Will I meet her soon?" Tristan had asked.

Zarius had pulled the covers up as he'd tucked Tristan between them. "That's the plan."

Tristan had fallen asleep, secure and confident in the knowledge that what Zarius said would happen always did.

"And the topic of the body fold defense was dropped," says Tess, a smile in her voice.

And Tristan never questioned why Zarius didn't teach it to him… If Tristan could feel his body, he'd blush.

Silence descends between them. There's the sound of the engine revving too high with each gear change, the odd squealing of tires as they take a corner.

But Zarius and Tess don't tell any more stories.

"We have to make him better, Zarius." Tess chokes the words out.

"That's the plan."

It's a good thing Tristan is paralyzed, or the thought he just had would've popped out of his mouth before he could stop it.

Let's hope that plan goes better than the one to find his Twin.

There's the sound of more rubber being left behind on asphalt and the engine shuts off. They must be home.

The car door opens. "Quick, open the door."

The rapid thumping of Zarius's heartbeat fills Tristan's mind. Zarius is carrying him inside. Who knows when the last time he did that was. When Tristan was three? Four? He frowns inside. There are no grunts to show Zarius is struggling with the weight. Time for more protein shakes.

Once he gets his body back…

The sound of boots down steps tells Tristan they're going down to the basement. He expected that. It's the safest place in the house. And where the nanites are.

"You open his mouth, I'll pour them in," instructs Zarius.

There's a pause and Tristan feels nothing.

"Dammit!" Zarius's voice has gone quiet. It only goes quiet when he's freaked out. "He's not swallowing. Quick. Turn him on his side."

"Get it out, Zarius!" Tess shouts. "He'll drown!"

Drown? There's more silence and Tristan curses the black void he's in. He's choking on nanites and he has no idea.

"It's fine," Zarius says with relief. "His mouth is clear."

"Why can't he swallow, Zarius?"

"We'll give him more. This time intravenously."

Tristan notices that Zarius avoids the question. He wills Tess to ask again. He wills his body to work.

Why can't I swallow?

"Here." Tess's voice is full of tension. "It's a double dose. Just in case."

It was only yesterday that Tess said they needed to be careful with the nanites. His pod didn't land with an infinite supply.

Which must mean they're worried.

To be honest, so is he…

"All done," Zarius mutters, as if his jaw is wired shut. "Now, we wait."

Tristan wills his mind to relax. The nanites won't take long. When his body is working again he's going to hug these two. Hard.

And then tell them to never tell stories in the car again.

Tess's perfume tickles his nose. "Why isn't it working?"

"I don't know." Zarius's voice is so quiet Tristan has to strain to hear him.

"What was he shot with, Zarius? This isn't normal."

"I don't know. It's not a weapon I've seen before."

Figure it out, Zarius! If Tristan could grab him by the shirt and shake him, he would.

"He's breathing," Zarius muses as if he's talking to himself. "Pulse is slow but steady." There's another pause. "He's paralyzed."

Paralyzed? But—

"Oh god. We need to get him to a hospital—"

"No," Zarius cuts Tess off. "He has nanites in his system. They'll ask too many questions."

Questions they can't answer.

"But…" Tess whispers. "He can't eat. Can't drink."

Last time Tristan checked, people don't survive so well without food or water.

Suddenly, Zarius is a flurry of motion. "I'll take some blood, study what kind of dark matter has poisoned him. There'll be an antidote we can program into the nanites."

"Is that possible? We only have a few days."

"Chardis can manipulate dark matter to his will—it's how Skins are able to turn invisible. It gives his weapons unique properties. It seems this poison freezes the motion of cells. I'll just have to find a way to reverse it."

Tess goes silent and Tristan wonders if she's thinking the same thing he is. Zarius makes it sound simple, but they all know it's not. He's talking about subatomic particles, here. Ones that don't behave the way anything else on Earth does. Heck, humans haven't even observed them yet.

If the technology Zarius needs isn't in the pod Tristan arrived in…

"I'll get started." Zarius's words are hard with determination. "Tess, you'll need to keep his mouth moist. A wet cloth wiped across his lips on a regular basis."

"Already got the cloth."

Of course Tess does. Caring comes instinctively to her.

It's why, seventeen years ago, she plucked a wailing baby from an alien pod out in the middle of nowhere and vowed to do everything she could to protect him.

But before anything else can happen, a beeping sounds somewhere behind Tristan. Instinctively, Tristan tries to leap into action. He's been trained to respond to that alarm.

It's the one alarm that means you act now, think later.

Except his body remains inert. Helpless.

It means Tristan has to lie there, motionless and vulnerable, as Zarius turns it off. The sensor is linked to outside the house. It detects dark matter.

Which means Skins are about to attack.

Zarius curses. "It's the poison. It led them straight here."

"They've found us?" gasps Tess.

"You stay here and protect Tristan," says Zarius. "I'll deal with them."

What? No! Zarius is still injured from the last fight! And Tristan is supposed to be the one who helps protect Tess. He struggles against the darkness holding him, but it's like fighting air...without a body. Mentally, he screams a denial. He should be beside Zarius, showing the Skins they don't ever want to come here again.

Zarius's heavy boots clatter up the stairs. The sound of Tess's breathing draws near, rapid and shallow. "Tristan, I don't know if you can hear me or not, but don't worry. Everything will be alright."

Tristan would give anything to be able to reach out and grasp her hand. Tell *her* it's going to be okay.

Then run up those stairs and actually make sure those words are the truth.

But he can't even feel if Tess is holding him. All he can do is lie here. Listening.

Like a trussed duck waiting to be cooked.

A clatter echoes from above them, followed by a *crash*.

Tess gasps, the sound even closer. More *thumps* then the sound of splintering wood carries down to them.

The Skins are inside. Zarius is fighting them.

Then there's silence.

Tristan strains to hear why. Has Zarius won?

Have the Skins…

But there's nothing. He can't even hold his breath, strain his neck, for pitch sake.

The *thumping* of boots on the steps finally fractures the quiet.

"Zarius?" Tess asks quietly.

But Tristan already knows the answer. The footfalls were too light, too slow. They're the steps of a man smaller than Zarius, one approaching with far more caution than a worried husband.

Tess's sharp intake of breath tells him she sees the Skin. "Don't you dare touch him."

"Oh, Chardis is going to do more than touch him," the man sneers. "It seems the poison did exactly what it was supposed to."

Lead them straight to them, like a freaking homing beacon. As Tristan lies paralyzed, waiting for them to carry him out.

Tess's feet shuffle beside him. She's moving into a fighting stance, just like she's been taught. Except she'll be no match against a man consumed by dark matter. A man robbed of soul and conscience.

Zarius! Where are you?

"Don't take another step," Tess warns, her voice low and determined.

The man chuckles. "The whole plan is quite clever, really. There's an antidote, you see. Once we have Gem secured, we want him to talk."

There's a subtle crunch as a boot scrapes over the concrete floor.

"Stay where you are! I won't let you touch him!"

"You won't be alive to stop me." The Skin's voice is cold as death, the words full of promise.

Tristan strains as he battles the invisible chains holding him down. But he's in a vacuum. Powerless as he hears the Skin leap.

As Tess's scream is cut short.

As something large hits the wall on the other side of the room and crashes onto the desk.

Tess!

14

BRIELLE

B rielle's feet are heavy as she climbs the front steps of the orphanage. All she wants to do is go to bed and let sweet sleep erase the day. But she knows she needs to write her paper so she can go to her big dinner tomorrow. That is, if the Pierces don't cancel because of what they just saw between her and Suki.

A sigh squeezes through her clenched teeth, and she opens the front door and walks in. She hugs the Abraham Lincoln book tight against her chest like a battle trophy, knowing it wasn't worth what she sacrificed. Brielle imagines many of the soldiers who fought in the very war she's supposed to write about probably felt the same way when they returned home.

She hears the whispers before she enters the common room, and she comes to a dead stop at the threshold. One of those voices belongs to Marie. After the recent confrontation with Suki, Brielle has no strength of will left to endure a verbal beating from Marie.

She stands in the shadows just outside of the common room for several long minutes, frozen with indecision. The paper needs to be written, but Brielle would do absolutely anything to avoid Marie. There's always the chance that the Brady Bunch won't see her, if she's quiet enough. But that's not a gamble Brielle is willing to take at the moment. She could just make a run for it, although that might inspire them to give chase, and she definitely doesn't want that.

Finally, Brielle adjusts the shoulder strap of her backpack, turns around, and walks back out the front door to sit on the steps. She takes out her spiral notebook and a pencil and cracks open the library book, resigned to write the whole thing out here in hopes that the Brady Bunch will be gone by the time she's finished. She can always type it up later, even if it takes her all night.

What a coward I am.

She tries her best to push her troubles to the back of her mind and puts all her focus on the task at hand.

The wall lamps cast a dim light, making it hard to read in the cozy evening darkness, but Brielle manages to find more than enough citations she can use. Blocking out the rest of the world, she spends the next hour or longer— there's no clock out here to tell time—writing what she feels is an excellent exposé about Abraham Lincoln's politics.

By the time she's finished, the sky above is completely black and star-spangled, her butt is sore from sitting on the cold hard cement, and her fingers are so stiff she can hardly flex them.

Satisfied and exhausted, she sets the notebook aside and leans back, enjoying the night air and wondering if it's safe to go inside yet.

She looks up at the stars, trying to keep her mind as open and empty as the vast expanse of space she sees. But so many things fight to get in, all the things she's afraid to face: Marie and her cohorts in the common room, whatever mayhem

Suki will inflict on her at school tomorrow, the fragile hope of the Pierces adopting her.

So when Tristan pops into her mind, as he so often does, she welcomes him.

He thinks he's an alien prince, and she has visions of bad things people have done. Maybe they really are perfect for each other. Two people on the outskirts of normal, albeit for different reasons. Does it really matter if he's crazy? Who is she to judge? There has to be a reason why she's so undeniably drawn to him. Despite his delusion, he's funny, sweet, sincere, and gorgeous as hell! If he's the best option she'll ever get, is that really so bad? Maybe after the adoption is finalized, she'll give him a second chance.

If the adoption goes through at all.

And if Cassandra hasn't gotten her claws into him by then.

The crunch of leaves nearby startles Brielle out of her daydreaming, and she whips her head in the direction of the sound. She expects to catch a glimpse of the tail of one of the stray cats skittering by, so she's even more shaken when she sees a large silhouette under the trees across the lawn.

Her heart rate spikes, flooding her veins with adrenaline and the urge to run, but she's stuck, unable to do anything but stare at the figure who she can feel is also staring at her.

After a few eternal seconds, her motor skills return enough for her to swallow and stutter, "W-w-who's there?"

The figure steps forward, and Brielle mentally prepares herself to use the thick library book as a weapon if need be.

His face comes into the light, and confusion mixes with the fear brewing in her chest.

It's Eye Patch Guy.

"Sorry, didn't mean to scare you," he says, his gruff voice softer than it was at the library earlier today.

Suddenly, every story Brielle's ever heard about him

replays in her mind, and she's filled with the morbid curiosity of which one she's about to experience first-hand.

"After that whole mess in the library, I needed to make sure you weren't on their radar," he says. "I needed to make sure you were safe."

Brielle isn't sure what she expected him to say, but that certainly wasn't it, and she's even more confused.

"On who's radar?" she can't help but ask. She knows she should just turn tail and run inside, Marie and the Brady Bunch be damned. Why doesn't she run?

He shakes his head, looking very much like an ex-soldier. "I can't explain that to you, yet." He takes another step closer, and Brielle flinches backward, which makes him raise his hands in a gesture meant to calm. "Trust me when I say I'm not the one you should be afraid of."

"If you don't intend to hurt me, then why are you here?" she asks, surprised by her own bravery. Or maybe it's just recklessness.

"Like I said, I only came to check on you, but since you caught me, I might as well warn you."

Check on her? Why would he care about an argument between her and Suki? Why would he care about her well-being at all? How does he know where she lives? Nothing about this makes sense, and everything about it seems wrong.

"Warn me about what?"

His one good eye locks onto hers. "Don't use your powers right now."

White hot terror flashes through her, and beads of cold sweat practically jump out of every pore. Brielle tries to feign ignorance, scrunching her brows in a way that feels like confusion, but she knows she can't remove the fear from her wide eyes.

"P-powers?" A nervous giggle trips out of her throat, then

quickly dies. "What are you talking about?" She shakes her head.

He looks down at the ground. "It's okay. You don't have to admit anything to me. I just need you to know that it's not safe to use your powers right now. They're looking for you, and you can't do anything to call attention to yourself. That is all. Have a pleasant evening."

And just like that, he turns around and walks off the lawn and down the sidewalk like he's just taking a nighttime stroll.

Brielle sits there, unable to slow her heart down as questions race through her mind. How does he know about her curse? No one knows, not *really* knows. Marie, Cassandra and Suki only suspect, with no real proof. So how does this guy, who might as well be a stranger, know anything about her at all?

And who does he think is looking for her? Her imagination really runs wild at that question. She entertains every idea from Shield Agents from the Marvel Universe to witch hunters who want to burn her at the stake. Or maybe scientists who want to dissect her and find out how her visions work.

Or could Eye Patch Guy be referring to Tristan? Tristan had noticed Brielle right from the get-go, had asked her out five minutes into meeting her. None of that made sense at the time, but if he's part of this, his interest would actually have an explanation. What if he's the danger that the crazy librarian warned her about?

And if so, does she have the restraint to stay away?

15

TRISTAN

"Chardis has been looking forward to meeting you," sneers a voice close to Tristan.

All the moves Tristan would use right now flash through his mind. An uppercut to the grinning man's jaw. He could swing his legs around and wrap them around the guy's throat. He could pummel the crap out of him like he was a punching bag.

But all Tristan can do is lie there. Waiting. Wondering if Tess is okay.

The Skin moves in closer, his voice sliding over Tristan. "One down. Twelve to go."

Suddenly, there's a gasp and a gurgle. The Skin grunts and his body *thumps* on the ground.

Tristan curses the still, silent blackness he's trapped in. What just happened?

"Fool," Zarius mutters. "Your impatience to get to a Zodiac Heir blinded you."

Zarius is here! And he killed the Skin! Relief floods Tristan's consciousness. A fist pump sure would be nice right about now…

"Tess? Tess! Are you okay?"

Zarius's voice is full of panic, something Tristan's never heard. Zarius invented cool, calm and collected.

But Tess has never been directly attacked before. The Skins have never come to their house.

Splintered wood crunches under Zarius's boots as he rushes to her. *Please, Tess. Please be okay.*

"Tess! Can you hear me?"

The softest of groans is the sweetest sound Tristan's ever heard. "Zarius?" There's a sharp movement. "Tristan! The Skin—"

"The Skin is finished. He never got to our boy, thanks to you."

"I didn't do anything—" Tess stops, gasping. "Zarius! There's an antidote! The Skin said there's an antidote!" There's more sounds of shuffling. "No, don't worry about me. I'm fine. We need to find it!"

They scramble closer to Tristan, then there's the quiet rustling of material being shifted.

"He'd have it in one of his pockets," says Tess.

"I've got it!" cries Zarius triumphantly.

"Quick, we need to get it into Tristan."

If Tristan's breath could spike with excitement, it would. *An antidote!* He listens as Zarius and Tess move around the room. They'd be getting a syringe from the monster-sized first-aid kit on the bench. Drawing in the liquid.

Then they're beside him.

"Hold on, Tristan," says Tess. "This is going to work."

For the first time since he was shot, Tristan believes her. He can't feel the prick of the needle or the sting of the antidote as it's injected into his veins, but he knows it happens. Both Zarius and Tess move back, releasing their breaths.

"How long will it take?" asks Tess.

"I don't know. I haven't come across this sort of poison before. It seems Chardis is becoming innovative."

"He's not moving, Zarius."

"Give it time," he soothes. "Tristan could be like this for a while yet."

A while? How long is a while? Tristan scans his body. Well, he thinks he does. As he reaches out with his mind, he finds he still doesn't know where any part of him is. There's nothing to feel. No sensations to experience.

Except... Was that a tingle dancing across his fingertips? Focusing everything he has, Tristan waits. Yes! Like a fairy is nibbling on his nails! Tristan tries to move them, except the link from his brain to his hand is still severed.

Feeling as if he's trying to move a mountain, he concentrates on where his fingers should be.

"Zarius! His hand!" Although Tess's voice is hushed, it's full of excitement.

Tristan didn't feel any movement, but Tess's words tell him he must've twitched. He tries again, this time sensing the flex of muscles and contraction of each knuckle.

"It's working," breathes Zarius.

Tristan gasps. And he feels it! He draws in a deeper breath and it's like air is being sucked into his lungs for the first time. It feels cool as it hits the back of his throat, the sensation dissolving as his chest expands. Man, that feels good.

He turns his head, finding Zarius and Tess exactly where he thought they'd be—right beside him. "I never want to hear about the body fold defense again."

Tess's laughter is powered by relief. She throws her arms around Tristan and he's never felt anything so amazing. His own arms feel like they're carved from stone, but he lifts them and hugs her back. Over her shoulder Zarius catches Tristan's gaze as he nods.

Tristan gives him a thumbs up. Zarius isn't big on physical affection, but the quiet joy in his eyes tells it all. Not to mention he looks like he just aged twenty years.

Feeling like he might've done the same, Tristan pushes himself to a sitting position. He looks around the basement, eyebrows hiking at the mess in the back corner. "Seems I missed all the action." He looks to Tess, heart jerking when he sees the blood trickling from a cut on her forehead. "Hell, Tess! Are you okay? Here,"—he shuffles off the table he was lying on—"lie down."

Tess rolls her eyes. "You're as bad as Zarius. You two have sustained much more serious injuries than this and still wanted to mow the lawn." She juts out a hip. "Are you giving me special consideration because I'm a girl?"

Tristan backs down faster than he ever has in his life, quickly straightening and stepping away. "Wouldn't dream of it." Give him an angry Skin with a gun, and he'll take him on in a heartbeat. Faced with Tess going all feminist on him, and Tristan knows when to admit defeat.

"Good, because we have some cleaning up to do." She glances at Zarius. "Was that the bookshelves I heard being demolished?"

Zarius grins. "We disagreed about whether he should go down to the basement or not." But then he frowns. "One got past as I was fighting the other two."

Tess places her hand on his arm. "You got here in time. We're all fine."

Zarius glances at the gash on her head but doesn't say anything. The protector in him would be disagreeing.

Tristan kicks the lifeless body beside him. "Everyone but him. We need to put these guys somewhere Chardis will get the message."

"We'll dump them back near the warehouse," Zarius growls. "He can see what happens when they get too close."

Tess wraps her arms around herself. "But they'll be back. They know where we live."

Zarius's lips flatline. There's nothing he can say to that. It's the truth.

Tristan steps around, shrugging. "Then we'll move."

Again.

But Tess shakes her head. "It'll take time to find somewhere in the area. We need to stay close to the school."

Because of Brielle. And Cassandra.

Even the Skins believed there are others...

Zarius hoists the Skin's body over his shoulder. "I'll get these in the truck. Then I'll dial up the security. Chardis won't attack straight away. He's going to need more men and a better strategy."

Because when Chardis sees the body count, he'll start to realize what he's up against.

Tess nods although Tristan can see the tension pulling down her brows. She follows Zarius to the stairs. "We'll start the cleaning upstairs."

Tristan follows her, noting the way Zarius doesn't even break a sweat as he shoulders the dead Skin. He heads straight to the garage, and Tristan is glad they managed to find somewhere that has an adjoining one. With a door going straight to the enclosed garage, they don't have to find a rug to roll these guys up in.

And he's pretty sure people don't fall for that nowadays, anyway.

Upstairs, the damage is worse than the basement. The living room is in disarray, the bookshelves and coffee table now little more than firewood. Two men lie lifeless on the floor, one right before them, the other by the door.

The first one didn't get far. The second one must've got the better of Zarius enough for the third to get past.

Zarius doesn't even glance down as he steps over the

sprawled body. "I'll get these next. You two get this place back to normal."

They don't need some nosy neighbor knocking on the door and catching sight of a lounge that looks like a wood-chipper vomited in it.

Tess turns toward the laundry. "I'll get the broom."

Tristan raises a brow. "Grab a bulldozer while you're there."

He starts picking up the larger pieces of wood while Zarius collects the other two Skins and Tess sweeps the rest of the debris into piles.

Evening is just creeping over the house when they finally finish. The lounge looks barer, and the basement no longer has a desk, but there's little sign that a battle between good and evil occurred here.

Tristan flops on the couch. "What a day, huh?"

He glances at the two people who are his parents. Zarius looks tired while Tess looks exhausted. "I'm thinking we order from that place down the road that does the kick-ass koftas."

Zarius stretches his shoulders. "You do that, I'll get rid of the Skins."

Tess moves a little closer to him. "Is it safe?"

Zarius presses a kiss to her forehead. "As safe as it's ever been, love."

Tristan rolls his eyes. Of course that's what Zarius would say—the truth. They've always lived with the danger of being found, of having to fight for their lives. But this is the first time it rocked up on their doorstep. But Tess doesn't need to be reminded of that. She needs the pretense of safety, at least for a little while.

Tristan throws a cushion at Zarius and it bounces off his surprised chest. Zarius spent the first sixteen years of his life on the Gemini planet. It seems subtlety isn't a strong trait among Tristan's people.

"At least point out that we kicked their butts."

Tess picks one up and throws it, too. "Yes, and promise you'll come back in one piece."

Zarius catches the second cushion, realization dawning across his face. He approaches Tess, slipping his arms around her waist. "Chardis attacked and lost. That is proof enough of our strength. And as we find each Zodiac Heir, we'll only get stronger."

Tess smiles and Tristan can practically see her melt. They lean in and touch lips, winding around each other.

"I want my cushion back so I can suffocate myself," Tristan calls out, hiding his face in his hands.

Tess and Zarius chuckle, and Tristan isn't surprised when two cushions pummel him one after another.

Tristan pushes upright, grinning as he heads to the kitchen. "At least the takeout pamphlets were safe," he calls over his shoulder.

He's just turned the corner when he freezes. A soft beeping has him spinning around and racing back. The sound is meant to be subtle, enough to let them know intruders are near, but quiet enough that no one outside the house would hear it.

Tess's stricken face is the first thing Tristan sees. "They're back."

Zarius curses. "Chardis regrouped fast. He must've decided to attack quickly, thinking we'd be unprepared."

And vulnerable.

"Well, he was wrong," mutters Tristan. "And this time, I won't be lying around thanks to his poison."

There's a loud knock on the door and Tess jumps. Tristan is in fighting stance, fists raised, before the rapping is finished. Zarius has done the same.

They look at each other and Tristan shrugs. "At least they're being polite and knocking."

It means the Skins want them to know they're here, alarm or no alarm. Tristan isn't sure what that means, but he knows it's bold.

Zarius draws in a slow breath, his body hardening as he exhales. He's centering. "I'll open the door. Tristan, I want you behind me. Tess, you move back."

Tess nods, not arguing. No one wants to see a repeat of how she got the cut on her head.

A few steps and Zarius is at the door. With a short, sharp movement he jerks it open.

Then, just stands there.

Alarm slams through Tristan. Have they shot Zarius with the same paralyzing poison? He's about to launch forward when Zarius speaks, his voice full of shock.

"Alden?"

What? Tristan knows that name! His hands drop an inch. "You've been to the library, too?"

But Zarius doesn't answer. Instead, he steps forward and the men clasp, thumping one another on the back.

They pull back and Zarius shakes his head. "It's good to see you, old man."

"Does someone want to tell us what's going on around here?" asks Tristan.

He doubts anyone's ever been happy to see Alden. He didn't even think the man could smile!

But smiling is exactly what Alden's doing. "It took you long enough, soldier."

Tess steps forward, frowning quizzically. "You two know each other?"

Zarius ushers Alden inside and closes the door. He grins at Tristan and Tess. "Alden is an elder from Gemini I."

Tristan's eyes pop open. "He's what?"

Alden's eye glitters with far more than crankiness. "I was there on the Gemini station when it was attacked. The King thought Zarius might need a hand so I was sent in my own pod shortly after."

"King Pharis always liked to think ahead," says Zarius, his tone saying he shouldn't be surprised by all this.

Tess steps forward, extending her hand with a smile. "Welcome. It's lovely to meet another person from Gemini I."

Alden glances at Zarius. "She knows?"

Slipping an arm around Tess's waist, Zarius nods. "Without her, I'm not sure I would've found Gem."

With that, all eyes turn to Tristan. He lifts a crooked smile. "I prefer Tristan."

Alden scans him from head to toe. "So this is why you were snooping at the library."

Tristan has to work not to frown. "Not that there was anything to find."

Alden chuckles. "That's because I've removed any shred of information about aliens or pods after Mirror Point had several land here."

Tess gasps as Tristan feels like his heart just tripped over itself. "Pods?" As in more than one? "Here in Mirror Point?"

Zarius is the first to break the stunned silence that follows. "Maybe we should all sit down and catch up."

He leads the way into the lounge and Alden looks around. All their houses look pretty bare because of the frequent moves, but now they're down a couple of bookshelves and a coffee table.

Tess smiles apologetically. "Please, take a seat. I'll bring out something to eat and drink."

Alden nods, sitting himself on the single armchair facing the couch. Zarius sits across from him but Tristan finds there's too much energy buzzing through his body to sit. He stands beside the couch, watching Alden closely.

Zarius leans forward, resting his elbows on his knees as he clasps his hand beneath his chin. "Tell me everything, Alden."

Alden brushes his eye patch. "Well, most of my pod was destroyed on impact. There must have been some sort of interference because I was knocked off course. It seems several others were, too."

Zarius and Tristan glance at each other. That's why they haven't been able to get so much as a whiff of another Zodiac Heir. Until now…

"Recovery was slow with this planet's primitive medical system. By the time I was able to start tracking the pods that landed nearby, the Zodiac Heirs were gone."

Tess enters, holding a tray with coffee and cookies. "Have you been able to find any?"

Tristan has to work not to frown. He's not sure if he likes Alden, and now the dude is eating his sweet treats.

Alden takes a biscuit, smiling in thanks. "I have my suspicions."

That has Tristan perking up. "There are others here?"

But Alden shakes his head. "From what I've pieced, they were taken to a local orphanage. Most were adopted out quite quickly."

"So they could be anywhere," Tristan mutters. Back to square one. He looks squarely at Alden. "We'll need to see what information you have."

"Your father had to learn patience, too." Alden turns to Zarius. "I've removed every shred of evidence about the pods from the public record. It's all at my house. I've been waiting for you to find me."

Tristan frowns. "You didn't think to go looking for us?" It took sixteen years to get here. That's a whole lot of time they could've saved.

Alden pins Tristan with his one eye. "I had to keep the

information hidden. If you couldn't find it, at least Chardis wouldn't either."

Zarius sighs. "He's right, Tristan. If there was a trail, Chardis could've found it before we did."

"I think he already has," states Alden.

The Skins asked where the others were...

Zarius shifts forward, his gaze intense. "The Skins have already attacked us, twice."

Tess's hand flutters to her throat. "The second time was here."

Alden straightens. "They know where you live?"

"We've increased security," says Zarius. "They won't be taking us by surprise again. In the meantime, we'll look for a new residence."

Alden nods, scratching his chin. "It will need to be close to the school."

This time, it's Tristan who moves closer. His whole body tingles with the need to ask the next question. "There are others there, aren't there?"

"At least one. I've been following her for a while now."

Her...

Every part of Tristan stills, hanging on what's about to be said. "Who? What's her name?"

Alden looks thoughtfully back. "Brielle. I believe she has powers."

The one word slams through Tristan. Brielle. A Zodiac Heir.

His heart thunders out one word, over and over.

Soulmate.

Alden glances at Zarius. "She's the only one who wasn't adopted when several babies arrived at the orphanage seventeen years ago. I've organized a couple who are... sympathetic to our cause to take her in. She needs protection."

Tristan starts to pace. That's his job. He's about to become Brielle's shadow.

Zarius pushes upright. "Tristan, we need her to see the stones. To touch them."

And if the second Gemini stone lights up, then what his heart suspects will be proven true.

Tess places her hand on his arm. "She'd need to come here. We can't afford for the stones to be unprotected."

"You're right," agrees Zarius. He turns back to Tristan. "Invite her over. We can talk to her, show her the box."

Uh oh.

Tristan rubs the back of his head, trying not to suck his head down into his shoulders. "That's probably not going to be as easy as it sounds."

All eyes turn to him and he shrugs sheepishly. "I kinda told her...ah, everything. She wasn't exactly receptive."

Zarius's head sinks into his hands. "Patience, son."

Tristan shrugs sheepishly. "Apparently a lack of it runs in the family." Which would explain why it's the one thing Zarius hasn't been able to teach him.

Alden stands, too, his face taking on the fierce lines he had in the library. "You have to befriend her, find a way to connect. How else are you going to ensure her safety?"

"Or find out whether she's one of us?" adds Zarius.

Tess is the only one brave enough to crack a smile through the tension that just replaced the air in the room. She looks steadily at Tristan. "You'll find a way."

Tristan nods. "Damn straight I will."

This is what he's spent his whole life preparing for.

Finding another Zodiac Heir.

Finding his soulmate.

16

BRIELLE

T he usual tribulations aren't fazing Brielle at all today.
        Not that any of the morning's events have been normal.

Suki apparently confessed her infidelity to Zayn, who dumped her in return. She came to school with no makeup and wet cheeks, and as soon as she and Cassandra spotted Brielle in the hallway, they scowled at her. If looks could kill, Brielle would've burst into flames. As if it was somehow her fault that Suki cheated.

"What's their problem?" Adalind asks as she catches up to Brielle in the hall on the way to Cooking class, noting the wicked glares.

"Who knows," Brielle says with a sigh. Because honestly, she doesn't care.

She can't stop thinking about last night with Eye Patch Guy. Is she really the target of some mystery danger, or is she merely the object of some delusion the crazy librarian has? She's not sure which possibility is more frightening.

Eye Patch Guy knows where she lives. If he really is just insane, he could sneak into the orphanage and abduct her.

And he's a very large man, she wouldn't stand a chance against him if he snapped.

But if he's not crazy… That opens up too many possibilities and unknowns, all of which have Brielle jumpier than a frog on a caffeine high.

"Brielle? Did you hear me?" Adalind nudges Brielle's arm as they enter the classroom.

"Huh?" Brielle shakes off her ponderings and turns to Adalind.

"I asked if you're ready for the big dinner tonight with your hopefully new parents," Adalind clarifies, climbing onto her stool at their station and letting her backpack slip off her shoulder and land on the floor.

"Oh, uh, yeah." Brielle sits on her stool so nervously that she almost slides off the other side. She takes a deep breath and adjusts herself.

Adalind frowns and raises an eyebrow. "What is up with you today? Everything okay?"

No. Nothing is okay. But she's not about to tell her only friend that. "Sorry. I was up all night working on my History paper so it would be out of the way and I could be clear-headed for the dinner tonight."

"Doesn't sound like it worked," Adalind says with a chuckle. "I don't think I've ever seen you this tired, or this jittery. I hope you didn't take one of those energy shots, they're horrible for you."

Brielle fakes a laugh, hoping to end the conversation there. How in the world is she going to get through the dinner tonight if she can't even keep it together for two minutes with her best friend?

"So you actually decided to show up today," Adalind says, making Brielle look up to see Tristan approach their station. His blue eyes twinkle as they lock onto her like they're made of diamonds, and her lungs stop working. "Or are you just going to randomly walk out again like you own the place?"

"Why, did you miss me?" He flashes Adalind a teasing smile that is nothing shy of delicious, then winks at Brielle, reminding her to inhale and get her lungs functioning again.

Adalind scoffs. "Yes, desperately." She rolls her eyes.

"How are you, Brielle?" he asks, as if forgetting Adalind is there at all.

"Fine," she says.

She's not sure how to feel about Tristan. The same time yesterday, he'd given her a cryptic warning to stay safe, and after last night, she can't help but wonder if he has anything to do with Eye Patch Guy. Her brain says to keep her distance, but her body can't help but gravitate toward him, like he's the magnetic positive to her negative. Now that he's so close, and she can smell him and feel his warmth, his proximity is fogging her senses and stealing her focus.

And he's looking at her with such intensity. Like she matters. Like she's important. No one has ever looked at her that way. It makes her want to let down her walls.

"Good." Tristan's smile widens. Does he have any idea how charming he is? "I was hoping we could have lunch together today."

Before Brielle can answer, Adalind interrupts with, "Uh, no, she's already got a lunch date, dude. Sorry."

For a split-second, Brielle is grateful for the road block her friend dropped. But the relief quickly fades as she realizes she needs to know once and for all what Tristan's agenda is. She can't keep being the rope in this tug-of-war between the massive red flags and her powerful attraction to him.

"I'm sorry, is your name Brielle?" he asks Adalind. "I believe Brielle is a big girl and can answer for herself."

Adalind's jaw drops and her brow creases, but Brielle interjects before Adalind can chew his head off.

"It's alright, Adalind. Can we skip lunch just this once? I actually would like to talk to Tristan about something."

Adalind scoffs and looks away, crossing her arms in silent rebellion.

"Great, it's a date then. And Adalind, I'm not trying to steal her from you. We can all have lunch together."

Brielle hardly even needs her lie-detection ability to know that his invitation is false and that the last thing he wants is for Adalind to join them. Brielle has to admit that she hopes Adalind doesn't take him up on it. She won't get anything out of him in front of an audience, and she's not sure she wants Adalind to hear the things he may have to say.

"Whatever," she huffs. "As long as I don't have to sit with the drama club, I'll be fine. Those guys never shut up."

Brielle laughs, relieved that Adalind doesn't seem too burned by Brielle picking him over her, even though that's not exactly the case. The air needs to be cleared. And Brielle needs to know if Tristan is someone she can trust.

Brielle's heart is bouncing off the walls of her ribcage like a nervous hummingbird as she waits for Tristan in the hall outside the cafeteria.

This isn't actually a date, she tells herself, resisting the urge to tap her toes. *This is just two friends having lunch at school. No big deal.*

But her body seems to have a mind of its own when it comes to Tristan, and her heart continues to ping pong inside her chest.

"There's the girl I've been looking for."

Brielle turns around and Tristan is walking toward her, his smile having the same effect on her as headlights for a doe foolishly crossing a nighttime road.

"I was thinking we could eat on the lawn," he suggests, waving toward the double doors that lead to the football field. "It's a beautiful day."

Brielle nods, hoping her smile doesn't scream love-sick school girl. "Sounds good to me." Being outside would get them away from the prying, accusatory eyes of Cassandra and Suki, and afford Brielle and Tristan the privacy to be more candid with their conversation topics.

She follows him out the double doors, her lunch bag in hand despite her complete lack of hunger. They walk quite a ways from the brick walls of the school, past the bleachers where a couple are sneaking in a makeout session. Heat rushes up Brielle's neck at the fantasy of her and Tristan in their place, but she quickly shakes the thought away. She can't allow herself to be blinded by her feelings for him. She needs to know the truth first.

"This spot looks perfect. What do you think?" He juts his chin toward a large oak tree by the fence.

The site looks a few notches more romantic than what she'd originally pictured when he asked her to lunch, but she shrugs. "Sure."

When he sits up against the thick brown trunk, she hopes he doesn't notice her knees quiver as they bend beside him. He withdraws a plastic Tupperware from his backpack.

"You bring your own lunch? I thought I was the only one left in our generation who did that." She chuckles, lifting her insulated lunch bag.

"School lunches don't cut it for me. I prefer healthier options. And no one cooks better than my mom." He takes the lid off the container to reveal a dish of sautéed veggies and some kind of fish, and even cold, it smells delicious. There's also a chocolate chip cookie cocooned in plastic wrap sitting on top of the concoction.

"And I suppose cookies count as a healthy food option?"

she teases. "I've been eating right all along and I didn't even know it."

He picks up the cookie, unwraps it and raises it to his lips. "We all have our vices," he says before taking a bite.

Brielle laughs, fingering her lunch bag and debating how to bring up the tenuous topic.

"So how are things going with your potential parents?" asks Tristan, catching her off guard. "You had a meeting with them a few days ago. Did it go well?"

Tristan's genuine interest in her is one of the things that makes him so irresistible.

"Yeah, the meeting went well, and I'm supposed to have dinner with them tonight."

"That's great!" He nudges her arm encouragingly, and even that slight brush of their skin is electrifying.

"If it even happens now," she adds, casting her gaze down at her still unopened bag.

Tristan frowns and tilts his head. "What do you mean?"

She sighs. "Last night at the library, they walked in on a… an argument between Suki and me. The scene did not cast me in a flattering light."

Tristan's brow smooths and he shakes his head. "Whatever happened with Suki, I'm sure that brief moment in time wouldn't override the things they already like about you. Have they mentioned anything to you since about cancelling the dinner?"

Brielle shakes her head. "No, but it's not like I'm the easiest person to get a hold of with no cell phone. For all I know, there's a message waiting for me at the orphanage from them."

"I'm sure you're worrying for nothing and your dinner will go off without a hitch," he says, his tone lighthearted. "If this couple are smart, they'll see you for the sweet, intelligent, captivating girl that you are." His eyes turn turquoise as they bore into her, like he can see right through her.

He's not just saying these things to flatter her, she can sense it. He really means it.

She lets go of her bag and puts her hands firmly in her lap. "Tristan, why do you like me?" Might as well be blunt.

He blinks a few times. "What?"

"You've only just met me," she clarifies. "And yet right from the first moment, you've shown way too much interest in me, and I want to know why."

He leans closer, and she gasps, unable to lean away. "I know you feel it, too. That pull. It's not something I can explain, or resist."

Brielle is both paralyzed and trembling at the same time. The intensity in his blue eyes, the truth she can feel in his words, it's all completely overwhelming, and her resolve is all but shattered. There's only a tiny whisper of doubt keeping her from diving in head first.

She forces herself to swallow to reawaken her motor skills. "That thing you said, about aliens. You were serious. You truly believe it, don't you?"

He looks down, his eyes darting over the grass around them, as if he's debating something. Then his eyes return to hers, and she tries to deny that under his gaze is her favorite place to be.

"I don't just believe it, I know it," he says, voice filled with conviction. "I have lived it every day for the past seventeen years."

"And you came here looking for others like you," she adds. "What makes you think there are others?"

He takes in a long, heavy breath. "Zarius, the man I call my father, was actually a palace guard and right hand of my real father, King Pharis of Gemini I, the Gemini Guardian. During the celebration of my birth, the space station we were on was attacked. All the other Zodiac Heirs aboard the station, princes and princesses like me, were sent in pods to Earth for their protection. I was lucky, sent with Zarius, who raised me with the truth of my lineage. But there are twelve other heirs on this planet, one for each sector of the universe, most of whom likely have no idea who they are. One of those princesses is the other Gemini Heir, my perfect match. My soulmate... My family and I have been searching for them my whole life, and so far, you are the closest we've come."

His story is completely unbelievable, the stuff of epic science fiction movies. Under any other circumstances, Brielle would never even entertain such a fantastical story. But how much more unreal are aliens than visions and curses? She knows her curse exists. Maybe other so-called fictional things do, too. And Tristan isn't lying about any of it, so he's either right or insane. She's not sure which one she's hoping for. Both come with their own dangers.

"What makes you think I'm one of these alien princesses?" Saying it out loud feels so surreal, like she's in a dream. And the possibility of being the soulmate he's looking for? Pure fantasy!

His eyes narrow at her slightly. "You're different. I can't explain it. I just sense it. Maybe the same way you can sense when someone is lying." He flares his brows, giving levity to the tension.

She nods. "And if I am one of your missing alien princesses, what then?"

"You get to know who you really are and where you really came from."

"How will you know for sure?" She's in so deep that she doesn't know if there's any going back, pretending this didn't happen.

"There's a test." He looks over both shoulders, as if making sure they aren't being listened to. "I can't go into detail, but it's a simple test. Not a question-and-answer or biological test. More like how they find out if a child is the Dalai Lama."

Her pulse spiked when he said test, making her imagine having her blood drawn, so she's relieved to hear that it's something more abstract. Holy cow, is she actually considering this?

"Why don't you come over to my house some time?" His invitation spikes her pulse once again. "You can meet my parents, ask them questions, or we can just hang out, eat something awesome my mom will make. And if you really want to know, you can take the test."

She takes a moment to respond, pondering. "And what if I take the test and fail?"

Tristan frowns, as if he hadn't even considered this possibility. "We'll cross that bridge if we come to it, but I'm certain you won't fail."

She nods and looks down at her still unopened lunch bag, whose contents she's nowhere near wanting.

"Does that mean you'll come over?" he asks.

Her heartbeat drums a cadence in her ears that gets louder and louder until she finally says, "Sure. Why not?"

All the colloquialisms she's ever heard ring in her head: down the rabbit hole, not in Kansas anymore… All she's ever wanted was to be adopted, to have a normal life with a family, a home, maybe a dog, and no bigger worries than school assignments or the latest celebrity gossip. Now she's actually considering going along with this whole alien thing.

She didn't expect to be as drawn to someone as she is to Tristan. The connection between them is so much more than a run-of-the-mill high school fling. And she's scared by how much she wants to explore it, to pass Tristan's test and be the girl he thinks she is.

Can she have both? A normal family *and* a whirlwind alien romance? Or will the two desires destroy each other?

You can't have both...Brielle pushes away the frightened whisper in her head.

There's only one way to find out.

17

TRISTAN

S he said yes!

Tristan has to mentally restrain himself from jumping up and giving a triple backflip a red-hot go. She must feel this, too—the undeniable draw from somewhere deep down in her soul. Instead, he allows himself a grin, the motion feeling like it stretches from here to Gemini I.

He leans forward, anticipation tingling over his skin. "Maybe tonight?"

Brielle's lips part, her body subtly angling closer. He can sense she wants to, but she's fighting it.

Tristan holds still, letting her decide, hoping she chooses what's happening between them.

But Brielle's eyes widen and she jerks back. "I can't. I have the dinner with the Pierces tonight."

Disappointment stabs Tristan like a blade, but he ignores it. She said she can't. That's different from a "no thanks." "Well, once that goes great, maybe the day after that?"

Brielle shakes her head ruefully, sliding a smiling glance his way. "You're an all-in kinda guy, aren't you?"

Tristan grins. When the fate of the universe depends on it, it's pretty necessary. "You noticed?"

"A little hard to miss," she replies, wrinkling her nose.

Tristan doesn't think he's ever seen anything so adorable. He finds himself entranced. Speechless.

Could it have finally happened? Could he have found his soulmate?

Brielle flushes, glancing at her watch. "We'd better get back. Lunch is almost over."

And yet something awesome has just begun.

Leaping to his feet, Tristan turns around and extends his hand. "Always the sensible one, huh?"

Brielle squints up at him, her smile returning. "You noticed."

Tristan's laughter starts somewhere deep in his happy place. It dances out, spinning crazily through the air.

But then Brielle places her hand in his. Instinctively, Tristan grabs it, and the laughter dies as he's flooded with awareness. And warmth. And something he can't name...

Without thought, he pulls her up. Brielle is as wide-eyed as he must be as they stand facing each other, hands clasped in the space between them. The mundane world around them fades away. All Tristan can see, all he wants to take in, is the girl before him.

It's like everything just realigned when he never realized how out of whack it was. Like the Universe itself is drawing them together. Like a new center of gravity has just formed between them.

When the bell rings, they both jump as they're yanked out of the bubble of awareness that had ballooned around them. Brielle jerks her hand back and Tristan rubs the back of his head ruefully. It seems the real world wasn't that far away after all.

"We'd better...ah...go," Brielle stammers.

Tristan picks up his lunch tub. "Yeah, don't want to be late."

From what he's seen, Brielle's spent her life trying to play by the rules. If she really is a Zodiac Heir, it's probably why she's struggled to blend in, to be normal. But until Brielle sees the truth for herself, she's going to shy away. He can't blame her. Although it's his normal, it's a lot for someone else to take in.

They fall into step beside each other as they walk across the lawn. Tristan wonders if his feet are even touching the grass. Their hands brush and warmth floods him again.

He wonders how her powers would tie in with his, if she's the Gemini Twin. He can't see the link between her lie detection and his visions, but he does know the Universe works in mysterious ways.

Tristan and Brielle. He can already feel it's going to be one hell of a love story.

They reach the lockers and Tristan leans against them as Brielle fiddles with the code on hers. "You've got History next, don't you?"

Brielle's brows contract as she flits a glance at him. "You know my schedule?"

Tristan's had to make sure he knows her every move. Because if Brielle's who he believes she is, then Chardis wants her just as much as he does.

And that sure as hell ain't gonna happen.

Tristan shrugs. "I figured if I've got Geography, you've got History."

Brielle nods thoughtfully. "Yeah, I've got History." She smiles. "I'm handing in an assignment early."

Tristan's about to point out that's impressive—he doubts he'll ever hand anything in early—when a voice skims over his shoulder.

"Rush job, huh? I bet that'll work out for you."

He spins around, surprised. He was so focused on Brielle he never heard Cassandra approach. Something frowns inside him. That's never happened before. He can't afford not to be on high alert at all times.

Brielle turns away. "It's none of your business, Cassandra."

Cassandra crosses her arms. "You make it my business when you break up my best friend's relationship."

Tristan's frown is strongly considering finding a way to the outside. What's Cassandra talking about? Nor does he like the snideness in her tone.

Brielle flushes as she slams her locker closed, her gaze flickering to Tristan. "I don't have time to talk about this. What Suki does with her own time is her choice."

"And yet you had time to talk to Suki and destroy her life *and* Zayn's."

Brielle spins around, her eyes flashing. "Did she tell you she cheated on him? More than once?"

Cassandra's lip curls. "She said they're exactly the rumors you'd start spreading."

Tristan slips in between them, raising his hands. "I doubt Brielle would—"

But Brielle steps around him. "I don't spread rumors."

There's an anger in Brielle's voice that tells Tristan that Cassandra just struck a chord. It sure isn't something he could see Brielle doing. Especially if she can see when a person's lying. Honesty is something she'd value.

But Cassandra meets Brielle's anger, possibly looking to raise it. "You're jealous of Suki just like you were of me, and you know it." Cassandra turns to Tristan. "Has she told you she tried to sabotage my adoption?"

Brielle gasps and Tristan instinctively steps between them again. "I think everyone needs to take a chill pill right about now." He relaxes as if to show them what he's talking about. "Plus, the bell's already—"

"Cassandra. Brielle. We do not tolerate tardiness here at Mirror Point High."

They all spin around to find Ms. Grotberg, the vice-principal, striding down the corridor, her hand already slipping into her skirt pocket. "This is unacceptable. The bell rang several minutes ago. I'm going to be forced to issue you a late slip."

Cassandra's entire demeanor changes, her body loosening as she hoists up a smile. "Ms. Grotberg, you're looking well today. We got caught up talking about our History assignments."

Ms. Grotberg turns to look at Brielle, who frowns as her gaze slides away. It seems she's not willing to back Cassandra up in her story, and if Brielle has to live with seeing people's lies, then Tristan understands why. There's enough untruth in the world as it is.

Ms. Grotberg raises a brow as her gaze settles on Tristan. He shrugs. "I'm in Geography. But what they were talking about was pretty interesting."

Apparently, there's a lot of bad blood still flowing under the bridge between Brielle and Cassandra.

Cassandra stiffens, although the motion is slight. Anyone else would probably have missed it. But Tristan's been trained to pick up on subtle changes. Cassandra ain't happy with how things are turning out.

Ms. Grotberg's hand dives back into her skirt pocket. "If that's the case, I'll be issuing you each with a late slip. If you hurry up, I'll reconsider giving your parents a call."

Even if this were Tristan's fiftieth late offense, Zarius and Tess wouldn't care about late slips. Ms. Grotberg obviously doesn't realize there are more important things in life.

Tristan thanks her as he takes the slip. At least Ms. Grotberg is taking her job seriously.

Brielle holds her hand out, accepting the piece of paper. Either the orphanage wouldn't care or she's willing to take this on the chin.

But Cassandra goes extremely still. Tristan glances at her from the corner of his eye, noticing she suddenly looks like she's been molded from steel.

Ms. Grotberg holds out the late slip and Cassandra stares at it, unmoving. Ms. Grotberg shakes it, raising her brows. "Cassandra? You're not showing that you're in a hurry to get to class."

Stiffly, Cassandra reaches out and takes it. There's a tiny flash of yellow light and Ms. Grotberg's eyes widen as she jerks back.

Cassandra flushes. "Sorry, static electricity."

Tristan glances down. They're not standing on carpet.

Ms. Grotberg frowns. "Of course. Now, back to class. I don't want to see you out here when I come back."

Ms. Grotberg strides away, her back looking like that little zap just shot a cranky-pole up her spine. Tristan turns back to Cassandra. He's spent his whole life looking for anything out of the norm...

She turns furious blue eyes to Brielle. "This is all your fault! If my dad gets a phone call—"

"So," Tristan jumps in. "I'm thinking class would be a pretty good idea right now."

He hears Brielle take a step back behind him as he watches Cassandra closely. His spidey senses are on high alert, even though he knows it's probably another false alarm.

Although Cassandra is an orphan...

Cassandra pulls in a deep breath, her eyes focusing on Tristan. Tristan scans down, noting the way her hand grips the paper slip. Maybe she was telling the truth. It could've been nothing but static electricity. When his gaze comes back up, Cassandra is looking at him with her brow ever so slightly hitched.

It's totally saying "So you had lunch with her, but you're checking me out…"

Which is about as far from the truth as she can get, but there's no way for Tristan to clarify that. Especially seeing as there's now a question mark bobbing over her head.

So he smiles. "I'm pretty sure no one wants to be here when Grotty gets back. Let's just head to class."

But Cassandra juts out a hip as she lifts her hand to it, the paper slipping out and fluttering to the ground. "I actually came over to see if you were planning on putting my number to good use anytime soon. Like for that date you promised."

Behind him, Brielle gasps and it's like a shot straight through Tristan's back. This isn't what she needs to see, not after the lunch they just had. With a sharp *slap*, one of her books lands on the ground.

Tristan frowns, bending down to pick it up, conscious she hasn't moved. Hurting Brielle was never part of the plan. He grabs the notepad and straightens. "I'm pretty sure that's not why you came over—"

The words turn to ash in his mouth. Cassandra's late slip flips up as the wind from the fallen book hits it and hovers as if it wants Tristan to get a really good look. A split second later, it flicks and flutters back down to the ground.

Tristan blinks, a whiff of burnt paper tickling his nose. The slip lays on the linoleum floor, the sight undeniable. The edges of the paper are singed. Burned.

And static electricity sure as hell doesn't do that.

Tristan gets himself vertical again, knowing this should be good news. But it's come at the worst possible time.

Brielle hasn't moved a muscle behind him. She's waiting to see what he's going to say to Cassandra's flirty question.

And he has no choice. He has to find out if she's a Zodiac Heir.

Tristan yanks up a grin. "But now that you mention it, no harm with the new guy wanting to make friends, is there?"

But Brielle's tiny intake of breath tells him otherwise. He spins around but she's already walking away, leaving him holding her notepad.

And a truckload of regret.

"Smart *and* good-looking," says Cassandra, her voice full of admiration. "I like."

Tristan turns back, telling himself if Brielle really is his soulmate, then something small like this won't get in the way. He angles his head. "What have you got against Brielle? She's not exactly the arch nemesis type."

Cassandra flicks her hair as she spins on her heel. "We'll have plenty of time to chitty chat over dinner. Tonight?"

Wow. And Brielle thought Tristan worked fast. But at least this way it'll mean he might have his answers sooner rather than later. "Sure. I've got your number."

After she scrawled it across his arm.

With a shining smile, Cassandra sashays past. "Looking forward to it."

Tristan pulls his hand down his face, wanting to groan aloud. Surely that didn't just happen. Maybe he should've said no, talked to Zarius or Tess. Maybe he's wrong.

Except the slip of paper is still on the floor. Tristan picks it up, and the burnt edge crumbles between his fingers.

He'll explain this to Brielle. Once she truly grasps what hinges on finding the Zodiac Heirs, she'll understand. He crushes the paper in his fist, striding down the empty hall.

Any other outcome isn't even worth considering.

That evening, Cassandra's already waiting at the restaurant, Chez Monet, insisting on meeting Tristan there. He'd joked that she doesn't want her parents knowing who she's going out with and Cassandra had giggled...but not denied it.

Tristan had shrugged it off, though. He's not out to impress her parents, or anyone else. He has more important things to do.

Like find out whether Cassandra's a Zodiac Heir.

As Tristan approaches, he's glad he went to the effort of a collared shirt and brushing his hair, because Cassandra has knocked it out of the park. She slinks toward him in a dark blue number that almost has Tristan's jaw dropping. How the hell is that thing staying up?

Cassandra smiles. "Hey."

Tristan's suddenly uncomfortable. Cassandra's gone to a lot of effort to look the way she does, when he's not interested in anything like *that*.

Unless she's your soulmate...

Tristan has to hide his startle. If Cassandra's a Zodiac Heir, there's a chance she could be.

Something in him screams a denial as Brielle's face flashes through his mind. But the Universe chose his soulmate, just like it chose each one of the Heirs. He doesn't get a say...

"Are you okay, Tristan?" Cassandra's brow crinkles in concern.

Get it together, man! He grins. "Sorry, my brain just flatlined for a second. You look amazing."

Cassandra's smile is dazzling. "Training six days a week means I get to wear dresses like this." She twirls and the layers of blue skirt fan out.

"Well, that's not fair. I train seven days a week and I don't get to wear anything as cool as that."

Cassandra laughs, the sound bright and bubbly and Tristan's grin grows. If he can keep things platonic, this date might actually be fun.

He holds the door open for her. "Shall we?"

Inside, the restaurant is quiet and elegant—kinda what Tristan expected when Cassandra suggested the place. It's obvious she comes from money. The waiter takes them to a back corner and pulls out a chair for Cassandra.

She sits down before Tristan can think of a reason to object. Having his back to a roomful of people always makes him uncomfortable—you never know who could be approaching you. When the waiter sees Tristan standing there, he comes around to pull out his chair, too. Tristan quickly slides in before he has a chance—he's never had anyone hold a chair for him, and he's not about to start.

"Nice place," comments Tristan as they both check out the menu.

"One of the few that my father doesn't own," replies Cassandra. She places her menu down. "I'm going to go with the Greek salad. No feta."

Tristan glances at her, thinking he'll have the steak. "For entrée or as a side?"

She folds the menu and pushes it to the side. "For mains, silly. My coach has me on a strict diet during training season."

Zarius tried that, except he likes Tess's baking too much.

"Isn't track season almost finished?"

Cassandra rolls her eyes. "Tell that to my dad."

Tristan makes a mental note. Cassandra chose to come to a restaurant her father wouldn't know about, and yet he's dictating what she eats. Obviously a rebel on a tight leash.

The waiter reappears and delivers their drinks—a soda for Tristan and sparkling water for Cassandra. He takes their orders and retreats with a stiff bow.

Tristan leans forward, focusing on the pretty girl across from him. "So, Cassandra. You're obviously popular. Quite the all-rounder, so a high achiever. Gorgeous. Confident. And a calorie counter thanks to a whip-cracking father." He smiles, angling his head. "What else should I know?"

Her eyes twinkle, impressed with his assessment. "That when I like something, I go for it," she purrs.

Tristan arches a brow. "And you like getting under Brielle's skin."

It's obviously why she took such a strong interest in Tristan.

Cassandra laughs again. "Maybe in the beginning. But I like you, Tristan." She shrugs a bare shoulder. "I get the sense we're going to click."

Tristan draws back, a little disarmed by her honesty. She's right. Talking to Cassandra is easy. She's fun, she's bold. Would this be what it's like with his soulmate?

Unbidden, Brielle's face comes to mind again. She's reticent, but she has layers Tristan is itching to peel back. And he's thinking about her as he sits across from Cassandra.

She props her chin in her hands as she leans forward. "So, what are you into, Tristan Ayers?"

Aliens. Finding the good ones. Learning martial arts so I can fight the bad ones.

Tristan knows this is his opportunity to put some feelers out. Usually he jokes that he's a film buff, particularly alien movies like *Men in Black*, *War of the Worlds*…*E.T.* Then he asks the person if they think aliens could be real.

But as his gaze flicks to Cassandra's hand wrapped around her glass of water, Tristan wonders whether he should ask what superpower she'd love to have. It's not so much her answer he'll be watching, but her body language. A widening of the eyes. Withdrawing her hand. Her blue gaze sliding away.

She's looking at him expectantly but then she focuses past his shoulder. Her eyes definitely widen and her hand withdraws as she sits back.

But then an unexpected smile trips up her lips, and her hand slides across the table as she leans forward. Uneasiness slithers up Tristan's spine. There's something about that smile…

Cassandra's hand doesn't stop until it's resting on his, her eyes flashing with something Tristan wishes they wouldn't —victory.

The uneasiness blossoms to dread. There's only one reason Cassandra would be looking like she just slam-dunked.

Brielle.

18

BRIELLE

F rank and Beatrice exchange flittering glances while their faces fail to hide smiles.

The dinner has gone so well. In fact, it couldn't have gone better! As Brielle sits across from them at the table at Chez Monet thirty minutes after everyone cleared their plates, she's certain they're a perfect fit for her, and that she's a perfect fit for them.

Now they wait for the waiter to return with Frank's credit card, and Brielle burns with curiosity as to what they're grinning secretly to each other about.

Beatrice gives Frank a subtle nod that Brielle wouldn't have caught if she wasn't watching them so intently, and he clasps his hands together in front of him on the white table cloth.

"We're just going to cut to the chase," he says, his smile shining as he speaks. "We want to adopt you."

Brielle's heart jumps into her throat, cutting off her oxygen supply.

"We want to be your mom and dad." Beatrice positively glows as she says these words that seem both difficult and natural at the same time to say. "Will you join our little family?"

"Yes!" The simple word jumps out of Brielle's mouth before she can even resume breathing.

"Really?" Beatrice squeals.

"Brielle, you don't know how happy you've made us!" Frank says, taking his wife's hands in his. "How about we celebrate with dessert at our house? Your new house."

Brielle's chest is so bursting with joy that it threatens to explode and ruin the nice white table cloth between them.

"I would love nothing more," she professes.

"Excellent! Ah, and just in time." The waiter hands Frank the receipt and his credit card, which is swiftly stowed back into Frank's wallet. He stands up and holds out an inviting hand. "Shall we?"

Brielle nods so eagerly she feels like a bobble-head doll, and she and Beatrice stand up and follow him to the front door.

But an impossible sight has Brielle slowing her pace behind her new parents, staring as if to prove to herself that what she's seeing is a trick of the mind. And yet, the longer she stares, the closer she gets, the sight only becomes more cemented in reality.

Tristan is sitting at a table in a dimly lit corner and *holding hands* with none other than her arch nemesis, the blonde beauty queen of Mirror Point High.

Cassandra.

And what's worse?

Brielle can't even duck out of view and pretend not to have seen them because Cassandra is sneering right at her, causing Tristan to turn and lock eyes with her.

She finally stops, frozen in a moment in time with Tristan, and not in anywhere near the same way they were earlier today. When he confided heartfelt hopes of his soul-mate, and insinuating she might be it.

How could she have been so stupid?

A sudden surge of determination cuts the moment short and rushes her out the door after Frank and Beatrice. She's not going to let Tristan ruin her night. She just got the family she always prayed for! Whatever he's doing here with Cassandra, she can't allow herself to care.

She's not two steps into the parking lot, however, when a hand clasps around her upper arm, igniting the electric sparks that she no longer wants to feel.

"Brielle, please wait," Tristan says.

Frank and Beatrice turn around midstep, and Frank's expression goes from jolly to guarded in an instant.

"Is everything okay, Brielle?" he asks, regarding Tristan with a look that says, "you'd better be careful how you touch my daughter."

Brielle is touched by Frank's concern, and she debates shaking free of Tristan's grasp and following them to their car without a word about what she saw.

But she can't. Not after their lunch together. Not after how amazing Tristan made her feel, only to betray her in the worst possible way.

She deserves an explanation, and she's going to get it.

"Yes, it's alright," Brielle says, amazed that her anger isn't seeping into her tone. "Can I just have a minute?"

Beatrice and Frank hover in place for a long moment, assessing Tristan to make sure he's not a threat, and an encouraging nod from Brielle sends them on their way to the blue Buick parked not too far away.

Brielle watches them until they get in the car and close the door before turning her righteous outrage on Tristan.

"So everything you said to me earlier today was a lie," she accuses. "Maybe everything you've ever said to me is a lie.

Maybe you're the one person who's immune to my lie-detection. And what a sucker I am for falling for all the—"

"It's not like that," Tristan cuts her off in a hoarse whisper. "I swear to you, on everything I have ever strived for, that I have no romantic interest in Cassandra."

"Oh, so it's just physical then? Why not, she's beautiful, sexy, everything a guy like you would want. So, what, she's the snack and I'm the meal? You have to take a little nibble of her while making sure I hang around, wrapped around your deceitful finger. I'm such an idiot!"

"No, you're not," he says, taking a step closer.

Too close. Too intimate a distance for what he just did. Brielle takes a step back.

That tiny gesture visibly stings Tristan, and Brielle takes a small bit of joy in that.

"I'm not into Cassandra like that," Tristan continues. "Everything I told you is true. I only came out with her tonight because…"

He bites his tongue, and there's no way in hell Brielle is going to let him keep his next words to himself.

"Because what," she demands, crossing her arms under her chest and jutting her hip like a dagger meant to slice.

Tristan growls under his breath, then says with some difficulty, "Because I think she may be a Zodiac Heir, too."

Brielle's not sure what angers her more. That Tristan is using his same tired old lie to excuse his actions with Cassandra, or that he thinks she might be his *soulmate,* too.

"Well, you know what? I hope she is. I hope you two live happily ever after in your little alien world."

"Brielle, please don't—" He moves closer again.

She puts her hand up like it's a stop sign. "Don't. I'm done with you, Tristan. Go back to your *Zodiac Girl* and leave me be. I have more important things going on in my life. Not like you care, but the Pierces just agreed to adopt me. And if you don't mind, I'm going home with them for a celebratory dessert. Good night."

She spins around and stomps to the Buick, refusing to look back no matter how much she wants to.

Time to close the book on the Tristan chapter of her life.

As soon as Brielle makes the decision to be in the moment and focus on this first time at the house she would forever after call home, thoughts of Tristan stay away.

Frank and Beatrice live on the outskirts of town where grass fields seem to stretch to the horizon. Theirs is a lovely two story colonial style house with white wooden walls and blue shutters on the windows. The house sits at the forefront of a property that's probably three acres, its boundaries marked by a charming white-picket fence.

Frank pulls up the sloping cobblestone driveway to the garage, and Brielle can't believe this is their house. Soon to be her house. It's exactly what she would have pictured for her dream home. She can already see herself playing catch with Frank in the backyard, or sunbathing with Beatrice on the deck chairs on the front lawn.

She opens her door and climbs out of the car, making her first steps on the property and she can't believe this is actually happening. Is this how Cinderella felt when Prince Charming brought her to the castle to live happily ever after?

"Come on in," Frank invites after he unlocks and opens the kitchen door inside the garage.

"I'll get dessert started," Beatrice says as she skips ahead of him, then pauses and looks at Brielle over her shoulder. "What do you like on your ice cream? Chocolate or caramel?"

"Both," Brielle answers, and Frank chuckles.

Beatrice lightly slaps him on the shoulder. "She really is just like you."

Brielle blushes at that comment and follows them in.

The house is just as perfect and cozy inside as it looks on the outside. Hardwood floors that shine like amber under the warm lighting, granite counters atop ornate cabinets and an island with stools she can imagine having breakfast at. Past the shorter arm of the L-shaped counters is the living room, furnished with reclining brown couches that look like heaven to sit on and relax in front of the huge flat-screen on the brick wall above the fireplace. And there are so many windows. It's night right now, but Brielle imagines they would look gorgeous with the morning light streaming in.

"Let me give you a little tour while Bea works her magic," says Frank, tipping his head toward the living room.

Brielle follows as he takes her through the house: the living room, the game room, his study, Bea's craft room, their bedroom, a guest room. And finally…

Frank places his hand on the doorknob of the last door across from their bedroom at the end of the hall. "We weren't super sure what style you'd like, but we figure you can always redecorate it however you want." He opens the door and ushers her inside.

The room is twice the size of her room at the orphanage, and the elegantly carved queen bed is three times the size of her current bed and covered in more blankets and pillows than she can ever imagine needing but can't wait to try out. There are two dressers that match the bed, and a long closet with sliding doors that takes up one entire wall.

"It's perfect," she says through a lump in her throat.

"Good, I'm glad," says Frank. Then after a pause, he says, "That boy earlier, is he your boyfriend? You seemed pretty upset with him."

Brielle shakes her head, her Tristan-free bubble popping.

"No, he's definitely not my boyfriend. Just some boy from school, apparently dating a girl I don't have the best history with."

"Ah, I see." He nods, obviously uncomfortable about the topic but pursuing it anyway. "Well, if you ever want to talk about him, or the girl, or anything, I want you to feel free to talk to us."

She smiles, the tense knot his question had formed in her stomach loosening. "Of course. I would like that." And in a gesture that's so natural she doesn't notice until it's happening, she hugs him, and he hugs back.

And it feels perfect.

"Dessert's ready," Beatrice calls from the kitchen, and they withdraw from each other to join her.

Brielle looks out the windows that line one side of the hallway, savoring the way the grass sparkles in the light of the mostly full moon and trying to see if the stars are more visible this much farther away from the big city.

Right as she starts to turn away, a cluster of shadows dash across the edge of the yard. She doubletakes, blinking a few times as she stares at the spot she thought she saw them. The grass is still, and there's nothing out there. Not even a breeze blows through the trees. Maybe it was bats or nightingales.

Or Eye Patch Guy following her again.

Her pulse pounds for an instant before she tells herself she's being paranoid. It's probably nothing.

She sighs, ready to turn away and continue down the hall when a dark spot she'd been staring at in the grass moves, followed by more dark blotches.

Those were the shadows she'd seen. They really had moved. And they're coming toward the house!

What she's seeing doesn't make sense. What's casting those shadows? They seem to be in the shape of a person, but there are definitely no people out there. Could they be invisible? Or has she just finally lost her mind?

"Brielle, is something wrong?" Frank's concerned question makes her head turn.

"Umm...no, everything's fine," she lies, her voice cracking with uncertainty. "Do you mind if I step out for a sec?"

He lingers for a moment, the concern on his face deepening.

"Really, it's fine," she reassures. "I just think I need some fresh air."

If it is Eye Patch Guy, she needs to make him go away. She can't have him interfering with the utopia she's stumbled upon, and she'll do anything to protect Frank and Beatrice from his strangeness. She's not quite sure what she saw, but it must have an explanation, and she'll be damned if she's not going to get to the bottom of it. Right now.

"Alright, if that's what you need," he says, one foot hovering on the threshold of the kitchen. "Like I said, you can always talk to us."

"I know." She puts on her best smile and hopes it's convincing.

He nods and continues on into the kitchen, letting her slip through the porch door to the back yard.

Summoning up every ounce of her bravery, she shakily calls out, "Hello?"

Nothing. Not even crickets. As if they, too, have quieted to hear the intruder.

"Look, I don't know what you want, but you'd better leave or..." she hesitates, feeling foolish for talking to the silence. "Or I'll call the police."

The night is so still, so completely devoid of all sound, that it disturbs her to her core. Maybe it's because she's grown up in town and the distant noises of dogs barking and cars driving is her idea of what night sounds like. But not even the grass hisses under the slightest breeze, as if the moonlight has put everything in this field into a trance.

And it's the eeriest thing she's ever experienced.

Suddenly, desperate to escape the nothingness that threatens to swallow her without a trace, she turns to go inside. Something heavy drops onto her shoulder, and before she can scream, a hand clamps tightly over her mouth.

"Don't scream," whispers her assailant, and despite the hushed tone, she recognizes Tristan's voice.

She nods, burning with both terror and curiosity as to why he's here.

He removes his hand, and she slowly turns to face him. She really should have avoided him from the very beginning. Like a moth to a flame. Maybe *he's* the real danger.

He puts his index finger to his lips. "You need to come with me. Now." His whisper is so silent she wouldn't have heard him if the rest of the world was still in motion.

Barely able to move, she manages to shake her head.

"Please, you're in danger," he hisses. "They've come for you."

That triggers a cannon in her nervous system.

"Who?" she mouths, unable to put enough wind behind her question for it to be audible.

"I'll explain later, but we have to go *right now.*"

A sudden anger simmers deep within her and quickly spreads throughout her extremities. First he tells her she may be the person he's been looking for his entire life, then he goes out with Cassandra of all people, and now he shows up at what might become her new home and tells her to abandon her one and only chance at a family.

"No!" she hisses back.

"Urgh, Brielle, this isn't a game!" he groans hoarsely, no longer as quiet.

She glares at him and stomps forward. "You don't get to

do this, Tristan. You don't get to manipulate me, fraternize with the one person who hates me most, and then demand I leave my only hope at a better life. No. I'm not going with you. Leave, or I *will* call the cops."

His head drops between his shoulders and shakes slowly from side to side before lifting back up to look at her. "I can promise you that if you don't come with me, you and your new parents will die. You want to save them? Then we have to go."

The word "die" strikes a chord, and the vibrations resonate throughout her entire body. She knows she's in danger. She wouldn't have come out here if she didn't. And with all the weirdness of the last few days—Tristan showing up, her powers growing, Eye Patch Guy's warning—she can't just leave this to chance.

"Then tell me who's after me," she demands, still whispering lest she broadcast the danger to Frank and Bea.

He clenches his jaw and exhales loudly, then holds his breath when he hears the sound it makes. "His name is Chardis. He's the greatest evil in the Universe, and he's the one who attacked my family's space station and sent the Universe into chaos. He has assassins everywhere, forever hunting for the children who were sent to Earth seventeen years ago. They can become invisible and are extremely powerful."

Invisible.

Like the objectless shadows she saw moments ago. The reason she came outside.

"And they're here as we speak. It's only a matter of time before they discover us and destroy us both. The only reason they'd be here is if you really are a Zodiac Heir. Now, do you want to be adopted or do you want to live?"

He holds out his hand.

She looks at it, a hot debate warring in her head. If she

leaves now, completely abandons Frank and Bea without an explanation, she can kiss adoption goodbye. But Tristan isn't lying. Even now, in her fragile paranoid state, she can sense the truth in his words and being. He really is here to help her.

And in this moment, her draw to him is more powerful than ever before. His open palm looks like a life raft, and she feels like she's been floating at sea for months.

What should she do?

A twig snaps nearby, and out of instinct, she grabs his hand and pulls close against him.

"I'll explain everything when we get to safety," he whispers, his lips brushing against her forehead. "I promise."

Brielle doesn't know what she's just agreed to, but every fiber of her being tells her it's not safe for anyone if she stays.

Goodbye Frank and Bea.

Goodbye happily ever after.

19

TRISTAN

Wishing he had more time to explain this, but knowing he doesn't, Tristan grabs Brielle's hand and runs. His truck is parked further up the driveway, as close as he could get without being seen.

Right now, it feels too far away.

Reminding himself not everyone runs five miles before breakfast, Tristan has to force himself to slow down. He can feel he's pulling Brielle as they break through the bushes and onto the drive.

Maybe they got away in time. Maybe he's overreacted.

"Brielle?" a woman's voice calls out. "Are you coming back inside?"

Brielle's hand jerks in his as she looks over her shoulder. "Maybe I could just—"

Except there's the unmistakable snap of a branch somewhere behind them.

Tristan grips her hand tighter, moving away from the house. "We need to get out of here."

He takes them across the lawn, no longer bothering to

stick to the shadows. Brielle doesn't know how to fight. That means it's his job to keep them both alive.

And getting the hell out of here is his best bet of making sure that happens.

The truck gleams in the dull moonlight, and Tristan opens the door for Brielle. "Quick. They're not going to want to chat if they catch us."

Brielle clambers in and Tristan runs to the driver's side. He's barely shut the door when he jams it into gear. "You'd better put your seatbelt—"

The *click* finishes the sentence for him. "What about yours?"

Tristan presses the accelerator. Just like Zarius taught him, he parked with a quick getaway in mind. Facing the road, no obstructions. He glances at Brielle. "What?"

"Your seatbelt. You should have it on, too."

Keeping his headlights off, Tristan drives as fast as he can through the shadowy night. "It's fine. I'll get it later."

Brielle's hand appears under his nose. "Pass it here. If I need a seatbelt, so do you."

Throwing an exasperated look her way, Tristan has to work not to smile. Reaching over his shoulder, Tristan grabs it and zips it across his body. Before he can click it in, Brielle takes it and does it herself. A quick tug and she makes sure it's secure.

Tristan blinks. "Ah, thanks."

Brielle turns to face forward. "It's a good thing you agreed. If you didn't, I was going to take mine off."

Tristan's smile is out of place considering they're trying to get away from Skins, but it flares anyway. Brielle's sweet... but plucky.

Quickly wiping it off his face, Tristan focuses on the road. He can figure out if these feelings mean what he thinks they do once they get back to the safety of his house. Just a little bit longer driving half-blind and he'll turn on the headlights. Then he's going to make like a shepherd and get the flock out of here.

The outlines of barns and houses creep by Tristan's peripheral vision. Of course, the Pierces have to live out of town. Everyone's seen enough movies to know what happens on backroads thanks to the lack of nosy neighbors. His hands flex on the steering wheel. Not much longer—

The sound of a roaring engine splits the air a second before Tristan's truck is rammed from behind. Brielle screams as the impact jolts them forward, the seatbelt stopping Tristan from slamming his head against the steering wheel.

"Bastards," Tristan mutters under his breath. "Hold on."

Flicking the headlights on, Tristan jams his foot on the gas. The engine roars and the truck leaps forward, Brielle grabbing the dashboard.

The SUV's headlights flash on, spearing through the rear window. The light retreats, but only for a second. The Skins accelerate, too, the yellow glow feeling like it's breathing down Tristan's neck. The next jolt has his teeth jarring.

"Tristan!" Brielle cries in alarm.

Pushing his foot all the way down, Tristan feels the wheels spin for a second before they grip. The truck's rear end fishtails then streaks down the dirt road. Wishing he could comfort Brielle, tell her everything's going to be okay, he locks his arms. Focus is what's going to keep them alive right now.

The roaring draws close again, but this time, the SUV pulls out as if it's trying to overtake. Tristan continues to accelerate, his heart rate matching the odometer. He's never driven this fast, and not on a backroad he doesn't know. He tries to remember what turns are coming up. Whether there's somewhere he could lose them.

But he was too focused on following Brielle and her adoptive parents, cringing at the lame excuses he'd given Cassandra as he'd cut their date short.

The SUV draws up beside them and a quick glance shows two sneering Skins. The driver jerks his hands down and the SUV slams into the side of Tristan's truck.

They careen off the side of the road, the tires sliding and bumping over the rough ground. His teeth gritted, Tristan fights the wheel with straining arms, stopping it from jerking wildly.

A quick yank and they're back on the road, only to find the SUV is still beside them.

"They're trying to kill us!" Brielle shouts incredulously.

"They'd probably prefer us alive, but injured wouldn't be an issue," Tristan growls.

He accelerates again only to find the SUV right beside him, joined in some sick dance. If it was just him, he'd ram the bastards back, but he has Brielle in the car. And his job is to protect her, not turn her into a canned sardine.

It means he has no choice but to wear the next attack. This ram has him slamming on the brakes as they bump over rutted ground. Brielle cries out at the looming length of a tree they're roaring toward. Tristan doesn't have time to see how much space he has, he yanks the wheel down, the broad trunk whizzing so close past Brielle's window that she jerks away from the door. There's the screech of a branch scratching the side and they're back on the road.

"There's still half a mile before we're on the main road," Brielle whispers hoarsely.

Too far. Too much time for the Skins to send them slamming into the next tree.

A side road, probably a driveway, zips past them. "I've got an idea. Hold on."

The SUV lines them up. The Skins sneer as they wait,

wanting to make them sweat.

"What idea? Tristan—"

The moment the Skin twists the steering wheel, Tristan slams his foot on the brake. The truck screeches and slides to a halt as the SUV streaks over the road, no longer having something to bounce off. It jolts over the verge, careening as it tries to change direction. Tristan holds his breath, only to watch the vehicle quickly right itself.

"Of course, they do," mutters Tristan. Crashing into the side of the road and exploding in a ball of fire would've been far too convenient.

A quick glance makes sure Brielle's still bracing herself, and Tristan accelerates as he jerks up the handbrake and twists the wheel. The rear end of the truck spins around, and in a blink, they're facing the other way.

Tristan's foot slams down on the accelerator. The driveway they just passed has got to be only a few yards away. A quick glance in the rearview mirror shows the headlights of the SUV swinging around.

The Skins are about to give chase.

"Are you holding on?" Tristan asks. Hopefully this is the last crazy move he's going to have to pull off.

"I haven't let go!" snaps Brielle.

Tristan flashes her a smile. "That's m'girl."

The turn he takes onto the sideroad is fast and aggressive. Gravel and dust spew out, rising like a cloud behind them as the rear end of the truck swerves wildly. Tristan straightens it up and powers down the side road. Ahead is just what he was hoping there would be.

A barn.

Cutting the lights, Tristan veers off the track and bounces over the grass. The moment they're behind the building, he turns off the engine. Hopefully the cloud of dust they left behind obscured their little detour.

The silence that follows is short-lived. The furious sound of the SUV rumbles toward them. Tristan and Brielle freeze, not even the sound of their breath puncturing the air in the cab. He almost shakes his head. It's not like the Skins would hear them breathing. They either saw them drive behind the barn, or the truck managed to slip out of view just in time.

Still, Tristan doesn't give his aching lungs what they want until the SUV zooms past and around the next bend.

He sags, his head thumping against the steering wheel. "Man, that was close."

Brielle doesn't move. "Are you sure they're gone?"

"We'll give them a few minutes, then get the heck out of here." Tristan straightens, studying her profile. "The irony that the Skins didn't see *us* will have us smiling one day."

Brielle swallows, keeping her gaze straight ahead. "I hope so. I'm pretty sure my face is forever frozen in a scream."

Tristan shifts across the seat, brushing a strand of Brielle's hair from her face. "That was one hell of an introduction to the Skins. Are you okay?"

Brielle rubs her arms as if she's cold. "They were trying to kill us, weren't they?"

"From what I can tell, we're worth more to them alive. But yes, dead is a close second."

She shivers and Tristan wraps his arms around her. "We need to get home. Things will be different once you have your stone."

Brielle curls into him, gripping his shirt. "Nothing's ever going to be the same again."

Tristan's chest aches at the truth in those words. "But we'll do it together."

Brielle nods into his chest and protectiveness engulfs Tristan. The feeling of connection with this girl is overwhelming. The sooner she has her tanzanite in her hand, the better.

He pulls back. "It looks like we've lost them. Let's get you somewhere safe."

Brielle nods, wiping at her eyes. Tristan presses his face in close, his heart jolting as his eyes connect with hers. "Together, okay?"

The smallest of smiles tips up Brielle's lips. "Okay."

Sliding back behind the wheel, Tristan drives them back out to the road with the headlights off. His eyes spend just as much time scanning his mirrors as he keeps them on their ticket out of here.

It feels like neither of them take more than a shallow breath until they hit the tarmac. The streetlights feel warm and welcoming, the sight of another car zipping past has the noose around Tristan's airway loosening.

He glances at Brielle's pale face. "The good news is my place isn't far from here."

Brielle's quiet for a moment and Tristan wonders exactly how freaked out she is. None of this would be easy to assimilate, especially when it's thrown at you in an attempt to kill you.

She angles her head. "Where did you learn to drive like that?"

Tristan turns to face the road again. It seems Brielle isn't so freaked out that she's not wanting some answers. "Driver training started when I was twelve."

"Twelve? That's not exactly legal."

"Neither is ramming someone off the road. Zarius figured that if I have to choose between death and dipping my toes on the wrong side of the law, we'd go for option B every time."

Brielle twists even further to face Tristan. "Zarius?"

"Zarius is the palace soldier who was sent to protect me. He's taught me everything I know—how to drive, how to fight, what we'll need to defeat Chardis."

"You sound close."

"Zarius and Tess raised me. It's a long story, but they've been the most amazing parents someone like me could have."

Brielle nods slowly. "You're very lucky, then."

Tristan knows she's thinking of her own chance at a happy family. He considers telling her the Pierces potentially know who and what she is, but he knows now's not the time. He clasps her hand. "I'm looking forward to you meeting them."

Brielle goes quiet but Tristan doesn't have time to ask what's going on. They've just turned onto his street, and his house is at the end of the block.

He pulls the car over, stopping.

Brielle straightens, looking around. There's nothing but a park on one side and a corner store on the other. "What's wrong? Where's your house?"

Tristan indicates with his chin, his eyes scanning the empty street. "The white one at the end."

Frowning, Brielle leans forward as she tries to see what has Tristan on edge. "Then why have we stopped?"

Tristan's stomach plummets as his suspicions are confirmed. It was the slightest shift of a shadow that had him pulling over. The whopping piece of information that he'd forgotten in his haste to get Brielle to the stones.

He was a fool to think that he was taking Brielle to safety.

That it would be easy to reunite Brielle with her gem.

The Skins know where he lives.

20

BRIELLE

B rielle's pulse pounds so furiously in her temples that she fears her head might explode.

How did this even happen? Only an hour ago, she was taking the first steps into her new cozy life with the Pierces, about to enjoy a simple dessert in what promised to be her new home.

Now, after a high octane car chase that almost killed them, she's in Tristan's truck up the road from his house with no clue as to who's after them or why she just threw away the one thing she's spent her entire life wanting.

"Tristan?" she prompts as Tristan stares toward his house, gritting his teeth, still not having answered her question.

"They have my house surrounded," he says quietly.

She looks at the houses in front of them, scanning each one for signs of bodies. But the neighborhood looks as empty and peaceful as any for this time of night.

"There's nothing there, Tristan," she says, barely breathing.

"Just because you can't see them doesn't mean they aren't there. They can become invisible whenever they choose. They were real enough to chase us down with that SUV."

She can't take it anymore. There's no more denying or trying to explain away. She has to accept what's happening. But first, she needs to actually *know* what's happening.

"Who are they?" she asks finally, hammering the final nail in the coffin of her normal life.

Tristan turns to her, then takes a steadying breath as if preparing himself for the long explanation that's to come. "We call them Skins. They're people who've been possessed by Chardis. They're his puppets, robbed of whatever choice and soul they had before he infected them in exchange for heightened strength and speed and the ability to go unseen at will."

She swallows, the gulp audible in the silence of the truck. "Who is Chardis, and what does he want with me?"

"Chardis is...damn, Zarius could explain this so much better." He looks at his house again, chewing his lip and combing his hand through his hair before turning back to her. "Chardis is basically a conscious mass of dark matter. He has no soul, no empathy, no concept of right and wrong. He's pure evil, and the most destructive force in the Universe. Do you remember I told you that I and the other Zodiac Heirs were sent to Earth after an attack on our space station?"

She nods, eager to hear more.

Tristan continues. "He was the one who attacked. The history of the Universe has been one long battle between Chardis and the Zodiac Guardians. We're the only thing powerful enough to fend him off, to stop him from destroying one planet after another. Centuries ago, previous Zodiac Guardians sealed him away in a prison that was supposed to be impenetrable, but he managed to escape, and now that he has, he'll stop at nothing to kill off every last Zodiac Heir before we can come into our true power. That the Skins are after you can only mean one thing—you are a Zodiac Heir."

Her head is shaking before she even realizes it. "You made this all sound so fantastical earlier. Princesses and magic and soulmates." Her eyes narrow at him. "You never said anything about people wanting to kill me. You lied to me, Tristan."

His shoulders slump. "I didn't lie, I just left some things out."

"Omission *is* lying, it's just a form that I can't detect," she retorts. "And you used that against me."

"I had to," he insists. "If I had told you about the assassins after you, about the fate of the Universe being in our hands, you would have shut me down for good. I needed you to want it, needed to get you close to the stones."

He'd said something about stones during the chase, when she was buzzing with too much adrenaline to ask about it. "What stones?"

"The Zodiac Gems are what allow us to access our full power." He pulls the purple gem at the end of his necklace out from under his shirt collar. "When a Zodiac Heir touches their stone for the first time, it glows, recognizing its new master. And it will only glow if its Zodiac Guardian touches it."

"That was the test you were talking about," she says. "The reason why you wanted me to come to your house."

He nods.

"And what does that whole soulmate thing have to do with anything?" she asks sharply, still sour about being manipulated by that topic.

"For all the regions of the Universe, there is one Guardian, one person endowed with unique powers to protect that region of space. But the Gemini sector has two Guardians, one male and one female. Both born at the exact time on each of the twin planets that govern the region. Two halves of one soul, they are destined to be each other's perfect match. And when their two powers come together, there is no force more powerful. I am the male Gemini Heir." His fingers absentmindedly rub the stone hanging from his neck. "It's my duty, my purpose, to find the female Gemini Heir."

Tristan's got that look in his eyes again, that look that bores into her soul, both seeking and filling a need at the same time.

"And you think I could be her." The hostility has left her voice, and her pulse has actually slowed.

Tristan nods. "There are too many signs. The way I feel about you, that pull... I've never felt anything like it. I know you're an Heir, now we just have to see if I'm right about which one."

Her breath is almost completely gone, but she summons enough to say, "And the way to do that is for me to touch the stones?"

"Yep," he says with a sigh, sinking back into his seat. "Which are in the basement of my house that's currently surrounded by pitch knows how many Skins."

Brielle cocks her head. "Pitch?"

He blinks, then his lips tip into a small smile. "Sorry. I hear it so much from Zarius that I forget it's not common on Earth." His smile drops and he inhales sharply. "Zarius. I need to warn him about the Skins. And I can only hope he and Tess aren't home." He pulls his phone out of his jeans pocket and starts to text.

Brielle looks outside, watching for any sign of the same shadows she saw at the Pierces. But the scenery isn't as open here in town as it was in the country. There are too many light sources and large shadows cast by houses and cars.

"How do you fight something you can't see?" she asks.

How can I fight them at all? Visions and lie-detection are about as useful in a fight as a sneeze.

"Luckily, I've been trained by the best to do just that," he says, looking down at his phone anxiously. "But there's no way of knowing how many Skins there are, not until they show themselves. And I can't risk you getting caught up in it, not until you have your stone." His leg bounces under his phone. "Come on, Tess, answer me!"

Concern for parents she's never met tugs at her gut, reigniting the concern for her own would-be parents. Would the Skins have left them after they chased her and Tristan away? Would the Pierces be safe? She'd never be able to forgive herself if something happened to them because of her.

"So what's the plan?" she asks, her ability to sit still fading with each passing second.

Gripping his phone, he growls under his breath. "They're still not answering. And we can't just wait." He quietly unfastens his seatbelt. "I'll sneak in. As long as I stick to the shadows and don't make a sound, I can get past them and go inside. I'll get the stones and get out. If anything happens before I come back, start the truck and drive to the most populated area you can get to. They don't like to make a scene."

Tristan's getting ready to leave the car, and the sudden fear that she might not see him again strikes through Brielle like a lightning bolt. Her hand shoots out to grab his arm. "Please come back," she whispers, her lower lip quivering.

He pauses and meets her fretful gaze, holding it for several breaths. Then he leans closer and reaches up to cup her cheek.

This caress. This touch is so much more deliberate than the handful of times they've made brief physical contact. It fills her with the most euphoric energy, and all she wants to do is melt into his warm hand.

She settles for putting her hand over his and savoring the feel of his skin on hers.

"I *will* come back. I promise." His hand lingers for a moment longer, neither one of them wanting to let go.

Finally, with one last sweep of his thumb over her cheek bone, he withdraws. But before he can turn away, he frowns and squints out the window over Brielle's shoulder.

"What is it?" She looks behind her, seeing a girl walking down the sidewalk. Wait, that's not just some stranger. "Adalind?"

"Does she live around here?" Tristan asks, calculation wrinkling his forehead.

"I'm not sure, I've never been to her house," Brielle answers, her tone escalating along with her anxiety. "She's only ever come to the orphanage."

They both watch as Adalind moves closer and closer to the house Tristan's been staring at.

"Will they hurt her?" she asks, unable to look away in case a shadow flies by and swallows her best friend into oblivion.

"They might. They've been watching you. They know who your friends are. And she's getting awfully close to my house."

Resolve driving her, she unfastens her seatbelt.

Tristan clamps his hand around her wrist. "What are you doing?" he hisses.

"I have to warn her," Brielle asserts. "I can't just let her walk into a trap she can't even see!"

"No way!" He pushes a button on the door and all the locks click. "Right now, the Skins don't know we're here. If you go out there, they'll see you. You have no idea how important you are."

She jerks her wrist but Tristan's grip holds. "I am not more important than she is."

"Yes, you are!" he argues.

She scowls at him, feeling the clock tick with each step Adalind takes toward her possible doom. "If I am a Guardian, then it's my job to protect people, and I'm not going to stop before I even start."

"I will not allow you to give yourself away," Tristan says, frustration rising in his tone.

The moonlight catches on the screen of his phone that had slid slightly under his leg on the seat.

"I may not have to." She grabs his phone and dials Adalind's number.

"Hello?" Adalind answers.

"It's Brielle. Stop walking right now, turn around and make the closest right," Brielle instructs.

"What?" Adalind stops and looks around. "Where—"

"Don't say another word," Brielle warns. "Just walk the other way right now and don't call attention to yourself. I'll meet you around the corner and explain in a minute."

There's a pause, the chirping of crickets coming at her in stereo.

"Okay." Adalind hangs up then starts walking in the opposite direction, turning her head all around in search of Brielle.

They wait until Adalind is safely around the corner just behind them before slipping out of the driver's side of Tristan's truck and creeping over the sidewalk after her.

Brielle has no idea what she's doing. What is she going to tell Adalind? Does she tell her everything? Risk losing her only friend?

If it comes to it, that's what Brielle must do. Tristan says she's a Guardian.

If she has to lose a friend in order to save her, so be it.

21

TRISTAN

A dalind is just around the corner of the next building, pressed against the brick wall. Tristan scans the shadowed alley, straight away not liking where they are. It's a dead end, meaning they're trapped, and there are too many shadows, making it harder to spot a Skin.

But before he gets a chance to suggest another location, Brielle grasps Adalind in a hug. "Thank goodness. Quick, we need to get back to the truck."

Adalind pulls back, shaking her head. "What's going on, Brielle?" She glances over Brielle's shoulder and sees Tristan, her gaze flaring. "Has he got you in some kind of trouble?"

Brielle shakes her head. "No. Tristan just saved my life." She moves closer to him. "I'll explain it all, I promise. We need to get back to the truck first."

But Adalind folds her arms across her chest. "Not happening, bestie. I'm not going anywhere until I know what's going on."

Tristan grinds his teeth. This is the least safe place they could be having this conversation. Another scan of the alleyway shows nothing but a few trash cans and some crates. But Skins could be plastered against the walls from one end to the other for all he knows. Moving to the mouth of the alley, he leans back against the wall. This way he can see the alley, as well as whether anyone's coming.

"Look, I don't understand it fully myself, but dangerous people are here." The urgent note in Brielle's voice is unmistakable. "We need to get to safety."

"I told you he's trouble, Brielle! What is it? Drugs?" Adalind steps forward, gripping Brielle's arms. "Has Tristan made you take something?"

Tristan resists the need to push off the wall and get these two out of here. Adalind is talking way too loud. "Keep it down," he hisses.

Adalind glares at him. "There's no one here."

Brielle steps between them, pulling in a deep breath. "We're not from Earth, Adalind. And there's an evil trying to destroy us…and the Universe." Brielle says the words quietly, hesitation apparent in her voice. This is hard for her to tell Adalind.

Although Tristan isn't sure why she's friends with this prickly, possessive girl who seems to be determined to put them in as much danger as possible. Not only is she not leaving, she's talking loud enough to get Chardis himself here.

"Oh my god, he did give you something. You're tripping." Adalind grips Brielle's hand. "You need to come with me, Brielle. Right now."

Tristan pushes away from the wall. "Like hell she does."

Brielle glances between Tristan and Adalind, clearly torn. Tristan wishes there was time for her to make this choice. Brielle's had enough thrust upon her over the past few days.

But then there's the unmistakable sound of a car door slamming. Tristan glances down the alley way, knowing he won't see anyone, but still locking his muscles when he finds the street clear. "We have to go." They should never have stayed here. "They're coming."

Brielle shakes Adalind's hand free. "The assassins trying to kill us can turn invisible. Please, Tristan can keep us safe."

Adalind's chuckle has Tristan spinning around. "You mean like this?"

In a blink, she disappears.

Tristan jolts forward, fury spearing through his veins. Adalind is a Skin! How did he not realize?

Brielle is jerked backward, her feet stumbling as if someone is dragging her further into the alleyway. Her gaze latches onto Tristan's, her eyes wide and terrified.

"Brie—"

Tristan's knocked to the ground before he can finish shouting her name. The Skin who bowled him over becomes visible, his face contorted with satisfaction as Tristan's slammed into the ground.

His back explodes with pain as every drop of air is rammed from his lungs. But it doesn't matter.

Brielle's in danger. And Tristan was supposed to protect her.

Before the Skin has a chance to make another move, Tristan slams his fist into the face above him. The Skin's head snaps to the side, and Tristan makes the most of the momentum. He follows through with an uppercut and the Skin falls to the ground beside him.

Tristan rights himself to see Brielle further down the alley, still being dragged by an invisible Adalind. A few feet away from him, five Skins appear, one by one. They form a line from one side to the other. A wall of assassins between Tristan and Brielle.

Raising his fists, Tristan knows they're wanting him to come further into the shadows of the alley. Fewer witnesses. Less chance for him to escape.

It's a trap, but he has no choice. Brielle's already captured. Without him, she's Chardis's prisoner.

She's better off dead.

The Skins wait, their faces cold and hard. Tristan's going to have to come to them.

Zarius's words whisper through his mind. *Never face more than you can handle.*

Well, Tristan's just going to have to handle it.

He drops his head, his hands clenched by his sides. "You wanna play? Then let's play."

Making like a bowling ball, he runs straight at the middle guy, which is probably what the goons are expecting. At the last second, Tristan hooks left and sends his leg flying wide. The guy closest to the wall never sees the roundhouse kick coming. Tristan's foot connects with the side of the Skin's head, slamming him into the unforgiving bricks beside him. He crumples, just like Tristan planned.

Spinning around, Tristan puts his back to the wall. Now, the Skins line up, one behind the other. He's no longer facing four, but just one at a time.

Tristan grins. "Actually, I don't mind this game." He beckons with his hand. "Your move."

The Skin lifts his fists, his face consumed with the desire to kill. The guy behind him tries to step around, but Tristan twists right and the first Skin follows him, blocking the view for the guy behind him.

One at a time. This, Tristan can handle.

The Skin comes at him, and all it takes is a duck and weave for the Skin's fist to slam into the wall behind Tristan. The Skin's howl of pain is cut off by Tristan's uppercut. Tristan shoves the man back, and his comrades have to jump out of the way of the Skin's unconscious body.

"Kill him!" Adalind shouts from further down the alley. "This one we'll keep, but he's not worth the trouble."

Tristan's grin returns. "I like that Chardis thinks I'm trouble," he growls.

When several more Skins materialize behind the others, Tristan blinks. It's like he suddenly has triple vision. The Skin he was facing steps back, joining the others as they spread out, forming a semi-circle around him.

Uh. Oh.

This time, they don't come one at a time. Two leap at him, fists ready, another three already behind them. Tristan gets in a couple of good hits, knocking one Skin to his knees, before the first blow hits him in the solar plexus.

His body wants to double over but Tristan won't let it. He throws out a kick, but it misses, and a Skin on his left jabs him in the kidneys. Pain explodes through Tristan as he staggers back, hitting the wall behind him.

There's no break from the beating though, because more punches come. They slam his face, his chest, his gut. Within seconds, Tristan's knees give out. He pushes away from the wall, falling onto all fours.

Zarius's words slice through Tristan's mind. *Never let them get you down on the ground. You're too vulnerable.*

Which is exactly how Tristan feels as he watches the boot sailing toward his ribs. He groans as it slams into his side with all the strength the Skin possesses. Tristan curls into himself as pain cannonballs through him. He could've used Zarius right now.

As the second kick connects, Tristan wonders if he's going to vomit up his shattered ribs. His suit could've come in handy, too.

The third kick comes from behind and Tristan goes from curled to arched on the filthy ground. His insides feel like they've been turned into mashed potato.

Brielle screams. It's the sound of terror.

And Tristan's failure.

He struggles to get up, knowing consciousness won't be with him for much longer. Another kick, maybe two, and there'll be no ribs left to protect his vital organs.

But the next kick doesn't come. Tristan looks up, pain turning the world blurry. The Skin who was standing over him is gone, sailing through the air and slamming into a trash can.

Alden moves into his field of vision, standing in front of Tristan like the soldier he is. "Get up!"

Using the wall as support, Tristan straightens, every muscle screaming an objection. Beside him, grunts and thumps tell him Alden is fighting off the Skins. Shaking his head, Tristan knows he has to get it together.

This is the break he needed.

This is what could save Brielle.

Throwing his shoulders back, Tristan stumbles forward. He slams his fist into the nearest Skin, relishing the sound of cartilage crunching. The Skin stumbles backward, blood pouring down his face, giving Tristan the opening he needed.

He steps in beside Alden, instinctively choosing the side with the eye patch. "Brielle's been taken down the end of the alleyway."

"Well, then. We'd better get her back," Alden mutters, determination hardening his voice.

"I think I might be in love with you, Alden."

There's no more time to talk as the Skins rush at them. Tristan fights with renewed energy and the first Skin drops quickly. Each punch that gets through his defenses feels like a wrecking ball, but Tristan ignores the pain. He can hurt later.

When they've got Brielle to safety.

Alden fights as well as Zarius would, making them a formidable team. Punches are dealt with precision, kicks with force. They slowly make their way down the wall, further into the alley. Closer to Brielle.

But the further they move, the more Skins appear. Tristan feels his burst of energy waning. His fists ache and it hurts to breathe. And judging from the grunts coming from Alden, this is taking its toll on him, too.

As a Skin lands a punch across Tristan's jaw, he realizes something. Chardis sent an army along with Adalind. There's no telling how many Skins there could be.

"Use your suit!" pants Alden.

"I can't. I don't know how!"

Doesn't Alden realize if he could, he'd be all decked out by now?

Alden jumps forward, taking a Skin by surprise. He spins around, his elbow aiming for the next one's nose. "You need to—" Alden never has the chance to finish the sentence. He stops mid-spin, facing Tristan as his back arches, his eye widening with shock.

And agony.

Tristan watches, horrified, as crimson blood blooms on Alden's lips, then trickles over the edge. He's shoved forward, Adalind materializing behind him.

Holding the bloody knife she just withdrew from Alden's back.

Tristan catches Alden before he hits the ground, his bruised body crumpling under the weight. Alden's mouth works as Tristan feels the gush of warm blood on his hands. "Hang on. We can heal you."

But Alden's shaking his head. The healing potion isn't going to help anyone because Tristan won't be able to get it. His house might as well be on Gemini I right now. They've lost.

Tristan's blood is about to join Alden's as it pools on the grimy cement.

Alden lifts a hand only to drop it again. "You need to hold…your stone," he wheezes. "Then say…*Akash*."

Akash? What does that even mean?

But that's the moment that Alden goes limp, his eye becoming sightless and glassy. Ice floods Tristan's veins. "No!"

Adalind's chuckle creeps down his spine. "Finish him."

Tristan watches as her feet turn and head back down the alley to where she left Brielle. So she can bring her to Chardis.

Tristan straightens, watching Skins appear all around him, knowing there's more behind him. He grips the gem hanging around his neck.

This is their last chance. Please let him have heard Alden right. Please don't let his death have been for nothing.

The tanzanite digs into his palm. He shouts the single word like it's a battle cry. "Akash!"

It'll either be the last thing he's ever going to say.

Or he'll finally stand a chance.

Heat blasts from the stone and Tristan releases it as it flares so bright, he has to close his eyes. Suddenly, sensation explodes across his skin. He tries to identify where it starts, but it's everywhere. All over him.

Encasing him.

Tristan looks down to find a metal suit the color of midnight purple enveloping him so fast, he knows he can't blink. It wraps around his chest, expanding down his legs. Simultaneously, it streaks up his neck and closes around his face.

For a second, Tristan feels suffocated. What if he can't breathe in here? But then his lungs fill with air. He looks around, registering details he hadn't noticed before. A moldy lettuce leaf protruding from a trash can. A scar on a Skin's cheek. The scent of Adalind's fear as she runs back down the alley.

Tristan flexes his arm—whatever the suit is made of, it's hard...yet flexible. He looks down, realizing the energy of the shift has him levitating a few inches off the ground. He's surrounded in armor. His senses are heightened.

And it's possible he can fly.

He looks at the open-mouthed Skins around him. "It's time for a new game."

22

BRIELLE

Brielle has never been more terrified in her whole life as she watches her once best friend stab a man in the back while Skins tug her out of the alley and toward a waiting car.

Things couldn't possibly get any worse. Tristan is being attacked by invisible foes, Eye Patch Guy just got murdered, and the one person she trusted most has been working against her all along.

Wait, no. Things *can* get worse. And they will, whenever they get to where the Skins are taking her.

She doesn't want to find out!

But she's useless. No matter how much strength she puts into her jerks against her captors, they don't budge, and every futile effort inflicts more and more pain, and soon-to-be bruises. How are her so-called powers supposed to help her now? How could they possibly help Tristan?

Her panic spikes when she hears the sound of the car door opening behind her and her feet are lifted up off the ground.

No, no, no!

She can't tell if she's screaming the words in her head or out loud as every muscle in her body clenches in refusal to be put into that car, her eyelids sealing as if believing the bad things aren't happening if she can't see them.

Then suddenly, everything stops moving, and even behind her tightly closed eyelids a blinding light flashes not far ahead.

Brielle hesitantly squints her eyes open, looking up at the Skins that have hold of her arms and legs. They've gone still as stone, their stunned faces all aimed down the alley at the fading flash. Her eyes follow theirs to the source of that light, wondering what could be enough to surprise them.

Tristan is at the end of the alley, surrounded by Skins that are ducking as if from an explosion. But it's not a blast that let out such bright light.

As the glow implodes on the stone hanging from Tristan's neck, some dark and shimmering purple material seeps out of it, covering Tristan's body in a pixelated kind of way. From this distance, the substance looks both inky and metallic, mercurial yet scaly.

What have they done to him?

"Tristan!" she cries, certain she is about to watch her potential soulmate die.

But the looks on every visible face that's frozen in his direction are not expressions of victory, but of dread.

The inky purple has completely covered Tristan from head to toe, and he stands tall, flexing his fingers.

It's not poison or some alien biological weapon.

It's a hi-tech suit of armor!

Looking like Iron Man, Tristan slams his fist into the closest Skin, the man's body flying backward and smashing through the Skins behind him.

Instinctively, Brielle takes advantage of her captors'

distraction and puts every ounce of force she can muster into one final buck. Her arms and legs slip from their grasp, and she scrambles out of reach as they try to snatch her back up.

She sprints at full speed back into the alley, swerving through and leaping over Skins, knowing only that her place right now is at Tristan's side. She slides on the dirty ground behind him like a baseball player who just made a home run.

Eye Patch Guy's body lays beside her. Her heart tugs for him, but there's no time for tears or questions now.

As Tristan uses the body of one Skin as a sling shot against the rest of them, she scans the alley floor for anything she can use to help him. There's a dumpster, dozens of old wrappers and fallen leaves of all colors. Then something catches her eye. A dented pipe that's a little over a foot long. That'll do.

She grabs it and gets into a batter's pose, ready to swing with all her might at any Skin who gets close. She refuses to be the damsel in distress, or let Tristan take on this burden alone.

Not that Tristan needs her help now that he's in his suit.

He's incredible to watch. She'd seen glimpses of the fight before when the Skins were carrying her away, enough to know that the suit isn't responsible for the skill and grace she's witnessing.

Before she's even had a chance to swing her pipe, Tristan dispatches the last Skin standing, slamming his head into the ground so hard it cracks.

Tristan gets back to his feet and turns all around, looking for his next opponent. After a moment, he realizes there isn't one.

The alley in front of them is scattered with bodies, and from what Brielle can tell, most if not all of them are dead. She finds herself searching the lifeless faces. Adalind isn't among them. She must have fled.

Tristan approaches her, putting his armored hands on her upper arms.

"Are you alright?" His voice doesn't sound muffled as she imagined it would. It sounds crystal clear, as if there isn't a layer of protective metal over his face.

She can't see his eyes, only a black glass-like cover over where they should be, but she knows they're blazing with concern.

She nods rapidly, too flooded with adrenaline to speak.

He exhales heavily and lowers his shoulders. "Thank pitch!" He pulls her into a relieved hug, and she's surprised by how firm yet flexible the metal is against her exposed arms. What could it possibly be made of?

Her motor skills a second behind reality, she hugs him back, a wave of relief and amazement that they're both alive washing over her.

When Tristan eventually pulls away, she finds her voice. "I can't see your face. Are *you* alright?"

"I am for now," he says. "We need to get to my house asap before I realize I'm not."

She peers down the alley. "Do you think it's safe?"

"I think I killed every Skin who foolishly stayed behind. The rest fled. Along with Adalind." He says her name through clenched teeth.

"I'm so sorry, Tristan," Brielle confesses, her heart aching with betrayal. "This is all my fault."

He shakes his head. "No, it's not. Adalind had us both fooled. I should have been able to sniff her out from the beginning."

Brielle looks away, knowing the truth—that if anyone should have been able to see through Adalind, it's her. She never pushed her lie-detection with Adalind. Maybe if she had, she'd have known long ago that the great pretender was just that.

Her wandering eyes fall on Eye Patch Guy's corpse. "So, he was with you after all."

"What do you mean, 'after all'?"

The memory from last night flashes in her mind. "He came by the orphanage last night, told me I was in danger. It scared the crap out of me. I didn't know if he was crazy or…" She slowly turns her head toward Tristan. "…if the danger he was warning me of was you."

"I didn't know until last night that he was a royal Gemini guard sent to help Zarius. He must have come by our house right after he scared you at the orphanage. Alden was a good man."

Alden. Much better than Eye Patch Guy.

Tristan kneels near Alden's face, then looks up at Brielle. "He cared about you, you know. I know you only knew him as the crazy librarian, but he's been watching over you your whole life, keeping you safe from a distance."

Blood floods Brielle's face, neck and shoulders, a fresh heat steaming the sweat beads on her skin. Some deep, longing part of her heart breaks.

This strange man she never really knew was the closest thing to family she had on this planet. How different would things have been if he'd gone the route of Zarius and adopted her, raised her as his own? She could have known her purpose all her life, could have understood the powers she always believed were a curse. And she'd have had a dad, or something like it.

Now he's dead and she'll never get to know him, never get to ask the questions that are buzzing through her mind.

Never get to thank him for watching over her.

Tristan must see her tears building because he turns back to Alden and closes his lifeless eyes with his fingertips. "Rest in peace, Alden of Gemini I."

Brielle is on the verge of breaking down, succumbing to the sorrow that's suddenly overwhelming her. And if she doesn't get a hold of herself soon, she'll crumble and be useless.

She turns her back on the two, wipes her eyes and sniffles, taking a wobbly breath. "What are we going to do with them? We can't just leave all these bodies here."

She hears Tristan stand and come up behind her. "The Skins will clean this up. They always do. Their secret is as great as ours. Alden will disappear without a trace," he says, his voice heavy. Tristan straightens his shoulders. "But he'd want us to get you safe and for you to be reunited with your stone, there's nothing else we can do for him. That's our top priority." He offers his hand. "Come on, they might come back with reinforcements. We need to get in and out of my house before that happens."

Brielle places her hand in his, hurting that Alden doesn't even get a proper burial, but knowing that there's no other choice. Together, they sprint out of the alley and down the road to his house. As they move, she still doesn't trust the shadows surrounding them, fearing one might jump out at them the moment she turns her back.

They approach his house with caution, wary of any Skins still hiding in the darkness. They tiptoe up the walkway, Tristan using his armored body as a shield in front of Brielle. He grabs the doorknob, hesitantly turns it and pushes the door open.

The house looks fine, nothing seems out of place. Tristan seems surprised by that fact, but proceeds forward anyway.

"Everything is too quiet, too perfect," he whispers as he tucks Brielle behind him. "Keep your eyes open."

Brielle follows close behind him. Despite the caution that sizzles through every inch of her body, it's anticipation that drives her forward. This is the moment that will truly change her life forever. The moment she'll find out who she really is.

As they make their way down the dark stairs of the basement, she holds onto one silly hope—that she is, indeed, the lost Gemini Princess Tristan has been looking for.

23

TRISTAN

Tristan opens the door, not sure why he's still so edgy. Maybe it was the fight. Maybe it was seeing Alden killed. But whatever it is, it means he keeps his suit on as he pushes the door open.

That, and he's not entirely sure how to get it off, yet.

Although, the thing is so cool he's thinking it might be his new go-to outfit. A couple of days practice, and Tristan's pretty sure he'll be joining Superman in the sky.

Keeping Brielle's hand firmly in his, Tristan pauses as he listens. All the lessons with Zarius on hearing the tiniest of sounds have become obsolete. Although the suit protected him from all but the biggest hits the Skins could throw at him, it's like walking around in a super-sensitive skin. Everything's in high definition.

But Tristan doesn't hear a sound coming from the basement, let alone anywhere else in the house.

"Zarius? Tess?" he calls out. Maybe that's why he's nervous. If they aren't at home, where are they?

There's no answer, but Tristan didn't really expect one.

Maybe the silence is a good thing. Maybe Zarius and Tess escaped before the hordes of Skins surrounded the place...

Two steps down and Tristan freezes.

"What is it?" Brielle whispers, panic creeping into her voice.

Tristan looks around the basement, his heightened vision taking in every shattered piece of furniture, every hole in the wall, every inch of destruction.

"Bastards," he mutters.

The Skins have annihilated the basement.

The next thought has Tristan releasing Brielle's hand and shooting down the stairs. "Zarius! Tess!"

Please don't let them be among the carnage.

Tristan reaches the bottom of the stairs, scanning frantically. There's broken glass, wood splintered everywhere, but no sign of his parents. Tristan lets out his breath, the panic seeping from his body.

They're not here. They got away in time.

Brielle appears on the stairs. "Tristan?"

"It's all safe. For a second there I was worried that Zarius and Tess..." He shakes his head. "But they're not here."

Brielle looks around, taking in the destruction. "The Skins, they've been here."

Tristan kicks at a chair leg and it skitters only to lodge into a pile of smashed who-knows-what. "Yep. They redecorated."

It's then that Tristan sees his pod. Or what's left of it.

He rushes over, falling to his knees as he picks up the largest piece remaining. Looking like an overgrown piece of eggshell, it's no bigger than his hand. Brielle comes to stand behind him, resting a hand on his shoulder. How odd that the suit protects him from damage, but he can feel that gentle offer of comfort. "What was it?"

Tristan's body sags. "My pod." He looks up at Brielle. "We all arrived in one of these."

But his has been annihilated.

"I'm so sorry, Tristan."

Remembering what else came in that pod has Tristan shooting to his feet. "No, no, no." He takes in the wreckage. Nothing has been left standing. "Please, no."

He ploughs through the broken furniture to the other end of the room, falling to his knees as he clears away the debris.

Brielle kneels beside him. "What? What are you looking for?"

"The gems," Tristan breathes.

There are no Zodiac Guardians without their gems.

He uncovers the vent placed low in the wall. It looks undisturbed, but the Skins are twisted enough to take what's behind it and put everything back so it wasn't discovered straight away. So that someone like Tristan would think everything's okay.

His hands, still covered in the dark suit, tremble a little as he reaches out. With a quick swipe he pulls the vent down, revealing the safe behind it.

It looks undisturbed.

Punching in the code, Tristan holds his breath. *Please let them be there. Please...*

The door pops open with a click, exposing the dark interior. Two black boxes sit within.

Tristan falls back on his heels. "Thank pitch."

He draws them out, feeling their familiar weight. He looks at Brielle. "This is what they were trying to find." Destroying everything in the process would've just been done for pleasure.

Brielle's face floods with relief. "That's good." She glances down at the slim cases, her eyes widening. "They're the stones?"

Tristan nods, realizing they're getting closer to the moment that could change his destiny. And Brielle's.

He stands, Brielle following him. "Half of them, anyway."

Brielle looks at him for long moments. "Do you think you could take the suit off before we…you know? I can't see your face."

"Oh, of course." Tristan grins but then realizes Brielle can't see it.

He raises his hand to his chest, feeling the gem that's embedded there in the suit. This time, he whispers the word. "Akash."

In a blink, the suit withdraws. Plate after tiny plate retreats, absorbing into the next. Before Tristan realizes what's happened, it's gone. Impossibly, undeniably, relegated back into the stone.

"Now, that's cool," says Tristan in awe.

A second before he collapses with a groan.

"Tristan!" Brielle falls to her knees beside him. She gasps when she sees him. "Oh god."

It's like all of the pain the Skins inflicted hits Tristan at once. His chest feels like it's been excavated, his face like it's been pulverized. He thought he was running on adrenaline, but it's quite possible the suit was the one holding him up.

Tristan picks up the second box, holding it out to Brielle. "Nanites."

Although she's confused by the strange word, Brielle takes the box and opens it. Inside sit several glowing vials. "What are they?" she breathes.

Tristan keeps his breaths as shallow as possible. "Alien biotechnology. They…heal."

Brielle slips one out, holding it up. The yellow-green liquid glows gently, seeming to move of its own volition within the glass cage. "What now?"

"Normally…we'd inject them." Tristan works not to

grimace. Who knew talking took up so much lung capacity? "But the first aid kit…" Is in about a million pieces. He holds his hand out. "I'll drink it."

Brielle's eyes widen again at the thought of ingesting the luminous liquid. "Okay." She draws the word out as she removes the lid and passes it to him.

Tristan doesn't give himself time to think. He throws the content of the vial into his mouth, his body stiffening as the liquid slips over his tongue and down the back of his throat. It's…warm and gelatinous…and gross.

He wipes his mouth. "They obviously don't have berry flavor on Gemini I."

He drops his head back and it clunks on the floor but he doesn't care. Right now, every inch of his body weighs a tone.

Brielle scoots around, gently lifting his head and resting it on her lap. "Is that better?"

"Mm." Tristan lets his eyes flutter closed as her fingers gently push the hair back from his face. It probably looks like an eggplant right now, but Tristan gives himself over to the sensation. There's something about Brielle's touch that feels like it reaches right down to his soul. It soothes him in a way nothing else has before.

"Tristan?"

"Mm?"

"I don't think now's the time for a nap."

He doesn't answer. Right now, he can't think of a better time for a nap.

Brielle's fingers stop. "Tell me about the nanites."

They don't continue and Tristan realizes he's being blackmailed. "Nanotechnology," he mumbles, realizing he's willing to do far more to have her hands touching him like that. "Teeny, tiny robots that run around mending and fixing. Zarius told us every other day that the technology on Earth is the most primitive he's ever seen."

"Will it take long?"

Tristan cracks open an eye, looking up at the concerned face above him. "I'm not sure I'm in a rush anymore."

Brielle's lips part, her eyes softening. Tristan's pretty sure he's never seen anything so beautiful in his life. His body stills. His chest warms. One word trickles through his mind.

Soulmate.

The tinkling of his cell phone fractures the moment. Tristan jerks out of the spell that was being cast around him. Zarius!

Instinctively, he reaches for his pocket only to find it empty. His cell appears in front of him, held in Brielle's hand. Oh yes, she borrowed it to call Adalind.

The traitor.

Tristan takes his phone, his heart leaping when he sees Zarius's name flashing on the screen. He swipes the screen and brings it to his ear. "Zarius, where are—"

"Tristan!" Zarius's voice is thick and urgent. "Don't come—"

Ice shoots through Tristan's veins a second before a new voice slides over his ear.

"Hello, Tristan."

Tristan sits up, fury replacing the frozen fear. "If you so much as—"

Adalind chuckles. "I think it might be too late to be able to promise that. Now, if you want to see them again, you might want to listen."

Brielle scoots around, her eyes wide as she recognizes the voice. Tristan's hand tightens around the cell so hard he has to consciously unclench it. "Talk, then."

"We're at the warehouse and we'd like to chat." Tristan wants to snort but he doesn't. They don't want to talk. They want more blood on their hands. "My bestie can come if she likes, but that's it. We see anyone else, and your parents' deaths are on your conscience."

"You bi—"

"The feeling's mutual, Zodiac filth," Adalind growls. "I wouldn't take too long."

The line goes dead.

Tristan drops the phone before he crushes it. He looks at Brielle. "They have Zarius and Tess."

She gasps. "We have to save them!"

Damn straight they do.

Kneeling among the debris, Tristan picks up the box containing the stones. "You'll need this, first."

Brielle's eyes go wide and round. They lock with his and she nods once. "It's time."

Tristan's glad the nanites are already working their magic, because his chest has gone all tight again.

It's time.

Turning the box around, it slides smoothly in Tristan's palm. Zarius would bring it out regularly to show Tristan. To remind him.

Your power is held within these stones. A power bestowed on you by the Universe.

He'd pick them up one by one, always finishing with the second Gemini stone.

When the Gemini Twins are united, their power is the greatest the Universe has ever seen. It is as good as Chardis is evil. It is the light to his night. It is the one thing he fears.

Tristan swallows. If the prophecy is right, then this might all be over before it started.

He holds the box out to Brielle.

They're about to find out.

24

BRIELLE

The stakes have risen considerably, and Brielle suddenly feels the weight of the world—no, the weight of the entire Universe—on her shoulders.

The slick black box lays open in front of her. Sitting on its cushy purple cloth interior are six beautiful gems all about the size of a walnut. She can't imagine how much each of them would be worth to a jeweler, but to her, to their cause, they're priceless.

Even though she knows the importance and urgency of making her choice, the impulse to stall this moment is undeniable.

She turns to Tristan. "How many Zodiac Guardians are there? Twelve, one for each of the signs, right?"

"Thirteen, actually," he replies quickly. "There are two Geminis, remember?" His tone implies that he wants to rush her but that he's holding back. He understands what this must be like for her, and she's grateful for his indulgence, even though she understands what his parents' ransom must be like for him.

"There are only six stones here. What happened to the

rest of them?"

Tristan shakes his head with an air of futility. "I honestly don't know. Maybe the older Heirs were sent with theirs, or maybe the stones still reside with their Guardians on their home planets, if any of them survived. I really can't say. Zarius has only ever had these six." He takes a step closer. "Which of them speaks to you?"

His eyes flicker to the stones, and she tries like heck not to follow them, terrified to pick the stone he wants and fail to make it shine. She has to follow her gut here. It would be terrible for her to grab the Gemini stone and turn out not to be her, to see the look of disappointment on Tristan's face. To deal with yet another heartbreak. And worse, what if none of them shine and everyone was wrong about her? Or her stone is lost in the cosmos somewhere? What then?

She can't think like that, she has to focus.

Closing her eyes, she takes a deep calming breath, then turns her full attention to the stones.

She scans each one carefully. Like a psychic, she decides to hover her hand over each gem to see if she feels a tug or an energy from a certain one. The brilliant golden citrine shines like the sun and is gorgeous, and the perfectly cut diamond that reflects any speck of light into beautiful rainbow flecks would make any girl faint. But it's not beauty she's looking for, and neither of those speak to her.

Sitting next to each other at the top of the case are a pale purple stone and a shimmering pink stone. For whatever reason, she feels drawn to both. Why? She can't tell if her desire to pick up the purple one stems from the fact that Tristan's is a deep purple and this one would likely be for his counterpart. But she knows nothing about Zodiac signs and gems associated with them, that could be totally wrong. She inwardly curses her social ignorance.

The sound of Tristan's harried breathing urges her to

make a decision. Thinking it better to try the pink one and fail than going for the purple and failing, she hastily grabs the pink stone.

To her surprise, a euphoric sense of warmth saturates not her body but her soul. The pink gem in her palm shines, illuminating everything in the basement with a sunset-like sherbet glow.

With the sense of rightness that just infused Brielle.

A glee that she's never known fills her chest like a balloon, and she wants to jump and dance for joy!

This is the reason for everything! Her visions, her lie-detection, her orphancy. This tiny yet beautiful rock holds within it the truth of who and what she really is. An alien princess destined to join a battle to save the Universe.

Alden wasn't wrong about her, he didn't die in vain! Tristan wasn't wrong about her. She really is a Zodiac Guardian.

With a smile so wide that her cheeks feel pinched, she turns to Tristan, expecting an equally joyous reaction.

It's not there.

Her smile falters.

The joyous bubble pops.

She's not the Gemini Princess.

A part of her says that shouldn't matter. She *is* still an alien princess, a Zodiac Guardian. She should still be outrageously jubilant to finally have the answers to every question she's ever had.

But she isn't, and neither is Tristan. They both wanted her to be the other Gemini. The other half to his whole.

If she's not, what does this all mean? The connection between them that feels stronger than the gravitational pull of the sun, the burning delicious feeling she gets when he touches her. None of it makes any sense if she's not *her*.

Tristan has a soulmate out there. He's destined to be with someone else.

That realization is crushing, squeezing out any lingering joy that had survived the popped bubble.

But if she's not the other Gemini, who is she?

As if seeing the unspoken question in her eyes, Tristan says with a heavy sigh, "Libra. You're Libra."

Libra?

Her shoulders slump. "Tristan... I'm so sor—"

"It's okay," he cuts her off. He forces a small smile, shaking his head fervently. "This is good news. Really. You are a Zodiac as I thought, as Alden thought. This means we're one step closer to reuniting with the rest of the Guardians and defeating Chardis."

She nods, even though they both know she can sense the lie in his words.

She's not his soulmate. So much for avoiding a broken heart. This is one wound she's certain will never heal, and will in fact deepen when he does find her.

She shuts her eyes and turns away from the thought.

They have more important things to worry about, like rescuing Tristan's parents.

She swallows her despair and asks, "So, as the Libra Guardian, now that I have my stone, what are my powers? You said the stones amplify things, right?"

He nods and rubs the back of his neck. "Honestly, I should have known from the start. Your ability to sense when someone's lying. It should have been obvious, but I didn't want to see it."

She ignores the implication. "I also get visions of people when I'm close, when they feel guilty about something. I can see the bad things they've done. And just recently, I discovered I can amplify their guilt. That's how I made Suki confess her infidelity to Zayne. I didn't mean to, I didn't even know I'd done it until it was too late."

Tristan slaps his hand to his forehead. "That's right! That's your offensive weapon!"

Brielle scrunches her brow at him. "I hardly see how making someone face their guilt is offensive. Psychologically, maybe. But it still makes me no good in a fight."

"No!" He shakes his head fervently, his blue eyes burning with hope. "Now that you have your stone, it's so much more than that. Zarius called it a Penance Burn. Basically, you amplify someone's guilt to such a degree that it inflicts physical pain. Depending on the level of guilt, it can even kill someone! With all the horrible things Skins do, you're likely to burn them alive! This is great!"

A miniature big bang erupts in Brielle's mind.

She's capable of killing someone just with guilt?

She's not sure she wants that power. What if she accidentally uses it on someone who doesn't deserve it? She doesn't have control of her powers as it is, and now they're considerably more powerful.

In the words of Tristan, it scares the pitch out of her.

"We actually have a real chance to fight against the Skins!" His excitement is so thick, she could scoop it with a spoon.

"I'm not so sure about this," she confesses. "I don't have control of my abilities. What if I accidentally kill an innocent person?" She looks down at the pink stone in her hand, and it feels like a hand grenade.

"That can't happen," he assures her. "If you turned your power on an innocent, they'd feel nothing. It only hurts them if they have done truly deplorable things. It depends on their degree of guilt. The more people they've hurt, the more wrongs they've committed, the more they have to feel guilty about."

"So if I used my powers now on Suki? What then? Would she burn?"

"For cheating on a high school boyfriend?" He frowns, then scoffs. "She may feel a bit of discomfort, but you wouldn't burn her alive."

"How do you know?" she pleads. From what Tristan's said, he was a baby when he came here. How can he be sure of anything? How can he be certain that she won't accidentally burn everyone to a crisp? Even him?

"Because Zarius knew," he says with finality. "Zarius worked behind the scenes of the Gemini Court. He witnessed the Guardians in action, and he passed that knowledge down to me. Which is why I should have linked lie-detection to your Libra powers."

"What does lie-detection have to do with Libra's power?" she asks, desperate for clarification.

"Libra is the epitome of justice and truth," he explains, locking eyes with her as if to make his words sink in. "Libra is the Judge of the Zodiac. So it makes sense that you'd be able to sense lies, sniff out the truth, and make people face the wrongs they've done. And when those wrongs are severe enough, Libra can punish them."

They sit in silence for a moment, letting Brielle come to terms with this knowledge. If Tristan's right, once she gains a firmer hold on her powers, she'll actually be able to fight for herself, to help Tristan. No one will ever have to die for her again. If only she'd gotten to her stone before Alden showed up. But then, if he hadn't, Tristan would have never figured out how to activate his suit.

"Now, let's put your stone to the test," he says, as if on the same wavelength. "Let's activate your suit."

Her leg twitches nervously, and she grips her stone tightly. "H-how do I do that?" Again, the fear that she might

fail, might somehow be unable to meet Tristan's expecta-
tions, slices into her, reopening the wound that will never
heal.

"Give me your stone," he says, holding out his hand.

She places it into his waiting palm, and he quickly affixes
it to a simple black cord like the one around his neck.

"May I?" He lifts the cord toward her with both hands.

She obligingly gathers her hair into a pile at the back of
her head so that he can clasp it around her neck.

He steps closer, a movement that feels so natural. His
hands gently lift the cord up, sweeping her jaw as he closes
the clasp. His hands linger after, and their eyes meet. His
fingertips at the base of her neck raise delicious goosebumps,
and the urge to close the small distance and kiss him is hard
to resist. His full lips look so inviting, beckoning her closer.

But it's not to be.

She turns away and lets her hair down, and Tristan
removes his hands, his disappointment like a mask on his
face.

"Now what?" she asks, her voice cutting through the
tension in the air like a knife.

Tristan takes a few steps back, giving her space. "Hold
your stone and say the word '*Akash*'," he instructs.

Lifting her hand to the pink gem now sitting against her
collar bone, she braces herself, unsure what to expect. She
wraps her fingers tightly around the stone and shakily says,
"*Akash.*"

A burst of light radiates from her stone, rays shooting
from the gaps between her fingers. Something cool and solid
starts to cover her chest, her arms, her legs, even her face.
The process feels like it takes an eternity, even though she
knows it must only take a few seconds. She's so preoccupied
with the encasing around her face that she doesn't realize her

fingers and feet, her entire body is fully enclosed, until she looks down.

Unlike Tristan's midnight purple suit, hers is a dark platinum pink.

"Excellent," Tristan says, his voice crisp. "Now, we're ready."

TRISTAN

B rielle's the Libra.
      Three words. And everything's changed.
Brielle's. The. Libra.

As Tristan holds the truck door open for Brielle, he finds he can't look her in the eye. He should be doing a happy highland jig seeing as he's found the first Zodiac Guardian. He wishes Zarius had been here to see the gem burst to life in Brielle's hand.

The pink tourmaline.

But the disappointment is heavier than Tristan expected. It seems to weigh down every cell in his body. And not only is it heavy, each shard is sharp and jagged, embedding themselves into the very fabric of his being. It tells him this feeling won't be leaving anytime soon.

Brielle climbs in, her hand wrapped around the stone at her throat. It would've been good if she had more time to adjust to her suit and newfound powers, but time is one thing they don't have right now. Once she'd relegated her suit back to its stone, they knew they had to leave.

The Skins have Zarius and Tess.

Climbing into the driver's side, Tristan clenches his teeth. Obviously, he wanted to find his soulmate so bad that the first Zodiac Heir he came across, he decided she must be it. It was his impatience at its best.

Or worst.

Because now his heart aches as much as the rest of him.

"So, what's the plan?" Brielle asks, her voice a mix of determination and apprehension.

Tristan pauses. If Brielle had been his Gemini Twin, they could've combined their powers. There probably wouldn't be a fight. Chardis would be running scared.

But Brielle's the Libra. They'll have to depend on his fighting skills and her ability to nuke the Skins with their own poor choices.

It's going to have to be enough.

"The warehouse is going to be surrounded. They'll want us arriving but not leaving."

Brielle nods, no doubt having thought of this.

"I've spent most of my life learning how to fight. The suit will only make me stronger. I'll go in first, you back me up."

Brielle nods again. "And we get your parents out of there."

Tristan turns the key in the ignition. It all sounds so simple. So straightforward.

But this is the most dangerous scenario he's ever walked into.

Before he pulls out of the driveway, he turns to Brielle. "If things get hairy, I want you out of there. I can fight, you can't. We can't afford for them to capture you."

Brielle tightens the hold on her stone. "Okay. But I'm going to do what I can to help."

Tristan was kind of hoping that she'd stop at the okay. "No heroics, okay?"

Brielle narrows her eyes at him. "Has Zarius ever said that to you?"

Turning away, Tristan starts the truck. That's exactly what Zarius has said to him in the past, but it's the fact that Brielle is intuitive enough to pick that up that had Tristan thinking they were soulmates in the first place.

And right now, that word isn't one he wants in his head.

They haven't gone far down the road when Brielle speaks up again. "What's your power, Tristan?"

He flicks a look her way. "I have visions of the future. Always two though, and only one of them is the truth."

Brielle's mouth forms a silent O. "And there's no way of telling which one is the future that's going to happen?"

"Nope."

Tristan's tried to see if he can tell. What's the point of seeing two alternate realities and not knowing which one will come to pass? He's spent hours looking back on all the dual visions he's had. Is it the first one? Is one vision longer than the other? More vivid?

But he's always come up empty handed. Nothing differentiates them apart from the ending. There's no rhyme or reason as to which vision turns out to be the future he'll live.

Like the two visions he had when he first arrived in Mirror Point. Cassandra, battered and bruised. Tristan refuses to think she's dead. And Brielle...One vision with a pool of blood.

Death is undeniable in that one.

Tristan's hands tighten on the wheel. At least there's no Cassandra where they're going. They have enough going on right now. And, when he has to face that reality, he'll just have to make sure it's the second vision that's the true one.

Right now, he needs to focus on Zarius and Tess.

The drive to the warehouse is a quiet and tense one. Tristan knows Brielle's not ready to face this. She's only seen a sample of what the Skins are capable of. But her powers could be the difference between freeing Zarius and Tess or… losing them.

Plus, Tristan doubts Brielle would've let him leave her behind. There's a tough streak in her that he's not sure even she knew existed.

They reach the bottom of the hill where he parked when he was here with Tess. "We'll walk to the top and scope the place out," he tells Brielle.

She nods, her face tight. "Makes sense."

Lying on their bellies, they peer over the rise. The warehouse looks exactly the same as last time. Big. Square. Unassuming.

Tristan watches closely, not surprised that nothing's moving. "The Skins would be invisible," he explains to Brielle. "Who knows how many are patrolling."

"There's going to be a lot of them, isn't there?"

"Like I said. They want us walking in, but not walking out. They've learned that's not as easy as they'd like it to be."

Especially now that they have their suits.

Brielle lets out a slow breath. "I suppose there's only one way to find out."

Tristan's about to reach out and squeeze her hand but he stops himself. Brielle's obviously scared, but she's not backing down. That, he can respect.

But she's not his soulmate and he needs to stop acting like she is.

Tristan turns and scampers down the hill a bit, then stands up. "I'll go in first and clean some of them up. Count to ten and then join me."

Brielle frowns. "What if there's a lot of them?"

Tristan grins for the first time since he found the basement trashed. "Ten seconds is enough."

He grips his stone as he looks at Brielle, waiting for her to do the same. Her shoulders squaring resolutely, her hand comes up, wrapping around the tourmaline that is her birthright.

They say the word simultaneously. "Akash."

This time, Tristan knows what's coming. As a purple just a shade away from midnight wraps around him, he welcomes it. He revels in the rightness of it.

He draws strength from it.

Looking at Brielle, he takes in her deep metallic pink as she faces him, legs slightly parted. She's sleek and kinda sexy and…Tristan looks away. Not his soulmate.

And right now, his parents need him.

Knowing the Skins are expecting him anyway, Tristan doesn't bother with sneaking up like he did last time. With a quick nod at Brielle, he leaps into the air.

Just as he suspected, it's like gravity's been dialed down. He arches high and streaks forward. As he surges toward the warehouse, he realizes he can hear the wind rushing past him, but he can't feel it. That he's not cold or hot or unsteady despite being several feet off the ground. He can't wait to take this baby for a spin.

He hits the ground several yards away. Another leap and he lands beside the water tank in a crouch.

He holds himself there, his breathing even as he listens for movement. A leaf skitters over the ground. A beetle scrapes its body over a pebble. But apart from that, there's nothing.

He's just done a quick lap around the warehouse when he stops. He's not alone like he thought he was.

Brielle is standing in the place he just left.

Tristan shakes his head. "That wasn't ten seconds," he mutters quietly.

She shrugs. "I wanted to be here if you needed help."

Tristan blinks behind his mask. Brielle's voice sounded as if she was talking directly into his ear. It seems they can talk directly to each other with these suits.

Brielle looks around. "They're all inside, aren't they?"

Tristan nods, trying to shake the foreboding that's swelling in his gut. "They knew we were coming, so they've concentrated their fighting power in one location."

Inside the warehouse.

Making this trap as inescapable as possible.

Tristan pauses. "Do you want—"

"I want to use my powers to help, Tristan."

Tristan nods, acknowledging the determination in Brielle's voice. "We'll go in carefully, then. Use any element of surprise we can."

Brielle doesn't answer, instead moving around to stand behind Tristan. "I'm ready."

The slightest tremble tells Tristan that despite the resolve, Brielle's scared. He's glad. It means she has some idea of what they're about to walk into. Reaching around he gives her hand a quick squeeze.

Soulmate or no soulmate, they're going to have to work as a team.

Keeping close to the wall, Tristan moves stealthily to the door. Grabbing the handle, he turns it as slowly and quietly as he can.

If he can take out even a couple of Skins before they're seen, then he'll use any advantage he can get.

But as he opens the door and peers through the crack, two things happen.

Zarius roars with rage. "Get your hands off her!"

Tristan sees his parents tied to two poles a few feet apart, the glint of a knife at Tess's throat.

Actually, three things happen.

His heart screaming with anguish, his mind exploding with fury, Tristan runs through the door.

"Tess!"

BRIELLE

B rielle is frozen in the doorway, left stunned by Tristan's roaring charge into the warehouse at the sight of his parents.

In an instant, Skins materialize all around to meet him head on. His fury fuels him, quickening his response time so that he catches every strike before it comes his way. He catches one Skin's fist and hurls him backward, then flips over two Skins that charge from both sides, sending them both flying with one roundhouse kick.

But even with his suit and his rage, Brielle fears there are just too many Skins for him to contend with alone. And he's not here alone.

Screw sitting on the sidelines waiting to be tagged in. She has these supposedly badass powers. It's time to use them.

Thanks to Tristan's sledgehammer entrance, no one notices her slip through the door before it closes. Brielle sneaks up behind the nearest Skin—the one farthest from the mosh pit circling Tristan. She's not sure how this is supposed to work, but she figures her best bet to make her power the most effective is by touch. She grabs the Skin's shoulder and, just like she did with Suki and Marie before, she wills the amplification of his guilt.

The Skin spins around so quickly, he has Brielle by the neck and off the ground in a flash. In desperation for her life, for the ability to breathe again, she slaps both hands on his wrists at her throat and pushes with all her will for him to feel his guilt.

Nothing happens. The Skin doesn't flinch. If anything, his grip tightens, and the blood in her face pounds with more intensity.

She can't feel his guilt. No visions of his past misdeeds invade her mind, even when she welcomes them in with her fast-fading consciousness.

None of it is working. Her stone doesn't work.

She's a failure. And now she's going to choke to death.

Just as her range of vision begins to narrow, the vice around her neck releases her, and she lands on her knees on the floor. Her starving throat sucks in air, and blinking rapidly, she looks up. Tristan has the Skin by the shoulder. He swiftly snaps his neck, letting him topple to the floor in front of Brielle.

"Are you okay?" he asks, his voice right in her ear despite him standing a few feet away.

She nods, even though she's far from okay.

"Keep yourself hidden," he says. "Remain our secret weapon." He turns around and returns to the fight, and she scrambles behind a stack of wooden pallets before she can be seen.

She should tell him it didn't work. She's no secret weapon.

It now makes sense why she couldn't tell when or if Adalind was lying. Why she never had visions of her. Adalind is a Skin, possessed by Chardis's influence. Someone who's not in control of their actions can't feel guilty for them.

Adalind might as well be a robot, and robots don't feel remorse.

Brielle's power is useless against their enemies. Tristan was wrong. About so many things.

"Tristan!" a female voice calls out.

Brielle quietly crawls to the edge of the pallet stack to peek at the two prisoners tied to support beams. His adoptive parents, Zarius and Tess.

"Why did you come here?" Zarius shouts angrily. "There are too many of them, it's a lost cause."

"As if I could ever leave you behind," Tristan says. She can't see him, but his panting tells her he's still fighting while he talks.

"Aw, what a touching family reunion." Brielle would know that voice anywhere.

Adalind steps out of the shadows and into the light of the fluorescent overhead bulb. Brielle's blood boils at the sight of her, at the wicked smile now spreading across her ex best friend's face.

"Where's my bestie?" she asks.

"I told her to stay behind," Tristan pants.

"Oh well, we'll find her soon enough," Adalind says with a shrug.

"Ah!" Tristan groans at the same time Tess and Zarius shout, "Tristan!"

Brielle's heart jumps, desperate to run out and take action, but she knows she can't do that. She needs to stay hidden. So far, no one knows she's here, and *that* is their secret weapon. She just has no clue how to use that to their advantage yet.

Considering her powers are useless.

Tristan comes into view, dragged by two Skins at each arm, and they bring him right at Adalind's feet.

"You said if I came, you'd let them go," he says. Brielle

can't see his expression beneath the suit, but she imagines his perfect teeth barred in rage.

"Ah-ah-ah." Adalind shakes her head and wags her index finger. "In fact, what I said was I'd kill them if you didn't come, not that I'd free them if you did. You really should listen more closely."

"Grr-ahh!" Tristan growls, trying to jerk free of his captors to no avail. "You have me, they're useless to you. Let them go and I'll do whatever you want."

"Tristan, no!" Tess pleads.

"We're not leaving you," Zarius shouts.

"Enough of this silly chatter," Adalind snaps. "Chardis will be here soon, and he'll decide what to do with all of you." She tosses her hair over her shoulder and smiles. "In the meantime, I have a little surprise for you."

She snaps her fingers and a door behind her opens. Two figures drag something in, but Brielle can't see past the thick curtain of fluorescent light between her and the shadows they're moving through to tell what that something is.

Then they come into the light and drop their cargo with a *flop*.

It's Cassandra!

Mirror Point High's queen bee is covered in scrapes and bruises, her once beautiful eyes swollen shut by purple flesh, and the hair she's always so proud of is mussed and tangled.

Despite their history, Brielle can't bear to see her this way.

"What did you do to her?" Tristan asks, his voice gravelly.

Adalind sways her hips to one side and waves a hand. "Well, we suspected her of being an Heir, so we subjected her to a series of…tests. But no matter what we did to her, she did nothing but cry and scream and beg for mercy. No powers whatsoever. Pity. We were hoping to kill three birds with one stone, so to speak, but Cassandra's no more a

Zodiac Guardian than I am. Oh well." She shrugs again, and Brielle's insides twist with a cocktail of hatred for Adalind and deep sympathy for Cassandra.

"She's not breathing," Tess gasps. "You killed the poor girl and she wasn't even an Heir?"

Dead? Cassandra's...dead? Every tender moment they ever shared in their childhood replays in Brielle's mind, and a resonating regret for not making amends saturates her to her core. Cassandra didn't deserve to die like this. She may have become somewhat of a bully the past few years, but she didn't deserve to be tortured for powers she didn't even have. Brielle's eyes well up with tears.

"I wouldn't worry about her. You'll all join her soon enough." Adalind closes in on Tristan and gets down to his level. Her back is to Zarius and Tess.

This is Brielle's chance. She can cry for Cassandra when this is over.

If they make it out alive.

"You may have been wrong about Cassandra, but you were right about my bestie," Adalind says as Brielle hunches low and creeps toward the captives.

Tess catches her approaching, and at the sight of the suit, she purses her lips and nods to her. Brielle swiftly gets behind the beam and works her fingers quickly and quietly to unravel the restraints. When Tess's release and fall around her, Brielle moves over to do the same for Zarius.

"So tell me, Prince Gem, who else do you suspect of being one of you?" Adalind asks, tipping his chin upward with her index finger.

Adalind is so busy reveling in her victory, she never sees the ambush coming.

Zarius swings a thick two-by-four right at the back of her head. "He prefers Tristan."

27

TRISTAN

The brief moment of surprise as the Skins watch their leader crumple is all Tristan needs. He leaps, somersaulting through the air and landing behind them. One sweeping kick and they're both knocked out cold.

Tristan streaks toward Zarius and they both form a defensive line in front of Tess and Brielle.

"Nice suit," Zarius comments.

Tristan lifts his fists as the Skins start fanning around them. "What were the chances it was going to be my favorite color?"

Three Skins run at them at once, but they don't stand a chance against Zarius and Tristan. Like two gears in a well-oiled machine, Zarius quickly dispatches one while Tristan's fist ploughs through the other two.

"Adalind?" Tristan asks quietly, noting the pool of blood circling her head from the corner of his eye where she lies beside Cassandra's dead body.

"I doubt she'll be getting back up again," Zarius states flatly.

Tristan can't bring himself to feel sad for the loss of the girl. She betrayed Brielle. She killed Cassandra and Alden.

She wanted to kill Tess.

The next punch aimed at a Skin is powered by the rage that thought sparks. The Skin sails through the air, landing in an unconscious heap a few feet away.

"And the girl?" Zarius asks as he rams his elbow into the next fool who comes at them.

"Brielle. She's the Libra."

The words slice straight through Tristan, the suit being no protection from the truth. The next kick slams straight through three Skins like a battering ram. Just as he lands, a piece of wood cracks across Tristan's back. The sound of it splintering is like a gunshot.

Tristan straightens and turns to face the man. "That could've hurt," he growls.

Using his fists like pistons, he pummels the Skin's chest. The man jerks and grunts over and over, before finally collapsing.

"Tristan!"

Brielle's panicked voice has him spinning around. Two Skins have used the distraction to work their way around and come up behind. One grabs Tess by the hair as the other sets his gaze on Brielle.

"Use your powers," Tristan calls.

The bastard will never stand a chance.

Except Brielle's stepping backward, shaking her head. She whispers the next words, but they're undeniable as they slide over Tristan's ear.

"My powers. They don't work on the Skins."

There's no time to ask what the hell she's talking about. To try and get his head around what that means.

Zarius is already running toward Tess. Tristan leaps into

the air, covering the distance in a flying arc. He lands behind the Skin, relishing the sound as his armored fist slams into the side of his head.

And then, there's no time to talk. To think. The Skins have finally figured out they need to rush them at once if they're going to stand a chance.

But there's no way they're getting through Tristan and Zarius as they come to the forefront again. Tess is behind them. Brielle with her.

And it seems Brielle's just as helpless as Tess is, armed with less than basic fighting skills.

Tristan and Zarius fight like they've never fought before. At times back to back, others side to side, they form an impenetrable barrier. Father and son. Guardian and Zodiac.

As Zarius grabs one Skin and shoves the guy at Tristan, he almost finds himself smiling. An uppercut and a kick to the chest, and the man's no longer a threat.

This is what being a Zodiac's about.

Being a team.

And winning because of it.

Suddenly, the handful of Skins left go still. Like puppets, their arms drop by their sides, their heads flopping down like the strings have been cut.

Tristan and Zarius straighten, glancing at each other. Instinctively, they take a couple of steps back, closer to Brielle and Tess.

"What's going on?" Tess asks quietly.

Tristan waits for Zarius to answer, but nothing comes. Which means he doesn't know.

Whatever's going on, it isn't good.

"I say we get the hell out of here," mutters Tristan. He reaches back, finding Brielle already coming up beside him. He grasps her hand tightly. "Now."

Zarius is running on adrenaline and doesn't have a suit to protect him.

Brielle's powers don't work on Skins.

Tess has been close to death enough as it is.

Suddenly, a click reverberates through the silent warehouse, and the door to their right opens slowly.

They all freeze. It was too slow for a breeze to have pushed it open.

Yet no one is coming through.

Tristan indicates the others stay where they are as he takes a few cautious steps to the side. It could be the door popping open at the wrong moment, but they need to be careful.

Tristan's taken two steps then stops.

A man enters through the door, his stride casual. He stops a few feet in, adjusting his cuffs as he maintains a side profile.

Tristan's breath disintegrates. It can't be...

The man is tall, ink black hair combed back from his pale face. Slowly, deliberately, he glances up at Tristan, half his head in shadow. A wide smile creeps up his flawless face. His gaze flickers past Tristan, finding Zarius, Tess and Brielle, but then quickly returns to him. A few more steps and the door whooshes closed behind him.

Instinctively, Tristan knows who he's facing.

Chardis.

Just like his hair, he's dressed in ink, from his collared shirt to his creased slacks to his polished shoes. Of course, he is. Chardis likes to think he's the new black.

Finally, he turns his face toward them. Tristan almost does something he's never done in his life. He has to physically stop himself from stepping back.

Chardis's left eye is missing. No, not missing. Nonexistent.

Nothing but a socket of nothingness, thin spidery veins the color of black blood extend from it, creeping across his face and disappearing into his hairline. It's the coldest, creepiest thing Tristan has ever seen.

He goes to step back beside his parents and Brielle when Chardis speaks.

"Don't move."

Like hell he won't.

Another step and Tess cries out. Tristan stills, fear spearing through him. Tess is clutching her chest, her eyes wide with panic and pain.

Tristan spins around, facing Chardis. "Leave her alone!"

"When I was told there was not one, but two, Zodiac Guardians here, I knew I had to come. I mean, what if you found your Gemini Twin, Tristan? Why, I could've been in a spot of trouble." His gaze flickers to Brielle. "But instead you found yourself a Libra." The black lines that are his brows hike up, stretching the spidery veins on his face. "I bet that was disappointing."

Tristan's teeth are clenched too hard to respond. He needs to get to Zarius and Tess. And yet the darkest evil in the Universe is right in front of him.

"You do know what dark matter is, don't you Tristan? It's the glue between atoms, the fascinating, mysterious substance that holds our Universe together. It's the foundation of everything, yet undetectable on this primitive planet." Chardis's lips twitch. "If you have the ability to harness it, there's no limit to what you can do."

"Enough of the physics lesson," Tristan growls. "What do you want?"

But Chardis continues as if Tristan didn't speak. "Considering it's tucked between every atom in this Universe, it means all I have to do is squeeze and it contracts."

Tess cries out again, and from the corner of his eye, Tristan sees her collapse in Zarius's arms.

"I can crush a can. A car." His black gaze flares with obsidian fire. "Or a heart."

Zarius roars an objection only for it to be cut off. Chardis chuckles. "Or a throat."

Tristan's hands flex helplessly by his side. "What do you want?" he growls again.

Chardis levels his cold gaze on him. "Remove your suits."

Brielle's gasp splinters across Tristan's ears. Just like him, she realizes they'll be far too vulnerable if they do that. They'll lose what little advantage they have.

It's Zarius's groan as he drops to his knees that propels Tristan into action. "We'll do as you ask. Just leave them alone!"

With a short nod to Brielle, he says the word. In a blink, his suit is gone, Brielle's disappearing a second later.

Chardis's smile grows. "Ah, what fine young Guardians you are." He angles his head. "And yet you have so much to learn."

Turning to look at Zarius and Tess, Chardis raises his hand. Insidiously, a black mist starts to form around him. It grows, creeping along the warehouse floor like coal-colored cancer. The moment it touches anything—poles, walls, the silent bodies of the Skins—it creeps up, defying gravity in its quest to devour.

Including the legs of Tristan's parents.

"What are you doing?" Tristan demands.

But Chardis is focused. Unwavering.

In his determination to kill Tristan's parents.

"No!" he screams, his hand reaching back for his stone. Except he can't lift it. It's like gravity has multiplied, chaining him with invisible bonds no matter how much he strains against it. It pulls down on him, anchoring his feet into the floor. Leaving him immobile.

Helpless as he watches Tess and Zarius collapse, gripping their chests. The black mist licks hungrily at them, tendrils winding their way around their waists.

"No," Tristan screams through his tight throat.

But there's nothing he can do.

Zarius looks up at him. He mouths two words. "Find them."

His face contorts with agony, and he draws Tess to his chest. His parents cling to each other as their hearts are crushed within their ribs. Blood appears at Tess's mouth as Zarius presses a kiss to her forehead. Their eyes close simultaneously as their bodies crumple into the inky mist that now covers the floor.

This time, the denial screams through Tristan's mind. Through his heart. Through the very core of his being.

But it does nothing to stop the reality of what's happened.

Zarius and Tess are dead. Killed by Chardis.

He turns to Tristan, one eye glittering with satisfaction, the other a black hole of evil. "I wanted you to see that before I finished you next."

The mist grows and multiplies, sucking any light from the room. The warehouse shrinks as it turns into night.

His whole body turns cold as Tristan realizes his vision has come to pass.

Cassandra's dead.

Everything's black.

Brielle will be next.

He doesn't stop the cry that explodes from his throat as he feels his heart compress. It's like a weight's just been slammed on his chest. Agony detonates from the inside out, the sound of Chardis's chuckle an unwanted poison in his mind.

As the pain has his legs giving out, Tristan wishes he 'd been strong enough. He couldn't protect Zarius or Tess. He couldn't save Brielle.

He's failed.

28

BRIELLE

Ah Brielle can do is watch as Tristan crumples and
screams. She's never felt so useless. Zarius and Tess
just died right in front of her, and the same thing is about to
happen to Tristan.

"Chardis, please stop!" she begs, running forward and
stopping just short of the black mist. "Take me instead. I'll go
without a fight. I'll do whatever you want. Just spare him.
Please!"

"No, Brielle!" Tristan groans, the words barely audible
through his clenched teeth.

Chardis aims his black, soulless eye on her, and she
suddenly feels heavier.

"Having a Zodiac Guardian as a pet *is* a tempting offer,"
Chardis says like a panther purring, stalking slowly closer.
"But what use do I have for Libra? Power of truth and justice,
eh? Was it your justice to let Alden die for you? Was it your
truth to befriend the girl plotting your demise just because
she cast a smile in your direction? You can't even save the
boy you love."

He waves his hand toward Tristan, who's doubled over at his feet, barely breathing and clutching his chest.

Desperation fries Brielle's nerve endings from fingertips to toes, threatening to burst through her chest. And yet all she can do is watch Tristan gasp to death. Hot tears stream down her cheeks, and she wishes she still had her suit, if only to hide her face.

Chardis is right. She's of no use to anyone. Alden died trying to save her from Adalind. Cassandra died because of the connection Adalind saw between them. Brielle came here to help Tristan rescue Zarius and Tess, and because of her failure, they're both now dead, too. She's nothing but a walking disaster, a living disappointment.

"There is no truth other than what I say there is, no justice other than what I will there to be," Chardis says, his chest puffing out. "I am the truth and justice in the Universe, and I will not be judged by the likes of you."

Brielle's body is all of a sudden so heavy that she can no longer stand. Her knees buckle and she lands on all fours. This is his doing. He's manipulating gravity.

"I must say, I do love seeing a Zodiac Guardian on their knees," he boasts, his thin lips curling in a wicked smile. "Bowing to the rightful power in the Universe, like a good girl."

A force tightens around Brielle's chest, cramping her lungs and making it impossible to fill them. Gasping, she looks over at Tristan, who's now laying on the floor in the fetal position. His face is puffy and red, like the blood is trapped there.

She knows there are only seconds left until he dies. And her, too.

"I do wonder which of you I should kill first, which of you I should make the other watch as they die," Chardis says as he paces around them.

Tristan's bulging eyes find hers, and he reaches out. But his arms are too heavy and don't make it more than a few inches. He nods, and she understands all the many layers of that small gesture even without him mouthing the words, "It's okay."

No, it's not. None of this is okay. Tristan has spent his whole life looking for her, or at least other Guardians like her. Fate has to exist. Brielle refuses to believe that the Universe would set them up to meet only to kill them immediately after and doom itself in the process.

Cassandra and Alden, Zarius and Tess, they can't die in vain. They just can't! She *is* going to avenge them and save Tristan, or she's going to die trying.

With every ounce of her strength, she pushes herself up enough to look at Chardis, her arm muscles shaking violently with the effort.

"If...not...me," she says between broken breaths. "Then...who?"

Chardis stops his pacing and looks down at her. "What?" There's a hike in his brow as if he's impressed by her ability to speak through his gravity intensification.

"Who...will...judge...you...for...all...you've...killed?" The last word exhausts her air supply and barely makes it past her lips. The lack of oxygen makes her arms give out, and she falls flat on her chest.

Chardis gives a low chuckle. "You're no match for me, girl."

A familiar tingle in her gut signals through the white noise of pain and suffocation. She would know that tingle anywhere. She's felt it her entire life. But it makes no sense. Not with him.

The tingle creeps up her belly, then her neck, and as she knew it would, the vision takes hold.

Brielle is suddenly spiraling through a whirlwind of faces

meeting their death. Whole planets destroyed, massacres on levels too horrible to fathom. Blood and blackness staining every flashing image.

When the vision fades, she feels spent, both physically and emotionally. The weight of all those stolen lives and mass extinctions crushes her more than Chardis's gravity.

Guilt. The most powerful guilt she's ever felt.

And it belongs to the man standing in front of her.

Brielle doesn't understand it, but she doesn't have the time to question it. She embraces the foreign guilt no matter how much it hurts her soul, her heart. She gathers it into a tight little ball inside her, and in one last ditch effort, she throws her hand out at him, imagining herself hurling it right at his chest.

Just like with Marie and Suki, her spirit feels lighter as soon as the guilt is gone.

"What…what is this?" Chardis's voice spikes with alarm.

Brielle cranes her head off the floor to look at him. His eyes are wide with panic as his hands roam his chest all over. The black veins climbing across his face stand out in stark relief.

"Urgh," he groans, clutching his heart.

She suddenly realizes it's not only her spirit that's lighter. Her limbs move more freely, their weight receding by the second. When she has enough strength to turn her head to Tristan, she finds the bright flush slowly leaving his face, his cheeks and eyes deflating back to their normal size.

Chardis's power is waning.

She turns back to him and wills the guilt to intensify. He cries out in pain and clutches his abdomen as if some creature is about to burst out of it. Is that a red glow beneath his hand? She doesn't believe it until a wisp of smoke rises between his fingers.

Brielle's weight is back to normal and she scrambles to

Tristan, and both of them stare in amazement as the flesh of Chardis's cheek, neck, hand, begin to char from the inside out.

"What's happening?" Chardis shrieks, flicking a sneer at Brielle.

"Your judgement," Brielle says, her shoulders rising and falling with each starving breath.

Chardis's face twists into a hideous snarl. "This is far from over, Guardians!"

The space behind him ripples and warps into a strange sphere that distorts the images beyond it. Before Brielle can make a move, he steps into it and blinks out of sight, the ripple smoothing immediately after.

"What the—" Brielle jumps to her feet and runs to the space where he disappeared. "Where did he go?"

"I think it was a wormhole," Tristan says, shakily climbing to his feet as well.

"Do you think the penance burn will kill him?" she asks, adrenaline still galloping through her veins as her lungs adjust to their full capacity.

"I really don't know, but I doubt it." He stumbles close, tripping and grasping her shoulder for support. "What happened? I thought you said your power didn't work on the Skins."

"It didn't." She shakes her head in confusion, looking around at the dead Skins that surround them. "They felt no guilt, so there was nothing to amplify. I think because they weren't acting of their own volition. You said they are possessed or infected or something, right?"

He nods, catching his own breath as well. "So your power doesn't work on the Skins because they aren't in control of themselves and feel no remorse. But Chardis did?"

"It was subtle and buried deep, but the weight of it was atomizing," she explains. "He's done so many horrible things, and I saw all of it." A shudder runs up her spine, and pressure builds behind her eyes of tears she's not ready to shed. "He's a monster."

Tristan looks down at the lifeless shells of his parents. "Yes, he is."

The tears she fights to keep inside push even harder to be set free. "I'm so sorry, Tristan." There are a million things she wants to say, but she knows that none of them will ease his pain.

He continues to stare at them for a long moment, then turns away and sniffles. "We'll take them back with us, give them a proper burial. They don't deserve to be disposed of by the Skins."

She nods, and her eyes find Cassandra. "Cassandra, too. She may have been a bit of a witch, but she didn't deserve this."

Brielle kneels over the body of her rival and brushes the matted blonde hair away from her bruised and cracked face. Why didn't she try harder to make amends with Cassandra? If they had stayed friends, Adalind wouldn't have been able to blindside them. Cassandra might still be alive. Brielle can't forget all the nasty things Cassandra's done since she got adopted, but things didn't have to be that way. Maybe she should have told Cassandra about her powers long ago. The powers that are not a curse as she thought, but a gift, a true way to protect those she loves. She's been so wrong, about so many things.

Cassandra's chest rises ever so slightly.

Is she breathing?

Brielle moves her fingers around Cassandra's neck to find her pulse, and sure enough the artery drums a weak beat.

"She's alive!" she shouts, waving Tristan over. "Cassandra's alive!"

Please don't let it be too late to save her.

29

TRISTAN

Tristan reaches Cassandra's side just as Brielle does. He ignores the ache that seems to have woven itself through his ribs. It flares hot and hard with each breath, but he doesn't care.

Cassandra might be alive.

They both kneel beside her, their breath held as they wait to see whether Cassandra has any of her own.

Yes! There it is! The slightest rise of her chest.

Tristan falls back on his haunches. "She's been paralyzed."

Brielle gasps. "What? How?"

"Poison. The Skins have used it on me before." Tristan looks around. "There's an antidote. One of these guys will have it."

Ready to use in case they wanted to interrogate Cassandra again.

Tristan stands, gritting his teeth as his head swims. "You stay with her, I'll find it."

He only has to go through the jacket pockets of two Skins before he finds it, relieved that it's in a syringe. Obviously the Skins needed it to be ready.

Brielle's holding Cassandra's hand, watching her closely. "What she must've gone through..."

"If she's lucky, she won't remember."

Uncapping the syringe, Tristan hesitates. All this first aid stuff was always Tess's domain. He's never injected anything into anyone.

But Cassandra's breathing is barely there. He doesn't have a choice.

Not when Zarius and Tess are...gone.

Tristan welcomes the stab of pain at his sharp intake of breath. It's only a fraction of the agony that's going to hit him when he finally allows himself to think.

Knowing he needs to do this, Tristan pierces the skin of Cassandra's arm with the needle and injects the antidote.

Sitting back, he lets out a breath. "Now, we hope to hell it works."

Brielle's hands flutter over Cassandra. "She'll just...wake up?"

If Tristan's right, she will. "That's the plan. The antidote worked pretty fast when...when Tess gave it to me. She was so good at that kind of stuff."

Talking about her in the past tense suddenly is far more piercing than he'd ever imagined.

Brielle nods, her eyes soft with understanding. "They both loved you very much."

Tristan looks away. They both died for him.

Brielle sighs. "It's probably a good thing Cassandra's not a Zodiac Guar—"

Tristan shakes his head vehemently. "When I was paralyzed, I could still hear everything."

She clamps her mouth shut. And Brielle thought she had secrets before...

From the corner of his eye, Tristan sees Cassandra's fingers twitch. She's starting to wake, which means they have to get her out of here before she sees the graveyard of bodies around them.

Including Zarius and Tess.

Clenching his jaw as he shoves away that thought, Tristan scoops Cassandra up. He can try and process that when this is all over.

Try to figure out how the hell he's going to keep moving forward.

Brielle holds the door open and Tristan carries Cassandra out, striding away from the warehouse of death and toward his truck. Outside, it's still dark and quiet. Tristan looks around, wondering how everything can still look the same.

Not when everything's changed.

Cassandra stirs in his arms and he looks down, finding her eyes fluttering open. Tristan stops, waiting to see what they'll be dealing with.

Her blue eyes groggily blink up at him. "Tristan?" Her hand lifts, brushing his cheek as if she needs to make sure he's real.

"Yeah, it's me. You're safe now."

Cassandra's brows crinkle, her body twitching as sensation returns. She's probably going to be sore in a whole lot of places, and yet he can't tell her she's lucky to be alive.

"I…" She swallows. "They…"

"We're going to take you home."

Cassandra's eyes widen. "We?"

Brielle steps in, her face soft with reassurance. "It's only the three of us. Like Tristan said, you're safe now."

Cassandra stiffens. Her blue eyes shoot to Brielle before returning to Tristan. "You can put me down now."

Lowering her gently, Tristan releases her slowly, making sure she doesn't collapse. Her body wouldn't be used to seeing such violence.

But Cassandra locks her knees. She throws back her shoulders.

Then narrows her gaze at Brielle. "Just before they…" She shakes her head. "They said your name. They asked me about you."

Brielle takes a step back. "I'm so sorry you had to go through this, Cassandra."

She takes a step forward, her body vibrating with anger. "I should've known you were somehow involved in this. Did you ask them to take me?"

Brielle gasps. "No, I'd never do that. I—"

Tristan steps around to face Cassandra. "We went for a drive and found you beside the road, unconscious. Despite what's happened in the past, Brielle would never wish this on you."

Cassandra's hands are clenched by her sides and it takes her a couple of seconds to tear her gaze away from Brielle.

Who's right. It's a good thing Cassandra's not a Zodiac Guardian. Brielle was probably thinking that her violent introduction to their world would leave scars. That Cassandra's perfect world would have been turned upside down.

But right now, Tristan's realizing they don't need that sort of conflict in their fledgling ranks. The Zodiac Guardians' strength is as a team. Cassandra and Brielle's history will only fracture that.

Tristan grasps her arm, in part to keep her focus on him, in part because Cassandra's trembling is morphing into shaking. He asks his question slowly, knowing her answer is going to make all the difference. "What do you remember, Cassandra?"

"I… I was walking back from the restaurant. There were men…" She closes her eyes then opens them again. "And then I woke up here."

Tristan watches her closely. "That's all?"

Cassandra lifts her hand to her temple, frowning. "That's all I remember."

Relief that something's finally gone right floods Tristan. They don't have a civilian on their hands who they have to explain why they were tortured and interrogated. That words like Zodiac and Guardian are more than science fiction. In fact, it's possible the Skins wiped her memory themselves in an effort to cover their tracks.

Tristan wraps an arm around her shoulder. "Come on, let's get you home. Your parents are probably worried."

Cassandra nods mutely, allowing Tristan to lead her to his truck. She climbs in the back seat and curls up, her eyes fluttering closed.

Tristan and Brielle glance at each other. Sleep is probably the best thing for Cassandra right now.

They drive back quietly, not wanting to wake her. As they pull up the wide driveway to park outside the large, double story mansion, Tristan frowns. No lights are on, there's no movement.

The monster-sized house is asleep, even though Cassandra has been missing for hours.

Cassandra wakes as the truck comes to a stop. "I'll walk the rest of the way." She opens the door, moving stiffly but determinedly.

Tristan jumps out, glancing at Brielle to let her know it's probably best if she stays in the car. Coming around, he grabs Cassandra as one of her knees gives out. "Your mom is going to ask some questions."

Cassandra snorts. "She's overseas." Flicking back a strand of matted hair, she angles her chin. "A shower, some strategic makeup, and no one will know."

Tristan has to keep his eyebrows from hiking up. It's not the response he expected from her. At the same time, if she's going to act like this never happened, that's a good thing.

He nods. "Okay. But if you get dizzy or anything, you'll need to see someone."

Cassandra's lips tip up. "I will. Thanks, Tristan."

Shrugging, he allows himself a smile. "Good thing I was at the right place, at the right time." Releasing her arm, Tristan's glad to see Cassandra stays steady. "Get some rest."

"I will." With a flicker of her fingers, she turns away, limping toward the house. Instead of walking through the front door though, Cassandra turns left and disappears down the side of the house.

Climbing back in the truck, Tristan sits and waits, although he's not sure what for.

He doesn't want lights turning on in any of those multitude of windows—it would mean Cassandra has to explain her injuries. Cassandra having to think harder about what happened to her.

And why.

But the house remains dark. Meaning no one's going to be there to help Cassandra wash away the blood. To *tsk tsk* over the bruises. To tuck her in and reassure her she's safe.

"Do you think she'll be okay?" Brielle asks quietly.

Tristan sighs, starting the truck again. "It seems she's tougher than she looks."

The drive back to the warehouse is silent. Heavy with the knowledge of what has to happen next.

Lifting Zarius and Tess's bodies. Putting them in the back of the truck like they have with Skins in the past.

Wondering how he's going to explain their disappearance.

Trying to forge a life without them.

But Tristan slows as they reach the final rise before the warehouse. Instinctively, he cuts the headlights.

Brielle leans forward, having seen it, too.

A soft glow rises into the black night, punctured by

flashes of red and blue. His hands tightening around the steering wheel, Tristan creeps the truck to the top of the hill and stops.

"Dammit," he mutters.

Several police cars have surrounded the warehouse, their lights flashing. Beside them, a single black car is parked.

Brielle frowns. "Does that car say FBI?"

Tristan works hard to carve out a short, sharp nod. His body feels like it's turned to stone. "Yeah, you read it right."

He scans the bodies moving in and out of the warehouse, quickly finding what he's looking for. The tall, thin frame. The balding head.

The nose poking around where it shouldn't be.

Tristan allows the truck to roll back, his mind screaming for him to go down there. To be able to say goodbye to the two people who were his world.

Who he now has to face his future without.

Brielle grabs the dash as if she's having problems letting go, too. "But—"

"We can't go down there. The feds will ask too many questions."

"Oh, Tristan," Brielle breathes, realizing what this means.

Tristan looks away, preferring to keep his gaze on the black night rather than the movement and lights. "It's probably better this way. I'll get a knock on the door. They'll get a proper burial. I won't be able to answer any questions as I was never there."

Brielle goes quiet. She knows the truth.

Tristan was there.

He saw Chardis murder Zarius and Tess.

"So, what now?" she asks, her voice tight with the pain Tristan's feeling.

If she were his soulmate, that would make sense.

But she's not.

Tristan grits his teeth. "I'll drop you off at the orphanage then head back to my house and wait."

Cassandra is home safe, with no memory of what happened.

They now know Brielle is the Libra, a Zodiac Guardian.

Chardis is gone…for now.

With a heavy sigh, Tristan allows the truck to roll back. Once they're far enough away, he starts the engine and heads back to Mirror Point. "It's over."

30

BRIELLE

The night seems so much darker as Brielle walks up the stairs of the orphanage. Her steps are heavy, and it's not just because she was nearly crushed by hyper gravity. This is going to be her permanent place, at least until her next birthday.

Now that she's thrown away her chance at a family.

But she can hardly feel that selfish loss now, knowing that Tristan's loss is so much greater. She only lost a possible family. He lost a real one. Somehow, that sting burns deeper than anything else.

At least she could be there for him. They may have failed to save his parents, but they discovered they have a major advantage against Chardis.

Her powers.

If she'd practiced more, been better prepared for the fight, she may have even defeated him tonight. She clenches her fists with the vow that the next time they face him, she will.

Then she opens the door, ready to face her solitary orphan life once more.

"Brielle!" The voice that doesn't belong here reaches her before she sees them standing next to Sister Agatha.

Frank and Beatrice.

Before Brielle has time to react, Beatrice rushes forward and wraps her in a tight embrace.

Shock has Brielle stupefied, unable to react.

She sees Frank's face over Bea's shoulder, and the emotions carved there are a mixture of concern and relief.

"Why did you run off like that?" Bea asks, still hugging her.

Brielle is speechless. There's no explanation she can give that will make any sense, or excuse her disappearance.

Frank closes in, putting a hand on her back. "We were so worried about you. We didn't know what else to do but wait for you here." He looks over at Sister Agatha, whose wrinkled face is fluffed in a loving smile.

Brielle finds her voice at last, though dry and cracking as it is. "I'm so sorry for leaving like that. There's no excuse for my behavior. I understand if you want to call off the adoption."

Beatrice pulls back enough to face her, a frown pinching her brows. "Oh, you sweet girl." She shakes her head, then smiles. "It's already done."

Brielle blinks and looks at each of their faces one at a time. "Wait. What?"

"We signed the adoption papers as soon as we got here," Frank says, looking and sounding the epitome of a father.

Brielle's breath catches in her throat. "R—really?"

They nod.

"It's understandable that you'd freak out," Frank says. "We shouldn't have rushed you over to our house. It was too much too fast. But we wanted to make sure you know that you always have a home with us. You can always rely on us. We aren't going to give up on you."

"Unless…you really don't want us as your parents." Bea's eyes mist up as she barely gets the words out.

Overcome with more emotions than she can name, Brielle throws her arms around Bea's neck, letting loose the tears she's been holding in all night. She feels Frank's large, warm arms close around the two of them as well.

"Thank you," she sobs. "There's nothing I want more in the whole world!"

They stand like that for several long minutes, holding each other, and Brielle can't tell whose tears are soaking whose clothing. A warmth ignites in the center of this hug-fest. It's the feeling of unconditional love, something Brielle has never known. It's a feeling that tells her everything is going to be okay…somehow.

When they finally pull away, Brielle and Bea wipe their faces and laugh out their relief.

"We'll be by to pick you up in the morning and help you pack your things," Frank says. Then he points a paternal finger and jokes, "But no running off again, young lady."

A shaky laugh rolls out of Brielle's lungs. "I promise."

Bea purses her smiling lips and rubs Brielle's shoulders, looking as though she's not ready to leave her. "Have a good night, my darling girl." She caresses Brielle's cheek, then finally steps away.

The two wave goodbye and head out the door.

Brielle is left standing there, bewildered at how events transpired.

She has a family now. A real family. Even after she ghosted them with no explanation.

The joy in her chest rivals the ache left by Chardis's abuse, and she wonders if her weakened ribcage can take the pressure of so much bliss.

Sister Agatha comes up to Brielle. "I had a feeling they were finally the right couple. I'm so happy for you." She clasps her hands in front of her, and Brielle almost believes the nun wants to hug her but is holding back. "I will be both sad and proud to see you leave in the morning."

"Thank you, Sister Agatha," Brielle says, her eyes stinging at the realization that she's truly leaving. "I'll miss you, too."

Sister Agatha's owl-like eyes seem to shine. Is she actually holding back tears? "You've had a long night and it's far past time for you to get some needed sleep. On with you to your room."

"Goodnight, Sister." And as she all but skips to her room for hopefully the last time, her oldest friend creeps up on her.

Guilt.

How is it fair that, on the night Tristan loses his family, she gets one? How can she allow herself to feel so grateful when he's so heartbroken? It's not fair that she gets to walk into a full and loving home while Tristan goes back to an empty one.

The Universe is a cruel mistress. And yet, they're doing all of this to save it.

The battle is far from over. Even though this night ended in a win for her, she knows there will be much more pain and loss to come.

All she can do is enjoy the good while it lasts. And right now, she's loving it.

31

TRISTAN

Two marble headstones.

Although they rise from the grass right in front of Tristan, the sun failing to warm their cold, hard surface, he still can't believe it.

In all the ways he saw this fight against Chardis playing out, Zarius and Tess were there, in every one of them.

Every. Single. One.

Except, now he's alone.

No parents.

No soulmate.

No clue as to who or where the next Zodiac Guardian is.

Tristan locks his knees as they try to give out. He's already discovered the tears don't help the loneliness. The hopelessness.

The what the hell do I do next.

Mirror Point Cemetery is quiet this early in the morning, which is what Tristan wanted. In the week since their deaths, he's visited them every day. He still talks to them.

Still waits for some sort of sign.

A movement from the corner of his eye has Tristan spinning to the right. He's been so caught up in his grief, in the assumption that Chardis is off licking his guilt-ridden wounds somewhere, that he's let his guard down.

Zarius would be disappointed...

But there's no one there. Just more rows of headstones, two much larger than the others only a few down. Tristan frowns as he peers closer. They're not tombstones, they're a memorial of some sort. And it looks like flames are licking across the top of them.

He rubs his eyes and looks again. The tendrils of fire are gone.

Turning away, Tristan's shoulders slump. The lack of sleep is getting to him.

And so is losing everything he owns in the house fire the Skins started. He'd returned to his house to find it ablaze, firefighters and trucks scrambling to keep it under control. They'd stopped it from spreading. But hadn't been able to stop the last home he shared with Zarius and Tess from becoming little more than ash.

Tristan hadn't been surprised. He'd considered whether he needed to do it himself. But still...it'd been the cherry that garnished the worst day of his life.

Now, he's homeless. Alone. And seeing fire where it doesn't exist.

"What do I do, Zarius?" he whispers.

Zarius had always been his guide, his mentor. The one with all the answers.

And Tess...she was their light, their hope. The one with all the smiles.

Tristan's hands spear into his hair, trying to contain the anguish. It's during these moments, it feels too big, too overwhelming.

Too impossible as Brielle turns to him, wondering what's next.

His cell phone rings and he answers it automatically, assuming it's her. Although they're not soulmates, their Zodiac Guardian bond is a strong one. They often do uncanny things like call only to find the other was just thinking of them.

But it's a male voice that jolts into his ear. "Good day. Am I speaking to Tristan Ayers?"

Tristan's instantly on alert. Someone he doesn't know calling him out of the blue can't be a good thing.

"Yes, you are," he says brusquely, not giving him any more than that.

"Wonderful. I tried coming by your house, but… Terrible tragedy, I'm so sorry."

Tristan doesn't answer. There's nothing to say.

The man clears his throat, introducing himself and the firm he's from—of course, both bearing the same name. "I'd like to coordinate a meeting as soon as possible."

"I'm pretty busy…" Tristan tries to figure out how to finish that sentence.

Busy doing what? Trying to find a comfortable position in his truck to sleep in?

Coordinating a team of non-existent Zodiac Guardians?

Never eating waffles again?

"It's to discuss Alden's estate, seeing as you're the sole beneficiary of it."

Tristan blinks. "I beg your pardon?"

"Yes, his last will and testament is very clear. The house, the contents, and his fortune are all yours, irrespective of your age."

House?

Fortune?

Tristan glances around, wondering if he's hearing things as well as seeing them. "Ah, sure. I can come around this afternoon."

"Wonderful," the man says warmly and Tristan realizes he should've paid attention to his name.

They coordinate a time and Tristan hangs up, staring at his cell for long moments. He turns back to the headstones.

Zarius would've known about this. He and Alden were Guardians. Their job was to ensure the fight could continue.

Zarius's final words echo through Tristan's mind.

Find them.

Tristan's arms fall to his side, his shoulders pulling back as he fills his lungs. He wanted a sign, and he just got one.

Zarius and Tess and Alden didn't just die for him. They died for the fight they believe in. A fight to save more souls than any one mind could ever imagine.

Their loss won't be for nothing. In fact, their deaths just made this personal. Chardis winning isn't an option.

It's not over, he vows.

The battle to save the Universe has only just begun.

Ready for the next installment in the Zodiac Guardians series?
Check out CAPRICORN CONJURED!

CAPRICORN CONJURED

**TWELVE TEENS. ONE TASK.
SAVE THE UNIVERSE.**

Jareth prefers to be alone. After losing his parents in a tragic accident, he knows it's the safest thing he can do. For everyone.

But when Veronica marches into his life, she refuses to leave him to his solitary existence, surrounded by nothing but his art. Vibrant and full of laughter, she won't take no for an answer. Despite himself, Jareth starts to wonder whether his heart could trust again…

Except two more strangers arrive, also refusing to leave. Tristan, determined to prove Jareth has powers, and Brielle, the girl who's searching for family just like Jareth is. They believe he's a Zodiac Guardian.

And that he must join them to defeat a great evil.

After a close brush with death, Jareth's safe world implodes. He discovers Veronica isn't who she claims she is. He learns that Tristan has foreseen his death.

And he begins to suspect that the loss of his parents may not have been an accident.

Jareth will be forced to decide. Run for his life? Or join a small group of teens claiming they're destined to save the Universe…

Be swept away by this epic 12 book Sailor Moon meets Avengers series from USA Today Best-Selling authors Tricia Barr and Tamar Sloan! Grab your copy HERE!

http://mybook.to/CapricornConjured

MORE EPIC ROMANCE TO FALL IN LOVE WITH!

ALSO BY TAMAR SLOAN

PRIME PROPHECY SERIES

KEEPERS OF THE GRAIL

KEEPERS OF THE CHALICE

KEEPERS OF THE LIGHT

KEEPERS OF EXCALIBUR

DESTINED DEMIGODS

ELEMENTAL GAMES

THE SOVEREIGN CODE

THE THAW CHRONICLES

ALSO BY TRICIA BARR

THE MATING GAMES

THE BOUND ONE SERIES

THE AMARANT SERIES

SHIFTER ACADEMY

HEAVENLY SINNERS

ABOUT THE AUTHORS

By day, Tricia is a full time mom to two beautiful girls and a wife/business partner to a handsome hard-working husband. By night—and nap times—she's a USA Today Best-selling Author of unique and thrilling teen and adult fantasies inspired by her vivid, somewhat creepy dreams and her own adventures around the world.

Tamar hasn't decided whether she's a psychologist who loves writing, or a writer with a lifelong fascination with psychology. She must've been someone pretty awesome in a previous life (past life regression indicates a Care Bear), because she gets to do both. When not reading, writing, or working with teens, Tamar can be found with her husband and two sons enjoying country life in their small slice of the Australian bush.

www.ingramcontent.com/pod-product-compliance
Lightning Source LLC
Chambersburg PA
CBHW050019180626
46810CB00002B/490